witch eyes

For Christina, and all the things you never got to see.

SCOTT TRACEY

witch eyes

flux
Woodbury, Minnesota

First Edition
First Printing, 2011

Book design by Steffani Sawyer
Cover design by Kevin R. Brown
Cover illustration by Shane Rebenschied/Shannon Associates LLC
Cover images © 2011
       house: iStockphoto.com/Kamo
       man: iStockphoto.com/ Алексей Егоров
       clouds: iStockphoto.com/Jeka Gorbunov
       trees and fog: iStockphoto.com/Peter Zelei

Flux, an imprint of Llewellyn Worldwide Ltd.

Library of Congress Cataloging-in-Publication Data
Tracey, Scott, 1979–
  Witch eyes / Scott Tracey.—1st ed.
     p. cm.—(Witch eyes ; #1)
  Summary: After a terrifying vision, Braden retreats to an old city divided by two feuding witch dynasties, where he learns that the head of one dynasty is his father and the guy for whom he is falling is the son of the head of the other dynasty.
  ISBN 978-0-7387-2595-6
  [1. Witches—Fiction. 2. Magic—Fiction. 3. Gays—Fiction.] I. Title.
  PZ7.T6815Wit 2011
  [Fic]—dc23

                    2011013996

Flux
Llewellyn Worldwide Ltd.
2143 Wooddale Drive
Woodbury, MN 55125-2989
www.fluxnow.com

Printed in the United States of America

ONE

Binding circles were bad news, my uncle said. Since I was currently *trapped* in one, the word *understatement* came to mind.

"You think it's going to be that easy to escape?" Across the field from me, the graying man snickered. The sun was just about to set, and the odds of help coming from somewhere in Middle of Nowhere, Montana, were slim.

Between him and me were a series of concentric circles dug into the ground, and I was in the center. Seven in total, and so elaborate they must have taken weeks to design properly. It was always important to be exact when tapping into powerful magics like a mystical prison cell.

That's what the circles were for. "You know all it'll take is one tiny flaw, and the whole thing breaks down," I bluffed. But the truth was, my casual glance around hadn't spotted a single flaw. That was bad.

"I've got you right where I want you," he said.

If I hesitated for too long, he'd know I was intimidated. So I smiled. Leaned back and stretched. Pretended like I had all the time in the world. But behind my sunglasses, I waited and watched. The stretching was starting to aggravate him. He started scowling, right on schedule. Arms crossed in front of him, his face getting red. I knew all the signs.

After all, the man was my uncle.

He'd been the one to design the challenge—get trapped in a binding circle and then figure out a way to escape. Weeks of design meant weeks' worth of energy building up the spell's power, making it that much stronger than my uncle's already impressive abilities.

For most practitioners, magic was like cooking. Mix the right ingredients in the right combinations, and boil for the desired effect. Uncle John and I were different—most of the time, if we knew the spell we wanted to cast, it was just a matter of gathering the magic around you and making it happen. Willpower.

But cooking had just as much a place in magic. Uncle John could have been listening to a book on tape or learning Swahili while he was putting the circle together, and the circle's power would be the same. But if he'd just forced it into place without any tools, the slightest crack in his focus and the whole thing would have fallen apart.

"When would you use something like this?" he asked.

I looked around me. "Never."

"And why not?"

"Because something like this takes a lot of work. It's

difficult to get someone to walk into a trap when there's a big X on the ground, right?"

"So why use them?"

I looked blankly back at him.

"Some witches use them for summoning spirits from the other side," he said, an unmistakable chiding to his voice. I should have known this. "And the most powerful spirits can only exist inside the circle."

This part sounded more familiar. "You mean like demons."

"Anything of a significant power," he clarified. "Their power is too great—it forces them back where they came from. The stronger the entity, the less they can remain in our world. A binding circle is one way to hold them here."

"Make them do algebra," I muttered. "They'll get so bored they'll forget to leave."

"Braden, now's not the time for games," he snapped. "What do we know about demons?"

I sighed, thinking back. Most kids took Math, English, American History. Mine was more Demons 101, AP Magical Defense, and Advanced Sorcery for Slackers. "Demons are too powerful to deal with, they can't be controlled, and they have hungers that can never be sated. They exist to destroy and consume."

"Tell me something that you didn't memorize out of a textbook," he chided.

"You can't control a demon, but you can contain it. Trapping them in the circle limits their power." I tried to think. "So if you could work out the properties of the circle, you could keep one trapped indefinitely, right?"

He didn't *exactly* smile, but that twitch of his lips was basically the same thing. He took the magic far too seriously. Like it was life or death, instead of just another lesson. "So how long do you think I can keep you trapped?"

I started to smile. "Five minutes, tops."

"How about all the laundry for a month?"

My smile widened. "Light it up, Uncle John."

The binding circle was currently only half done. Anyone could walk in or out. In effect, it hadn't been turned "on." That changed the moment Uncle John struck the match and flicked it into the third circle.

As the fire started to circle, the magic started to spiral from one layer to the next. Each ring of the spell added its own unique energies. Fire, water, a ring of quartz, tree branches, and some I couldn't see. I had seen glimpses of Enochian, some Latin, and even some Sanskrit scratched into the packed dirt of the field when I first stepped inside.

"Wow, you really went all out."

His reply was distorted, warped like there was a curtain of water between us. "It's even got an infinity charm," he said, sounding far too smug. "Anything you throw at it will only make the bindings stronger."

"And this'll really trap anyone stupid enough to walk into it?"

"Slacker nephews, demons, and anything in between," he confirmed. "Are you ready?"

I glanced around one more time, still not seeing the

flaw that would get me out of this. Uncle John had been teaching me all about magic circles and their many purposes for the last month. Summer was winding down, and lessons outside would be fewer and farther between.

He preferred the outdoors, and not just because he was a nature lover. Magic that went awry was a lot easier to contain if it didn't have walls to incinerate or a roof to tear through.

My magic, in particular.

"I'm not a slacker," I said, hoping to buy myself some time.

He threw back his head and laughed. The fact that the distortion between us made him sound like a hyena was comforting. "When's the last time you wrote in your journal?"

My journal, the bane of my existence. Uncle John was all about the organization. The house had to be perfectly in order, the refrigerator had to be stocked just so, and every spell had to be documented. How you cast it, what you cast, what tools you used. I could only imagine the indescribable glee he'd gotten from note-taking each stage of the jail-cell circle.

"Oh, come on!"

"Everyone else does it," he said.

"So if everyone else jumped off a building, I should, too?"

His retort was almost instantaneous. "Well, if someone had written down the gravity-countering spell like they were told, that question would be rhetorical, wouldn't it?"

"Like every other witch out there spends hours writing out all their spells."

The smile eased back and he got serious again. "Quit stalling."

"I'm not stalling!"

"Braden!"

Fine.

I looked down, one last time, looking for the flaw. But nothing jumped out at me. If I was any other witch, Uncle John's binding would have trapped me perfectly.

Good thing I wasn't like other witches. I pulled off my sunglasses and heard my uncle shout "Noooo!" before my eyes cleared and my vision exploded.

two

There was a moment where time seemed to fracture, a crystalline snapshot of the world where Uncle John had started raising his arm, his face full of fear and alarm. Where motes of sunlight lay poised above me, and the westerly breeze was tangible and tangled up against my skin. It was as if the world around me had called a time out.

Then the landscape expanded into something larger than four dimensions, the binding boiled itself down to an alphabet of magic, and the visions swallowed me up.

So many hunters, tracking weary feet on sullen soil brown with disappointment and impotence. The animals avoided this place of strange magic; ancient ways worked into the stone down to the very bedrock. Silver songs under the full moon, dark music of the fallen things when the sky grew dark. And a man, hiding and running and running and hiding. His fear soaked up into the roots like water.

The sunglasses were meant to keep my powers in check. With the ability to see the world as it truly was— not the filtered world that most people saw, but the true world—I soaked up everything like a giant sponge. Everything that has ever happened in a place, to a person, or because of an object leaves an imprint. The stronger the emotion, the more violent the death, the darker the spell, the impression will be likewise as strong.

My eyes—my power—was also my curse. Witch eyes, my uncle called them. A "gift." I was "special."

Sometimes being special wasn't a good thing. It was every short-bus nightmare come to life. Normal people had eyes that stayed a solid color. Blue. Brown. Hazel. Their eyes weren't on some sort of permanent screensaver, always moving and shifting around, never the same shade twice.

Every time I unleashed the power of my vision, it was only a matter of time before I was overwhelmed. Hundreds, sometimes thousands, of memories were in a place, and all of them funneled into me all at once. For as long as they ravaged through me, I'm at their mercy.

But my eyes also had another use. Magic had its own distinct presence in my visions, and spells had their shapes and forms. To look at the magic was like swallowing it up with my brain, dissecting it until I understood exactly what the spell did and why, and storing that information for later.

I could duplicate almost any spell I'd seen, but spells were fragile things, and they couldn't hold up after being poked and prodded by my brain.

My eyes tore through the binding circle like it was no thicker than a blade of grass.

One hundred twenty-two hours. Seven thousand, three

hundred forty-one minutes. Four charms buried to prepare the path, eleven spells to empower, thirty-nine pieces of quartz all mined from Arkansas, four candles hand-dipped by the woman who was so desperate she'd do anything. Ordered and neutral and everything has a face the facts he's outstripped you with caramel drums pounding at dawn bursts of thundering waterfalls that used to filter through here.

Faster and faster, images and memories and distances pulsed in front of me as the spell unraveled and laid its essence down in supplication. The fire shot up around me, rivaling the sun, and then was snuffed out. Beyond the spell, I saw the field for what it was.

Lavender air wafted down the path he shouldn't have taken if he knew what's good for him leaving me for that dark angry sun red hate working here everyone's so rude with their cowboy hats and expensive jade ambivalence like anything really makes a difference anyway, you're never getting out of the darkness.

"Focus on the spell," someone called out, their voice ringing like it was coming from down a dark hallway. But their advice was sound. I looked, and remembered, and felt.

Seven layers to the spell, seven different elements and in different numbers. Frequencies and patterns and words and lines that draw a picture in the air. I could see how all the pieces fit together, and how they'd been so carefully arranged. Magic was normally paint by numbers, but this was very nearly a masterpiece. It was the design that caught my attention and allowed me to focus until John could react.

Blessed quiet settled over me, and my eyes settled behind darkened shades. "You cheated," my uncle whispered, his hand against my head.

I counted my breaths, getting to twenty before I tried to move. Or think. I realized something was pressed against my nose, and my eyes closed involuntarily. Another nosebleed? My gift came with a price. Headaches were the least of it, then nosebleeds, then migraines, and then unconsciousness.

I tried to sit up and started coughing instead. It was like I'd suddenly inhaled a tobacco farm. "Not such a badass spell after all."

He started rubbing my back like I was a toddler needing to burp. "I should make you put it all back together," he said. "Any idea how long that took me?"

"Seven thousand, three hundred forty-one minutes," I managed, through another round of coughs.

"Migraine?"

I closed my eyes and focused. Usually, the migraine came blistering forward, like a flag corps in a parade. But there wasn't anything at the moment. "Nothing yet."

"Good, because I'm not carrying you back to the house," he said, grabbing my arm and helping me back to my feet, before adding, "Slacker."

"You're just mad everything fell apart so quick." I kept

my hand on his shoulder as we headed back toward the house, my eyes on the ground watching every step I took.

"That spell could have held a demon for days. The point wasn't to use your power to break the spell apart," he said, his voice again taking on that chiding tone I hated. "It was to try doing it the hard way. To try to rely on yourself, instead of your gift."

"But you say that like I'm going to wake up someday without the curse. It's always going to be there."

My footing grew surer the closer we got to the log cabin. We'd lived in Montana since I was thirteen, moving away from the hellacious summers in Arizona where I'd grown up. In Montana there was actual snow, and trees, and rain. We still lived in the middle of nowhere, but at least we were hermits with actual weather.

Uncle John stopped suddenly, and I almost ran into him. "You know what using the witch eyes does to you," he said, looking away from me. "That's why we have to work so hard at containment."

As long as something can create a filter between me and the visions, I can look out at the world like everyone else. Sunglasses are the only real option—the dark lens focuses my attention. If I wore regular glasses, it would be almost impossible not to look out of the corner of my eye, or at things just outside the lens. Once the visions started, it was harder and harder to pull away.

"I get it."

"Do you?" He shook his head and chuckled. "Your

grandfather would have beat the ever-loving piss out of me if I'd ever tried to take the easy way out. Nothing worthwhile came without adversity."

We climbed the stairs and headed inside the covered deck. "You don't talk about him very often."

Uncle John looked back at me, almost as though he was remembering I was there. "No sense in dwelling in the past. Nothing there but bad memories and regrets."

I hesitated, wanting to push but afraid of shattering the moment. He didn't get in one of these sharing moods very often. "Like...like my dad?"

Whatever he was about to say was cut off by the shrill ring of the telephone. I watched his face close up, all those secrets about his life before me locked back up in the vault.

"I'll get it," I said, hurrying into the house. Just as much to get away as anything else. Family was one of those things that Uncle John got funny about. I knew he didn't get along with his father, and I knew my dad was his brother, but that was almost all I knew. My dad hadn't wanted me, was going to give me away, and Uncle John stepped in and took me himself.

"Hello?" I cradled the phone against my ear and reached for the refrigerator door.

Static hissed on the other end of the line.

I repeated myself, louder this time. "Hello?"

There were faint sounds in the background, the only reason I even knew someone was actually on the other end of the line.

"Hello!"

Another few seconds and no response, and I slammed the phone back on the cradle.

"Another hang-up phone call," I said, once he finally followed me into the kitchen. Almost on cue, the phone started to ring before cutting out halfway through, and then was silent.

He brushed past me, glancing into the open refrigerator. "How's your nose?"

I tentatively touched underneath the nostril. "No more bleeding. Why?"

"Good. Can you run down to the store and get some more milk?"

"Sure," I said automatically, before realizing something wasn't entirely right. The gallon of milk in the fridge was almost full, for one thing. And Uncle John's eyes were unfocused. "Everything okay?"

He blinked, and turned back around. The door closed behind him. "You run to the store and I'll order us a pizza. How's that sound?"

Now the false enthusiasm. I grabbed a twenty-dollar bill out of the change jar we kept by the door, but by the time I was slipping my shoes back on, Uncle John had vanished into the house.

That was weirder than normal, I thought on my way out the door. And that was saying something, considering I'd been raised reading grimoires instead of Grimm's fairy tales.

three

Even though we lived in a remote area, our house was just off the main road and there was a convenience store just a few minutes away. Dark had finally settled in as I walked, and I found myself thinking about school.

Being homeschooled had always been a burden. Regular schools were dangerous on a realistic level—one accidental spell and my secret would be out. And with my vision problems, it would only get worse. Every time the two of us rented some high school movie about growing up on the wrong side of the tracks, John would look at me and nod, as if to say *see, you wouldn't want that life anyway.*

I did, though. A normal school, a normal life. Our magic lessons were year-round events, six days a week, rain or shine. Homeschooled kids didn't have football games to go to, parties to attend. John didn't like people, so it wasn't like we were social around town. He kept to himself, but I wanted more than that. I liked talking to people. Hiding out in the middle of nowhere wasn't my idea of a life.

Before I knew it, I'd arrived at the convenience store,

and stepped from the dirt path onto old, worn concrete. A giant, fluorescent chicken presided over the parking lot.

I slipped inside, murmuring a thank you as an older woman with sad eyes and blonde hair stepped out and held the door.

The store was busy: a couple of older men hung around the register, a mother with two small children was fighting with them about candy, and two girls all in black had surrounded the coffee machines.

I walked through the aisles and the hairs on the back of my neck stood up, preceding a shiver down my spine. *Just an air vent*, I tried to tell myself.

Someone was staring at me. I could feel it. Most of the locals still saw me as the "weird kid" or the "disabled kid." The one who never took his sunglasses off, even inside.

One of the fluorescent lights above me flickered, a heartbeat-like sound that buzzed in rhythm. There was murmuring from the next aisle; words I couldn't hear. I peered up over the top of the aisle, but couldn't see anyone.

You're being paranoid, Braden.

Maybe I was. But I'd be a lot less paranoid once I had the milk and was back outside. I hurried down the aisle, and that's when it happened.

I slipped, or I tripped. My legs went one way, my body went another, and my glasses were ripped in a third. I pitched forward, my elbow smacking against one of the metallic shelves, and I just barely caught myself before my nose slammed against the ground.

The aisles rippled around me, and I realized, too late, that the visions were starting. Shapes and colors that shouldn't have existed slipped into my sight as the veil dropped and everything came into focus.

There was a moment where the visions began to start, thrusting themselves forward with their stories and pictures... and then something changed.

Black and white tiles were marred with spots of blood. My vision started to narrow, homing in on just those droplets until they were puddles, then lakes, and then oceans below me. The ocean turned to glass, then became a reflection of me staring down into it.

That's when the images began.

A normal vision is a thousand conversations, five hundred sonnets, ten thousand songs, and every sight and sound and color all flooding forward at once. This time what I was seeing was different. New. It was like a slideshow.

Flashes and shapes pulsed before and after each other, in some sort of sequence. Uncle John running as something slithered after him. A forest. A clock counting down. A lighthouse. A woman, standing on a rooftop over a sleeping city, her face completely shrouded in white lace. Things digging themselves out of the *ground*. Lightning. A sign. *Welcome to Belle Dam.*

A voice superimposed itself over the vision. *I want the boy.* Uncle John waving his hands as he ran, looking directly at me before the thing—the monster—finally overtook him. It was like watching the strings on a puppet get slashed, the way he fell to the ground.

And then the monster turns and faces me, and the voice returns. *Finally*, it said, with disquieting delight. *He's ours.*

Shock and fear allowed me to free myself from the vision. I scrambled on the ground for my glasses, eyes closed. My fingers wrapped around the plastic, and relief pressed up against the fear.

What *was* that?

This wasn't how the witch eyes worked. They didn't show me random images, they showed me people, places. This was like…some sort of portent. A warning. But the certainty of what I saw was something in my bones. I *knew* it was true, and real, and on its way.

Something was coming. Something that was going to kill my uncle before it came for me.

Forgetting about the milk, I picked myself off the ground and hurried out of the store.

¤   ¤   ¤

The parking lot and main road stretched before me, but once outside I glanced to my left. Tucked back against the woods was a path that led all the way to the rear of our house. Right now, the last thing I wanted was to be out in the open. So I hurried into the woods.

All along the way, I was whispering misdirection spells while fingering the silver chain around my neck. It was a Christmas present. A circle of silver could help restrain a witch's power, in theory, helping them maintain control. But silver was also useful in truth spells, and illusions like the misdirection spell were a way of bending the truth.

I slipped in the back door, about to announce myself when Uncle John's voice cut through the house. "I told you it's not going to happen!" I crept along the covered porch, inching my way toward the kitchen. "I don't care about what's going on in Belle Dam. Things change. Braden's not going anywhere."

Belle Dam? The image of the Welcome sign flashed into my mind. Gooseflesh erupted along my arms.

"Whatever my brother's gotten himself into isn't our problem. I'm his family now. You're not taking him."

My father? Was he in Belle Dam, too? "I don't care what he's saying now," John roared, close enough that I jumped. "Braden isn't suited for that kind of life, Lucien. He hasn't had an episode in weeks, and we're keeping it that way."

The phone was slammed into its cradle. Hard, raging breaths were still coming from the kitchen. I waited.

What was I supposed to say? "Hey, Uncle John, what's going on? I had a vision that something's coming to kill you. Oh, by the way, I know my dad's in Belle Dam."

That wouldn't go over so well.

I sat down in one of the plastic patio chairs we kept out here. He hadn't left the kitchen yet, so I pitched my voice over my shoulder. "Who was that?"

I was disappointed I couldn't hear the sound of his startlement. "Braden?"

Mimicking his tone, I replied. "Uncle John?"

"It was nothing," he started, "just a phone call from an old—"

I interrupted him. "I heard you."

He appeared in the doorway, but I kept looking out into the backyard. Along the path I'd watched him run—running from who knows what.

"Braden," he said again. "It wasn't anything important." He tried changing tactics. "What happened to the milk?"

"You never talk about Belle Dam."

"Of course I don't. I—" He realized his slip almost immediately. "It's nothing. Just an old town with a lot of bad blood."

I turned to look up at him. My uncle. Growing up, he'd never allowed the illusion that he was more than he was. He never let me call him Dad, Pop, or any other variation in between. He'd accepted he was my uncle and nothing more.

"What's he want with me? Why now?"

There was no response. Uncle John's eyes were trained on the dark outside.

"It's dangerous, isn't it?" I pushed. "If they decided to come and take me?"

"That won't happen."

"But what if—"

"It *won't* happen, Braden." He had that "stop pushing" tone to his voice.

The headache had started slowly, so inconspicuous I didn't notice the growing tension behind my eyes at first. It had probably started some time after the vision, but now that I was in a dark, quiet room, it was making its presence noticeable.

It went from minor discomfort to painful stabbing in my brain almost immediately. My hands were sweaty and gross, my heart was pulsing so hard I thought my head would explode, and a thousand knives were finding fresh places to stab my skull.

This was going to be a bad one.

Uncle John noticed too. Before I even realized what the whirlwind of activity around me *was,* he had picked me up and taken me into the rec room. It was the only room in the house with no windows, and no light—the safest place for me once the migraines came.

I leaned into the couch once he settled me down, and through the haze I heard the sounds of all the lights being shut off, one by one. I drifted, wanting to whimper but not remembering how. The migraine started spreading down into my shoulders, and from there into my arms. Later into my legs.

The only thing that existed was the pulsing pain. Even thinking was too difficult. Someone lifted my head, put something in my mouth, told me to swallow. Then a glass was pressed to my lips, and I did.

Eventually, the red haze started muting into vermilion, then into burgundy. Then back to black. Sleep didn't come quickly, but it eventually came.

It was bliss.

¤　　¤　　¤

It was still dark outside when I woke up. I moved gingerly at first, but the migraine seemed to be completely gone. I slid my glasses on and sat up, no longer tired.

A few hours ago, everything had been so different. And now my vision, and the phone call … where was Belle Dam even located? That was the first thing I needed to know.

I crept through the house, despite the fact that Uncle John would have slept through almost anything. The computer was in his office, which was really just a room with a desk in it. I booted it up, then waited, eventually typing Belle Dam into a search engine.

"'Belle Dam is a town in Jefferson County, Washington,'" I read aloud. Population eight thousand. One high school. One community college. Harbor. Lighthouse.

I scrolled down the page, finding a picture of the lighthouse during the day. The angles and proportion were all wrong—I couldn't say for certain if it was the same one from my vision or not. Only that it could have been.

The visions had told me that something was going to be coming for me, and that Uncle John would be in the way. But what? I hadn't been able to see what it was exactly. Or who it was.

I knew Uncle John well enough to know that he wasn't going to listen. The more I kept pushing, the less he'd listen. But something *was* coming. Something that would kill him to get to me.

Unless you get to it first.

Could I do that? Just … leave? There had to be something I could do. The vision showed me that Uncle John was completely overmatched—whatever it was would tear right through him. And as long as I stayed here, it would get closer and closer.

He'd do the same for you. Uncle John gave up everything for you. That was all the motivation I needed.

I shut down the computer and snuck up the stairs. In my bedroom I scanned the bookshelf above my bed, pulling down my journal. "You shouldn't have made me write everything down," I whispered aloud, flipping to the slumber spell he'd shown me a few months ago.

It was supposed to work like a sleeping pill—making it easier to fall asleep and stay that way. Every time I cast it, the spell always came out too strong—instead of a gentle lull of magic, it was like a sledgehammer taking effect almost instantly. We'd never figured out how long the spell would last, always reversing it before that happened. But now, it was a blessing in disguise.

I hesitated outside my uncle's room. Was I really going to do this? He was going to be so pissed when he woke up.

I cast the spell. Packed a bag. Tried not to look back.

four

The bus jerked back into motion. It was the middle of the night, a full day after I'd left Montana—and my uncle. A pair of older women sat right behind the driver, whispering to themselves. It didn't sound like Spanish, but I was too far away to figure out what it was. A couple of college kids were still working their way toward the back, trying to find a seat.

I squirmed down. *Just pretend you're sleeping,* I whispered to myself. *Ignore them.* Every time we stopped, I was sure that someone was going to get on the bus and call out my name. Or that they'd look at me and know somehow that I'd run away.

The shorter of the two took a seat in the middle, but the other one kept moving down the rows. He started to pass my row, and I exhaled with relief. Just like that, the motion in the aisle stopped, and I glanced up. He was staring down at me, with brilliantly light eyes that almost seemed to shine.

And then he swiveled around and sat himself in the chair next to me. There were two open chairs across the aisle, but it was like he *knew* I didn't want anyone to sit there.

I shifted against the window, pulling the top of my hood down over my eyes a little further. Twice already, someone had tried talking me into taking off my sunglasses. My tongue kept fumbling as I tried to tell them why I couldn't. Usually, I had Uncle John there to do it for me.

Trying to explain *anything* to the Adonis in Abercrombie sitting next to me? Damn near impossible. I shifted my head a little so that I could study him. It was bad enough that random college guy sat down next to me, but did he really have to be model-hot?

My uncle seemed to believe that no one could really know they were gay until they were "an adult." Like once someone turned eighteen, a switch was flipped in their brain and suddenly everything changed. Being gay wasn't something that we talked about—he didn't like the subject. He didn't exactly *hate* it, either—it just made him act all funny.

The first time I told him I thought I was gay had been a few years ago. What I thought would be one of those television moments where the parent smiles and nods knowingly turned ugly real fast. His face had gone white at first, and then just as quickly flushed red.

"You're not … *that.* You don't even *know* what you are yet." He had very nearly started snarling. "Do you even understand the kind of potential you have? How important you are? You do *not* have the luxury of wasting your life."

Abercrombie didn't say anything at first. This was a good thing. It gave me time to acclimate myself to him sitting just a few inches to my right. To try and focus on something other than the way his lips had this permanent smirk—almost a sneer—to them.

There wasn't much to see in the middle of the night except streetlights zooming past. It was easy to zone out on the bus. With the lights down low, nearly everyone took the opportunity to have an hour-long nap, before the next rest stop reared its ugly, unwanted head.

"You're heading to Belle Dam? Me too."

I shifted to see Abercrombie leaning over, staring at my bus ticket. I'd left it tucked in the seat pouch in front of me, the destination boldly printed on the front.

"Visiting family?" he asked.

"Not exactly," I muttered in reply.

Abercrombie shifted closer to me. I could smell something like sweat and cologne, a musky smell that went straight to my head. I pulled myself even further into the shirt, drawing the sleeve up to my face. His voice dropped to a conspiratorial whisper. "Belle Dam's not a good place for people like you."

I straightened up, my skin going cold from the inside. I tried to keep my voice steady. "People like me?"

"People like you," he agreed. "Which side are you on?"

I wondered if this was some game, to trick me into talking to him. "What are you talking about?"

"The feud," he said, still keeping his voice low. He

made it sound like I should already know what he was talking about. "You're either bowing down to Jason Thorpe, or you're sucking up to Catherine Lansing. So who is it? Who convinced the naïve little teen to come to town?"

"What are you talking about?"

He stretched his arms out in front of him, linking his fingers and pushing them forward until they started to crackle like popcorn. "The feud," he reiterated, like I was slow to catch on. "You're either a Montague or a Capulet." When I didn't immediately say anything, he rolled his eyes. "Romeo and Juliet? What's the education of this country coming to?"

"I know Romeo and Juliet. But that's about the only thing you've said that makes any sense."

Abercrombie sighed. "Some of them are ... different. Like you. Special. And they hate each other with a vengeance."

Some of them are like you. Witches? It wasn't so much that there were witches in Belle Dam as the fact that Abercrombie had singled me out. "You don't even know me. You don't know anything about me."

Abercrombie leaned forward, inhaling deeply. Sniffing. His whisper grew a little more audible. "You smell like fire. Same as they do."

"I don't know what you're talking about." My first instinct was to jump up and run off the bus right then. But there was nowhere to go as long as it was in motion.

Witches might be known for being burned at the

stake, but their connection to fire was deeper than that. A witch's aura was always burning: fire was action and power and energy, just like magic. When I looked at a witch, really looked, the first thing I saw was flames.

But I'd never once met someone who saw it the same way I did. Or smelled it, I guess. Let alone so flippantly. The bus felt like it was growing smaller, and having a giant sitting next to me made it impossible to jump out of my seat and get away. I was stuck.

"Relax," he said, suddenly pulling back in his seat. "Secret's safe with me." His lips curved upward, his smirk bordering on a sneer. "For now."

I could feel his eyes on me, but I curled into a ball, and my eyes never strayed from the view outside. Before a few miles had passed, he got up and moved to the front of the bus. I wondered just what I was getting myself into. *Maybe I shouldn't have run. Like running away will really keep him safe.* I stared out the window until I finally started to doze.

The next thing I knew, the bus driver's monotone voice woke me and announced that we'd arrived in Belle Dam ahead of schedule. I couldn't see Abercrombie anywhere on the bus, but the lights were already on, and people were getting off.

It didn't take long to gather my things together. When I'd bolted out the door from Uncle John's, I'd only taken what could fit in my backpack. Priority for my journals and road food, and barely a thought for anything else.

I was the last one off the bus. Dawn wouldn't come for at least another hour, but already there were threads of color on the horizon. Belle Dam wasn't a scheduled rest stop, so a few moments later the bus pulled back onto the road, its lights flashing.

I wish I'd been paying attention. I spun around the parking lot trying to get my bearings, but I could have been in the middle of nowhere for all the good that did me. The bus station itself was a squat, brick building with all the lights off. Industrial buildings covered both sides of the street, ruining the image I'd had in my head of the quiet, quirky small town.

Now what? Getting to Belle Dam had kept me going for the last twenty-four hours, but now that I was here ... I was at a loss.

A car whizzed past me as I headed for the building. I was the only one left standing around, with my backpack slung over one shoulder and no idea of what to do next. Everyone else who had gotten off had already gone. There was no one to ask for directions.

"You lost?"

I nearly jumped at the voice. Leaning against the building, intentionally in the shadows, was a guy. With his foot propped against the wall, and the shaggy brown hair, he looked like some sort of James Dean homage.

"What? No."

"You look lost," he said, stepping away from the wall. At least *he* was dressed for the weather. Jeans and a sweatshirt. All I had was my backpack, and a hooded long-sleeved shirt that wasn't doing much for the Pacific chill.

"I'm not," I said, adjusting the strap of my backpack.

He made a show of looking all around the empty parking lot. "You sure about that?"

He's making fun of you. "I know where I'm going." I glanced to my left. There were a few larger buildings farther down that way ... maybe that's where the rest of town was.

"Good." He didn't move from his spot, like he was rooted in the ground. But his eyes never left me.

"Great." I started heading in that direction.

"You sure you don't want some advice?" he called out, his voice now oddly humorous.

"What are you? The welcome wagon?"

"Nah. I'm Trey."

Whoever he was, he was kind of a dick. His silence grew more pronounced, and I turned back around to see him smiling. "What?"

"Town's this way," he said, using his thumb to point in the opposite direction.

"Thanks," I muttered, changing directions. Trey pushed himself off the wall and jogged ahead of me.

"You always this friendly?" he asked cheerfully. He turned around and started walking backwards, staring at me. The streetlights cast his face with shadows, but at least it was visible now. *Something in the water here?* I thought faintly, as I got a better look at him.

The guy on the bus had been all dark-eyed smolder and

danger, but Trey was more like marble and gold woven together. Under the streetlight, his dirty blond hair started to shimmer; he was tall, and moved like someone with all the confidence in the world. Even his face was taut with cheekbones, hard lines, and angles. Sadly, I was a sucker for geometry.

My breath caught in my throat.

"Easy there, kiddo," he said, his blue eyes sparkling.

"I'm not a kid."

"Of course you're not," Trey said. He sounded just like an adult, when they were trying to be patronizing.

My stomach was starting to rumble. The last thing I'd eaten was some stale pretzels a few hours before Seattle.

We were coming to the end of the parking lot, and Trey in particular was heading for a row of those concrete curbs at the end of parking spots. He still hadn't turned back around, preferring to annoy me.

I was about to open my mouth, to warn him to watch his step, when he took one large step to the side and passed between two of the curb stoppers.

He didn't even turn around. He couldn't have seen them. I looked down at them, and then up at him again. His smile had widened, if that was even possible.

"Did you see a friend of mine on the bus?" he asked, although he tried too hard to sound nonchalant. I realized that *this* was what the conversation was all about, what he'd been building up to. I wasn't sure how I knew, exactly, but my gut was certain.

"A little taller than me," he continued, holding up his hand for reference. "Dark hair, kinda cranky looking? His name's Drew."

Only one person I'd seen that fit the description. The other college kids had been light-haired. My mouth opened before I could catch it, and I asked, "Abercrombie?" I wanted to slap my forehead. Stupid nicknames should never hear the light of day.

So his name was Drew. It made sense that the two of them were friends. Pretty people hanging out together. Belle Dam wasn't much different than anywhere else.

"Abercrombie?" Trey looked puzzled.

"Sorry," I said, shaking my head. "He just reminded me of an Abercrombie model or something."

His expression turned curious. "You talked to him?"

I shrugged. "Yeah, so?"

"Did you see him get off the bus?" he asked, his voice tightening.

I shook my head. "I was asleep when we got here. He must have gotten off before I woke up." I thought about it for a second. "If he's your friend, why didn't he wait for you?"

His smile grew strained. *Drew's not his friend at all,* I realized. Trey was looking all tense, wound up like Uncle John did when I couldn't master the "easy" spells.

At the fringes of my mind, the throbbing was starting again. Even with sunglasses, tiny impressions still got in around the corners, flashes of light that just begged for my attention. It was impossible to avoid looking all the time. Sometimes I slipped.

Normally, the auras I saw around people were pretty boring. Anger, envy, apathy. The things I saw around Trey were new, however. They were like golden embers, occasionally catching fire and sparkling before the flame died out.

"What's your name, kid?" Trey reversed his position and slowed to match my pace.

"Braden," I said, and then closed my mouth before I said anything else. Asking him about the images around him was out of the question. This wasn't Uncle John, who I shared everything with.

"I'll see you around, Braden," Trey said, and then turned back the way we'd come.

five

Ten minutes later, I'd found a city, a harbor, and a whole lot of water. I'd followed the direction Trey had pointed out, and there really was a city here. At the far end of the street, the water was glistening, and I could see a few glimpses of boats on the water.

This was a town in the midst of some feud? It looked more like a town trapped in New England colonial times. I kept waiting for the threat of danger to pop out from behind the perfectly manicured rose bushes, or the sculpted ferns lining some of the sidewalks.

My stomach started to rumble again as I crossed another street. Luckily, there was a little diner in the corner of a three-story brick building. Helen's Kitchen.

A motherly looking woman with red hair greeted me at the door. "Just one?" Her voice was clipped as she led me to one of the wood booths along the window. She used the tops of the booths as a cane when she walked, easing a limp in her step.

"To drink?" She clearly wasn't the type to waste words.

"Uhm ... coffee? With cream?"

"Hello, Braden." A masculine voice chimed in behind the waitress.

I froze. *He found me.*

The man walking toward me wasn't my uncle, though. Or anyone I'd ever seen before. He was dressed in a full suit, had light brown hair, and couldn't be much past his twenties.

"Do I know you?" My hands gripped the sides of the table. *Okay, maybe there's a feud after all.* He didn't look much like the guys off of *The Sopranos*, but he might have been one of their accountants or something.

The man raised an eyebrow. The suit was tailored. The eyebrows tweezed. The fingers manicured. The shoes polished. The smile painted on.

"It's been awhile since we talked." He turned to the waitress. "Coffee please, Helen. Braden here and I have a busy morning in front of us."

Helen hesitated for a moment, the strain of working the night shift easing into maternal concern. "You okay, darling?"

The man in the suit chimed in first. "Braden's uncle and I are old friends."

"You know my uncle?" In my head, I was running through spells I could use to get out of here on a moment's notice.

The man dipped his head. "Lucien Fallon. He retained my counsel from time to time."

"So you're like a lawyer or something?"

"Indeed. You know he's incredibly worried, don't you?" There was a hint of a British accent, the sound of someone who'd spent a summer there and affected an accent for the rest of their life.

I shifted. "Guess so." I had a flash of insight. "You're the one who was always hanging up on me, weren't you? The one Uncle John was talking to."

"Of course," he said, dipping his head. "Providing counsel and cleaning up messes are only a few of the services I provide."

"Cleaning up messes?"

Lucien's eyes gleamed as he sat down on the other side of the table. "Dealing with teenage runaways is a new one, I'll admit."

"I'm not going back," I announced.

He started to laugh. "Who said anything of the sort?" Lucien didn't look all that old, but he talked funny. Almost like an old man instead of a young one. "Let's start with you telling me why you're here."

His eyes darted back and forth, like he could see through my glasses and one eye would reveal secrets the other hid.

"I'm just here," I said. Lucien gave me the creeps. I pulled away and tucked my arms close to my chest.

"How fortuitous," he said. "And here I thought it was the impending sense of doom coming for you."

I stiffened instantly. My poker face was nonexistent. "What are you talking about?"

Lucien acted as if he hadn't noticed. "It's alright, Braden. I know about what you saw. And I'm going to help you."

He can't know. No one can. I never said anything. I was paralyzed, trying to wrap my head around Lucien's big reveal.

"It will take a day or two to get everything situated. You know better than to go around town showing off, yes?"

"Wait. What?"

"There's a room waiting at the Belmont. Just down the street from here, on Washington. My secretaries stocked it for your arrival. I imagine you traveled light."

"Wait..." I trailed off, and Lucien picked right up on the silence.

"There's time for all that later, Braden." He held the mug between his hands. "But first, I have to make your arrangements. We can't have you missing out on your schooling. The local high school will have to do. My office will take care of your enrollment."

School? A normal school? Really? "Uhm...yeah."

"Excellent. For now, play the part of the ordinary teenager. Keep your ears open, and get to know the town. I'll take care of what I can. When I have some answers for you, I'll make sure you know." He paused. "It's remarkable, really."

Nothing about the situation was remarkable. I was

still trying to pull myself together, but Lucien kept throwing more and more at me. I couldn't keep up. "What is?" My mouth was dry, but it didn't even occur to me to drink the coffee in front of me.

"Your eyes. I suppose there's a bit of poetry in there after all. Connection to old wives' tales."

My eyes? Instinctively, I reached up to touch the glasses, make sure they were still in place. It was pointless, since the world still had the normal black film over it, keeping the truth at bay.

"You've heard of the Lansing family already, I imagine. You're not the first with your particular gift to step inside the bounds of Belle Dam. There was another, once."

I straightened. I couldn't help it. There was someone else like me? All my life, I'd thought I was the only one. "Who?" If there was someone else, maybe they knew a way to control it, to keep the power in check.

"Just a silly superstition," Lucien said with a wave of his hand. "Pay it no mind."

"Tell me!"

"A woman named Grace. They said she could see things that no one else could. That she had the Sight."

"The Sight?" Visions of what was to be. That wasn't what I could do. I only saw the now, and the then. At least, I had until the convenience store. *That* had been something like the future. My heart fell back into my chest. She "had" the Sight. Not has. So I was still the only one like this.

"So they say. She never went out into town without

37

her face completely covered. I can't imagine, living your life through a veil like that."

A woman with her face covered. Like in my vision?

Lucien was still talking. "For now, enjoy Belle Dam. This could be your life, Braden. Normal school, friends, football games and pizza? Do I have it about right?"

I was supposed to trust him, but he still made me uncomfortable. "What's your angle?" I asked carefully. *This isn't normal*, part of me wanted to say, but the rest of me was already considering the possibilities. High school. Hanging out with friends.

The lawyer flashed another smile, and for the first time, I saw shadows in the depths of his eyes. "Angles are for people playing games." He stood up from the table, pulled out his wallet, and dropped a bill down. "Lawyers deal in agendas."

s i x

Once he was gone, I ordered and immediately devoured my breakfast. Lucien's money had covered not only the two cups of coffee, but my meal and a generous tip on top of that. The whole conversation with Lucien had happened so fast, and he'd thrown so much at me... I'd been manipulated, I just wasn't sure how.

Helen had given me directions to the Belmont, which really was just down the street, closer to the water. It was an old hotel, but well kept. Belle Dam looked like the kind of town where everything worthwhile was restored to its original glory.

As Lucien had promised, there was a room already waiting for me. There'd been a box on the nightstand, with a cell phone inside. I pulled out the card beneath it. *You'll need this. Lucien.* I flipped the phone open. Already charged.

How did he have time to get me a phone already?

I threw my bag down on the floor, and leapt onto the bed the moment the door closed behind me. The hotel room was too quiet. There was silence, except for a faint buzzing from the television and its associated electronics. But the comfort of the bed was slowly seeping into my skin, and I drifted off.

I'd like to say I had crazy dreams that made sense in a few ways, but still managed to leave portents of the future all wrapped up in a nice and neat little bow. Instead, I dreamt of hamburgers.

It was afternoon when I finally climbed out of bed and started to get cleaned up. Taking a shower with sunglasses on, and keeping them from falling off, was a struggle. But I didn't dare take them off. People did really nasty things in the bathroom, things that could scar an innocent boy like me.

I found out what Lucien had meant by "fully stocked." The room was already lived in. By me.

There were clothes in my size in every one of the dressers. And if they were any indication, it was a much more confident, showy me that lived here. All bright colors, which I never wore, khakis and polo shirts. An entire shelf was filled with all sorts of designer sunglasses.

It was late afternoon by the time I left the hotel. Out of habit, I hung close to the buildings and the shade they provided. I wasn't really allergic to sunlight, but it was still uncomfortable. The lighter things were, the more my attention was pulled outside the safety zone of my glasses.

I saw a sign for a sub shop down the block and headed that way, coming up behind a girl about my age with a thick streak of pink in her short blonde hair. She laughed into a cell phone. "Yeah, he dropped me off. They're waiting to see what my mother has to say." She spoke so confidently her voice carried, and I had no choice but to be a silent partner in her conversation.

"She hasn't said anything about it at all," the girl continued. "She's probably still strategizing. If she tells me to change it, and I don't, then she loses. And if she tells me she likes it, or doesn't say anything at all, then I win."

I turned to head into the sub shop just as the girl announced to me, "No no, we don't eat in there. That place is off-limits." I glanced at her out of the corner of my eye. Big mistake.

The girl with the pink streak was dressed in a white T-shirt and jeans, her hair pulled back behind her. A pair of sunglasses was tucked in the front of her shirt. None of that made the slightest impression compared to the rest, though. All at once, the world seemed to shove itself forward, cramming every ounce of data it could.

She exploded right there in front of me into crystals of turquoise and orange. The girl was still there, but part of me saw a giant sculpture of ice-cold gemstones—precious things, virtually priceless. Slivers of turquoise hummed in the light, thriving on every last touch and word. An inner core, like orange mirrors, reflected back every facet and crevice upon one another until the whole thing glimmered like a diamond.

Spotlights everywhere, the stage is wherever she goes, the exterior may be glass but the core is diamonds. The loyalty she has isn't the loyalty she was expected to have. The heart scarred, tough, fragile, and caged. Excitement, tingling in the fingertips, just laugh and it's all okay.

Once it started, it was hard to stop. Like watching a car accident, or reality television. My head started pulsing, a throbbing that seemed to beat faster than my heart. Finally the images started to slow, and I pulled myself away. Focused on the black, on the darkness of the shade.

"I'll call you back," I heard her say from ahead of me. My skin grew cold as sweat pushed its way to the surface, covering my face and my arms.

If I didn't take some medicine soon, it would get a lot worse. If I slipped up again, then it would turn into a migraine. It would hurt to move my eyes; it would be agony to even keep them open. Push it much further, and I wouldn't even be able to walk soon after that. Let alone try to do anything as insane as lift my head to change the TV channel or pick up a book.

"You okay?" she asked, leaning into my personal space.

"Just a migraine coming on." I tried to keep my voice steady, as though this was any normal illness.

I was a terrible liar, and she was too perceptive for my own good. "C'mon, inside." If it bothered her to be going into the accursed sub shop, she didn't let it show on her face.

Out of the sunlight, it was a little better. The shop was built for ambiance, which meant all the lights were dimmed low. I took a seat at one of the tables, fishing for the pill bottle in my pocket.

"Here's some water," she said, setting a bottle down on the table between us. I took it, shaking a few pills out. "I'm Jade, by the way."

Once I'd swallowed them down with the icy liquid, I closed my eyes. "Braden." It would help a little bit. I focused on my breathing, and imagined I could see inside my brain. If I could see where the problem was, maybe I could crinkle my nose and make it go away.

"New here? Or just visiting?" Jade asked.

"New. I start tomorrow." If I could even get out of bed then.

"Belle Dam High? You're already a week late, you know," she said.

"That's the least of my problems today." Even the migraine couldn't match up at the moment.

"Is there somebody I can call for you? Make sure you're okay?"

I tried to fake a smile. When I opened my eyes, the pain was still there, but the more distance I put between myself and the visions, the better off I was. "I just need to go lie down. Thanks … for the water." I reached for my wallet, but she waved me off.

"Please, don't. It's not a big deal. You sure you're okay to get home?"

I nodded. Slowly. "It's not the first time. I'll see you around."

"Tomorrow. At school."

¤   ¤   ¤

Half an hour later, nothing was working. I used all the usual tricks to curb off the migraine—the medication, the towels, the total darkness. It was a low pressure that spiked at random parts of my brain.

The first thing I'd done when I got into the hotel room, after fumbling for minutes with the key they'd given me, was to pull all the curtains shut. The second thing I'd done was to call home.

"What's wrong?" The familiar tone of concern only made me feel that much worse. John knew the moment my hesitant "hey" cracked in the middle.

"Migraine," I whispered. *I'm sorry.*

"Focus on your breathing," Uncle John said, not sounding angry or hurt in the least. Why was he being so nice? I'd abandoned him.

I wanted to apologize, but I couldn't make the words come out. Every few seconds of coherent thought were ripped away, replaced with raw and savage red haze, and then just as quickly with calm again.

"Just keep breathing," he murmured into the phone, and I pictured him sitting on the edge of my bed, whispering the same things. I curled up against the wall, my head against my knees.

I did what he said, focusing on the in and out of my breath. Making each breath a conscious act, something I could control. I couldn't control the pain, so this would have to do.

"You'll be okay, Braden," he said, but his voice sounded farther away than it had a moment before.

I fell asleep to the sound of his voice, sounds of comfort. But as soothing as his voice was, part of me wondered why he didn't ask if I was okay. If I'd made it to Belle Dam. Or if I wanted to come home.

SEVEN

On my way out the door the next morning, when my mind was filled with this overwhelming concept of *high school*, the strangest thing happened. I got off the elevator in the hotel lobby, and the manager fell in line with me.

"I just wanted to assure you, Mr. Michaels," he said formally, and then he stopped.

So I stopped, too. "Huh?"

He leaned forward—he was young and prematurely bald, only a few sparse hairs left on top. "Everything is being handled with the utmost discretion. Mr. Fallon indicated that you were to be left alone." And then he winked, like we shared a secret or something.

"Uhm ... that's great," I said, since I really wasn't sure what I was *supposed* to be saying. I headed for the door, and the manager didn't follow, so I figured that was the end of it.

I bought a bagel at the corner café near the hotel, but skipped the coffee. I was already nervous and a little jittery, and I figured the coffee would make it worse. The high school wasn't far from the downtown area—there wasn't anything in Belle Dam that was really far from the downtown area.

The high school was one big, long rectangular prison of dark bricks and somber windows. It looked more appropriate for a funeral home than a high school, but no one had asked me for my opinion.

I glanced at myself in the main building's glass windows as I shuffled my way to the door. The sunglasses were fine for now; the sun was beating down already and the sky was clear. I thought I looked the part of any normal high school student. Maybe my hair was a little long, and my clothes still had that brand-new, never-been-washed look. I looked like I was trying too hard. But there was hope.

No one paid me any attention. There seemed to be more going on than interest in an unfamiliar face. It meant I still had a little time before I had to be on my game. I tried for a cool and casual expression, but my mouth didn't seem to want to twist that way.

Checking in at the office was easy, but I had the sneaking suspicion that everyone kept staring at me. And they couldn't get me out of there fast enough—it was almost like they were afraid of being seen with me.

People in this town are strange. It was like they thought I was someone else. I headed back out of the office and nearly ran into someone.

A girl decked out in some sort of gypsy attire cut me off and was nearly galloping back toward the school's front doors. "Jimmy!" she called. "Did you hear about Drew? My sister swears she ran into him at the grocery store yesterday."

Drew? As in the Drew from the bus? My interest was piqued. The guy she was talking to was leaning against the side of the building. "Armstrong?" He sniffed. "Doubt it. He's not showing his face around here *anytime* soon."

"My hand to God," the girl replied. She wore an army of bracelets that clacked their way down her arm every time she moved.

"Riley, let it go. You know he's not coming back. It'd be suicide."

The girl swiveled around suddenly, as if she could feel me walking up behind her. "You're new," she said abruptly. There was no question, no hesitation.

"Uh, y-yeah," I stuttered, looking away. I wasn't intentionally eavesdropping. She moved frenetically, always in constant motion. Clack. Clackclack.

"I'm Riley. Newspaper editor extraordinaire, fashion wunderkind, and resident expert on all things beautiful and damned." She shook her wrist, settling the bracelets all to the bottom. "Belle? Dam? Get it?"

"Braden." I looked away again to watch a throng of kids entering the building. "How much coffee did you have this morning?"

"It's all natural, I'm afraid," she confided. "Drives my mom nuts."

"Nice meeting you." I shoved my hands into the pockets of my jeans and tried to turn away. There was no easy way to break free of her.

"Right, right. So is that Braden with an A, an AI, or an AY?"

Braden with an AY? I shook my head, trying to focus on the conversation at hand. "Just an A."

"The classic," she said with a nod. "I approve." Riley swiveled around and looked over my shoulder. "Jimmy, we're not done yet!" she called. He'd apparently wandered off while we were talking. "Okay, you," she said, swinging back toward me. "Give me your schedule."

It caught me off guard enough that I did it without question. She looked it over and handed it back.

"So you know Drew?" It occurred to me once I said it that there might be more than one Drew in this town.

"Everyone knows Drew," Riley murmured, her eyes downcast. She started heading into the main hallway of the school and I followed. "He used to be all that anyone could talk about."

"Why's that?"

She shook her head and didn't answer. I got the impression that whatever happened, it wasn't pleasant.

And then just as quickly, it was like a switch flipped, and she was all smiles and energy. "I heard about you," she announced. "They said you've got some sort of . . . condition."

"They did?"

"You're not blind, so what is it? You're too dark to be an albino. What are you, some sort of modern-day pirate?"

49

She brightened considerably. "Are you wearing eyeliner?" She tried peeking underneath the glasses.

"No." It was really hard not to smile.

"Then what's the deal?"

Riley was like some sort of ferret on speed. I started to laugh. "They don't raise you guys with manners in this town, do they?"

"'Course not." She smiled. "They get in the way of getting the really good dirt."

For what was sure to not be the last time, I said, "My eyes ... I get migraines." All true, in a manner of speaking. For some reason, I felt bad about lying.

"Hmm." She nodded. She seemed to be thinking that over. The way her eyes sparkled, I could almost see the hamster inside her head going into overdrive, his wheel spinning uncontrollably.

"So you're the go-to girl for the gossip around here?"

Riley snorted. "Gossip? Boring. I'm a journalist. The school paper's basically my baby. And sometimes I can get my name in the local paper, if I'm in the right place at the right time."

Riley said she was an expert on local things. Maybe she'd be able to help me find out something about the mysterious Grace that Lucien had mentioned. If there really had been someone with my curse before, maybe there'd be some record. Anything that might give me an idea about how she controlled it. *If* she'd controlled it.

"You're going in there," Riley said swiftly, and then

pushed me toward the door. By the time I had turned around to ask her again, she was already power-walking her way down the hall.

The first few classes passed by in a blur. Like I'd suspected, public school was a lot different than what I was used to. I'd seen enough TV to know most of the basics. You don't get up and leave the room without permission. You don't talk out of turn. But some of the rules were a little more surprising. Debate wasn't encouraged. It was the teacher's way, without question. And most importantly—the seating chart seemed to be based around some unwritten social bylaws. The only seats available in every class were right in front.

Riley met me after fourth period. "How's it going so far?" She was scribbling something in a notebook as we talked. The hallway started to clear quickly as students rushed for the cafeteria.

The door behind us swung open, and a girl in a black and white pantsuit stepped out. The outfit slid around her like silk and screamed money. I didn't need the flash of pink in her hair to recognize her.

"Jade," Riley greeted her tightly.

My smile was tempered by the tone in Riley's voice. The notebook had disappeared, and all her energy was channeled into gripping her book bag strap.

"Nice to see you up and around. Headache's all gone?" Her voice was full of sugar. Jade wasn't even looking at me, her eyes were narrowed thoughtfully on Riley.

"Much better."

Riley rolled her eyes, offering nothing more than an irritated huff. "Come on, Braden, we're missing out on lunch."

"Guess I'll see you around," I offered.

"Photophobia?" Jade asked, in lieu of walking away. The thick eyeliner seemed to magnify the dark blue of her eyes. "I did a little looking last night. Bright lights cause migraines, and things like that?"

It caught me off guard, that Jade would have been interested enough to do research. "Yeah," I said. Something like that.

Jade turned away, looking to Riley. "You can run along. Braden and I are going to take a walk."

Riley shook her head. "He's following me around for the day," she said stubbornly.

"He'll be back later. You can sink your claws into him then. I know how status-hungry the newspaper staff is," Jade replied lightly.

I had to say something, to stop this little argument before Riley's feelings really did get hurt. But when I went to speak, I saw Riley's face. She looked defeated.

"Fine. I'll see you later, Braden," she said quickly.

"We don't get along," Jade explained while Riley headed down the hall. She moved stiffly, but never looked back to the two of us.

"Clearly."

"Come along. There's a whole new world to explore, new boy." Jade's smile was infectious.

So I followed.

eight

At first, I thought Jade was leading me off campus. I didn't even know if we were allowed to do that or not. I didn't think we were.

Instead, she led us to an alcove somewhere in the rear of the building. I hadn't been this far back yet, but there were windows looking out on one of the main streets in town. A trio of vending machines lined the walls, offering a sundry of soft drinks and prepackaged foods. We both got a few things from the vending machine and then sat on one of the couches.

"So what brought you to Belle Dam?"

"You know, family stuff." I tried to shrug it off.

"You have family stuff?"

I had to think about that for a second. "It's kind of a divorce thing." Which it was ... if you squinted real hard and looked off to one side.

Jade nodded, looking reserved for a moment. "Divorce is always hard, or so I've heard from friends."

"What's your story?" I wondered. "You and Riley didn't look like sleepovers were in your future anytime soon."

Jade chuckled. "If there are any skeletons in your closet, better check the locks. The girl finds out an awful lot of secrets."

I didn't know what to say to that, so I went with silence.

"You're a little like her, I think." Jade's voice was thoughtful.

"What's the problem with the two of you? You hate each other?"

Jade shook her head. In the direct light, the pink in her hair was even more bubble gum colored than I'd noticed before. "Riley thinks outside her reach, that's all. She's always off hunting the next big story. She wants to challenge the status quo."

"And you like things the way they are?"

"No," she admitted. "Not always. But it's safer that way. Making trouble just to make trouble doesn't do anyone any good."

"So you're saying she's trouble?"

"Riley's just a girl. I'd rather not waste my entire lunch period talking about *her*. The point of this was to find out all about *you*, remember?"

"I don't remember agreeing to that."

She threw her head back and laughed. "You'll figure out I get my way an astounding majority of the time."

"So what do you want to know?" I leaned in a little, equally fascinated and curious. Jade was all confidence and charm—not to mention the things I had seen with my sight the day before.

"What do your parents do?"

"Uhm, my uncle," I said. "No other parents to speak of." I noticed her wince, but went on as if I hadn't. "He's … kinda doing his own thing."

After that it was a good deal of small talk where she asked me more about where I'd grown up, life with my uncle, and all sorts of things that I had to think about carefully, or gloss over, before answering. The idea of being homeschooled amused her to no end, as did the fact that we'd really lived in a log cabin.

"And if anyone gives you a hard time," she announced, "just tell them you're a friend of mine. Give it a couple of weeks, and word will get around."

I laughed, thinking that she was joking. "Why would anyone give me a hard time?"

"Not everyone in town is a friend of the Lansings. And sometimes people get … overzealous when someone new comes in."

"Wait … you're a Lansing?"

Her smile widened, showing two rows of perfect teeth. "Of course."

I shook my head. No one had gone out of their way to point out the local celebrities yet. I heard crinkling, then looked down to see the empty bag in front of me. I hadn't even remembered eating the pretzels, but the bag was empty.

"Come on. I'll show you where you're going next.

Show me your schedule." As we walked through the halls, Jade started to give me a rundown of the teachers to avoid, and the ones to impress.

She did as promised and led me down into the bowels of the school for art class. The teacher prattled on for the entire period about "finding the natural light," whatever that was supposed to mean. I tuned out for the forty minutes, until someone dropped off a note from the office, from Lucien. Apparently, he wanted me to stop by his office after school.

"Braden!" As I left the classroom, Riley was in the hallway, heading in my direction. She stopped short, her forehead creasing as she peered up at me. "What's wrong?"

"Nothing," I said after a second. Did I look like something was wrong?

"Oh. Well anyway, I've decided to forgive you for going off to lunch with Jade, even if you did make me sit by myself." Her face scrunched up in distaste.

"What about that kid you were talking to this morning. I thought you were friends?"

"Not quite friends," she amended immediately. "Not quite something else."

"Oh." Relationship drama.

"Art, Braden? Eww," she said suddenly, making the connection with the room I'd just left. "You couldn't find a better class choice?"

"You're not into art?" I asked her. Personally, I was more interested in photography. A way to look at the world and see it without all the other layers swarming in at the edges. But Belle Dam High didn't have a photography department. Uncle John must have told Lucien that I was interested. So I got art instead.

"Of course not," she snorted. "I don't have an artistic bone in my body. And don't be like my mom and argue that writing is artistic. I want to be a journalist—that's not about being creative, it's just about what's true." She blinked, almost as though she realized the conversation had turned back to her.

"Tell me more about the Lansings?" I asked. Finding out about Jade had made me more curious.

Her expression frostened. "Ask Jade."

I tried a different tack. "Isn't there another family in town? The Thornes or something?" Playing dumb wasn't really my strong suit, but it seemed to work.

"You mean Mr. Thorpe?" Riley brightened. "Do you know he bought the school brand-new computers, and arranged for the paper to get printed out at the Gazette?"

"I thought I heard he wasn't a nice guy?"

Riley shrugged. "Maybe not to some people. But he's got a soft spot for kids. Y'know, since he couldn't have any of his own."

"Why not?"

She shook her head. "His wife died, and he never remarried. There were rumors, but..." Her voice trailed off.

"Rumors about what?"

Riley twirled one of the bangles around her wrist. "That

she killed herself. I don't think she would, though. My mom saved all these old society pages with her picture in them. She didn't seem like the type."

"People usually don't seem anything like they really are," I said with a shrug. "At least in my experience."

"I'd hope not," she said. "If even half of what they say about Mr. Thorpe or Mrs. Lansing is true…"

"Why, what do they say?"

Riley looked away and started moving down the hall. "It's not any of my business," she replied.

"But…?" There was a "but" there.

"It's like someone drew a big invisible line across the town. Jade's mom on one side, and Mr. Thorpe on the other. But every time something happens in town, people act like it's more about the feud than about what's really going on. It's all anyone seems to think about."

"You make it sound like they're in the mob."

Riley shrugged. "That's how Drew always describes them."

"So he's not a fan of theirs?"

"Would you be?" she scoffed. "They practically ran him and his mother out of town after his dad died. The Armstrongs used to be another one of the important families in town. Then Bennett Armstrong died in a car accident, and everyone turned on Drew and his mom. He used to get picked on a lot in grade school."

"So what's that have to do with the Lansings or the Thorpes?"

"I don't know," she said quickly. "Nothing. It's just a stupid local rumor." The clacking increased in frequency, and she started moving even faster down the hall.

"I thought you were the expert on all the stories around here, Riley. So what's the deal?" I didn't have to hurry much to keep up with her—even at her quick pace we were still walking in tandem.

"Ask your new friend, Jade. I'm sure she's got a great perspective on the situation."

It was the silence of the bracelets that clued me in to the fact that she had suddenly stopped. I was already several paces ahead of her before I turned. "You don't want to get involved with them, Braden. They're not like you or me. They think the rest of us are just pawns to toy around with."

"So they get together and hatch nefarious schemes to ruin our lives?"

Riley bit back a laugh. "Hardly. Catherine and Jason hate each other. Like classic English nobility hatred. I heard it used to be a lot worse, before Jason's wife killed herself."

Riley's words didn't make me feel any better about being here. If the vision I'd seen had anything to do with the Lansings and the Thorpes … what was I getting sucked into?

¤   ¤   ¤

Once the school day was over, Riley offered to take me to the editorial meeting for the school paper, but I declined. Her face was more than a little anxious when she asked,

"I'll see you tomorrow morning, right?" as though I was going to vanish in the night.

"Ugh! Not again!" Jade's shriek rang out clearly as I stepped out the side entrance. Riley had explained that senior parking was located on this side of the building. And Jade's parking space was front and center.

It was another few steps before I saw what was wrong. Sprinkled across the surface of her car were white splotches that shone against the black metallic paint. I glanced around. Every other car in the line was free of bird droppings, except Jade's.

"Just like last year," she said as she looked at me. "It's the first time since school started, though."

"Birds not a big fan of the sports car?"

"It's my brother's car. She held a hand to her forehead, dark manicured nails against the pink streak in the front.

"Why do you have your brother's car in the first place? You don't have your own?"

She stared at me like I'd just asked her to wear spandex. Then she cracked an unsure smile. "I've had three. After the last one, my parents said no more. So I borrowed my brother's. He doesn't mind." She grinned then, a look of pure mischief and princess attitude. "He might start minding once he finds out, though."

"So you stole your brother's car. After you did ... what? To the other ones?" Three cars? If that wasn't a warning sign, I didn't know what was. I had a sneaking suspicion of what she was going to tell me. I was right.

"I've got this thing about stationary objects," she admitted. "I kind of attract them."

Bad driver. Check. "And you've managed to piss off every pigeon in a hundred mile radius. Nice," I said. "Plus, now you've got to get your brother's car clean before he realizes."

Jade pulled a pair of sunglasses out of her purse and slid them on her face. "Look. We match." Of course, hers had a designer's logo crafted on the side, and mine were more about total eye coverage. "I'll just tell him I don't know anything," she went on. "I was at school all day, and his car was in the garage where he left it."

"In the garage. Where an army of angry birds attacked it," I pointed out with a straight face. "Unless you've got someone else to blame, he's going to know it was you, won't he?"

She thought that one over for a couple of seconds. "There may be a flaw in that line of thinking." She sighed. "I guess that means driving to the car wash and waiting for them to detail it. It's going to be too clean. He'll know something happened then."

"Well, if you're as bad as you say you are behind the wheel, then he can't blame you, can he? Assuming you can get the car home in one piece. The only way he'd know is if there was a giant dent somewhere on it. Right?"

She tapped a finger against her lips. "You might have something there." Jade opened the car door and gestured to the other side. "C'mon. I'll give you a ride. Only the outside's dirty. You can keep me company at the car wash."

"I've always wanted to ride in a car covered in bird crap," I said. Jade laughed, checking her face in the rear-view mirror. "But, I can't. I've got to run by the library."

"I'll drop you off, then."

"Why?" She was a very strange girl. They all were.

"Because maybe there's some use for you yet," she said with an enigmatic smile.

Nine

It didn't take us very long to arrive in front of the public library, but finding a parking space proved more difficult. Jade had to circle the block, which didn't seem to suit her.

"I'll just jump out here," I offered, as we came to another corner.

"You sure?" She blew an absent strand of hair upwards.

I nodded and pushed open the door. From the driver's seat, Jade's mysterious smile made a reappearance. "Don't worry. Your secrets are safe with me. For now."

¤   ¤   ¤

The library was an old classic. Elegant white stonework framed the two-story building, having dulled only marginally after years of faithful service. Large bay windows exposed row upon row of books inside and a hint of hanging lights that looked better suited to a fine-dining restaurant than to a library. There weren't any giant stone lions waiting outside its doors, but I loved it immediately. It just *looked* like a library.

I hadn't really figured out what I was going to do in the grand scheme of things, but before I did anything else I wanted to find out a little more about Lucien Fallon. All I knew so far was his name, and that there was something about him that made me nervous. His note said to be at his office at 5:00.

The computers were tucked away in a corner behind a series of bookshelves that only came waist-high—a nice little nook where people could surf the Net. I slid down into one of the chairs and started my research.

A quick Internet search proved that Lucien was well educated, European, and some sort of legal powerhouse. University in England, then law school in New York. There were tons of details about how he grew up and where he went to school, but there was almost nothing on his life after graduating.

The problem came when I glanced at one of the dates attached to a law school journal he'd been included in while he was in New York.

The dates are over twenty years ago, I realized, tracing my finger along the screen as if that would make it suddenly make sense. But the man I'd met wasn't in his forties. It'd be hard to say he was even in his thirties.

Before I could really hash out what the hell that meant, there was a looming presence above me. I glanced up. The narrow-eyed blonde blocking out the natural light took a second to recognize.

"I thought that was you," Trey said.

I closed the browser and got up from the desk. Trey cut around me and headed for the stacks, glancing at me over his shoulder for a moment before he disappeared. *Is he stalking me?* Then why did he show up and then start wandering off?

"Something I can help you with?" I finally managed to say, as I followed him.

"Not today," his voice whispered from a different row. He was clearly enjoying himself. "I never pictured the library as a great place for runaways. Interesting choice."

"I'm not a runaway," I lied. I turned a corner and found him waiting for me.

"Whatever you say. Who am I to judge?" Trey's tone suggested otherwise. "So what's your interest in Lucien Fallon?" He'd seen what I was looking up on the computer.

"He's my uncle's lawyer. That's all."

"Fallon's never quite that simple," Trey said. "But most of the time he's Jason Thorpe's lapdog, so what do you expect? What's your uncle do, anyway?"

"Computers." Later, I'd have to wonder how it was that the lies came to me so easily. I pointed at myself. "Custody stuff." What he said bugged me. Lucien worked for Jason Thorpe? One of the town bigwigs? He hadn't mentioned it.

"Ahh." Trey ran his fingers along the row of books, looking distracted.

"You know anything else about Lucien?" I asked, my curiosity piqued.

"Not anything that would help. He's scum."

"So if he and Jason Thorpe are so terrible, how come no one's stood up to them before?"

"Yeah, you're definitely new," Trey said, with a humorless laugh. "That's not the way things work around here. So where is this mysterious uncle, anyway," he said, switching tacks.

"My ... uncle?" I winced, and tried covering it up by pulling one of the books off the shelf and pretending to study the cover. It was some sort of haunted house novel, with the creepy-looking mansion all in black and gray. "He's ... coming. But I had to start school."

"Ahh." He plucked the book out of my hands and flipped it over to the back cover. "If you're in some kind of trouble, maybe I can help."

He said it so offhandedly, like it was nothing to him. *He probably thinks you're just another runaway, afraid to go back home.*

"I'm fine," I said, my voice tightening. "I don't need anyone's help."

Trey nodded absently, his eyes still on the book. Apparently it didn't suit his taste, because he slid it back on the shelf where it belonged and glanced down at me. "So what's with the glasses? You're not blind."

"My eyes don't see things the same way yours do," I said carefully. "It's like being allergic to light. I get these migraines, sometimes nosebleeds ... but it's nothing."

"Doesn't sound like nothing," Trey said, after a minute had passed. "So you've had it all your life?" I nodded, and he went on. "That's a rough gig. Must make you appreciate that you can see at all, huh?"

Doctors, and people I'd run into with my uncle, always said things like that. Thinking that sight, at any cost, was worth it. I used to fantasize about what it'd be like to wake up completely blind one morning. My best guess was that it was like stepping into a lake in the middle of a hot summer day.

I didn't know what to say to Trey's assumption. "I've got … stuff," I said awkwardly, with a gesture back toward the computers.

"If I were you? I'd tell your uncle to get a new lawyer. Fallon's just going to cause you both some trouble." There was a twinge to the way he said *both*, like he knew Uncle John wasn't anywhere near Belle Dam.

"Don't really have a choice in that," I said. Murmured voices picked up somewhere behind me, and I turned. When I looked back, Trey was already wandering away, to a table with books and papers scattered on it.

I checked the clock hanging above the computers. There was a little more than half an hour left until I had to meet with Lucien. Maybe I could find something out about Grace. Whoever she was, Lucien seemed to think I'd be interested in knowing about her. Which begged the question, why?

¤　　¤　　¤

"I'm sorry, hon," the librarian murmured. "The only information we have on local history is what's already over there. Everything on the Lansings would be there. If you're looking for something more, then I'd suggest the historical society, or the display they have in City Hall has a few old documents. Is this a report for school or something?"

She was seated behind the desk, her copper hair frizzed from one too many perms. I tapped my fingers restlessly against the edge of the desk. "School just started. I was just curious, I heard a story someone was talking about in study hall," I said with sudden inspiration. "But I'm not interested in the Lansings. Just about this Grace woman, and some sort of story about her."

"Grace *Lansing*," the woman emphasized. "The Widow of Belle Dam. You probably heard that old ghost story, about how she wanders the Lansing estate on a full moon night, didn't you?"

Grace was one of the Lansings? "Right. Something like that."

"They say that she's been waiting for her lost love to find her. Depending on who's telling the story, sometimes he's a ship's captain, other times just a captain of industry. The woman in white is a fairly standard ghost story."

"Really? So it's kind of like gossip? Someone picks up a story, and then goes home and tells their spin on it?"

The librarian chuckled, shrugging her shoulders. "I like to think the legend started here with us. Wouldn't that be exciting?"

Oh, yes. Riveting. "Is there a copy of Grace's story somewhere so I can read it?"

She shook her head. "I'm afraid not."

Why hadn't Lucien just told me that Grace was supposed to be a Lansing? "So there's nothing in the library that can help me?"

"There might be a mention of her in one of the books about local legends," the librarian said helplessly. "But I don't remember anything else."

"I'll just ask Jade. I'm sure she can tell me something. But I didn't know the town was all that big on legends and historical stuff."

"Oh, it's a big part of Belle Dam, hon. There's a Founder's Fest in the summertime right before Labor Day. You just missed it." She sighed wistfully. "Then there's the Key Festival in the spring. It's like an Easter egg hunt. The City Council hides a hundred keys all over town, and whoever finds the most wins a prize. My uncle won a year's supply of firewood from the Thorpe company one year. At the awards ceremony, they tell the story of how Grace Lansing hid a number of keys all over town, and if anyone found them all, they'd find a hidden Lansing treasure."

"Treasure, huh? No wonder everyone likes the key hunt."

I thanked her for the help and headed for the exit. Nothing useful.

Lucien's address had been on Washington, which was the same street as the Belmont. All I had to do after leaving the library was turn toward the water and head in that direction. I cut across the street, behind a line of cars waiting at a light, and crossed over a corner of the town square.

It only took a few minutes to reach Washington,

where the traffic was much more serious. I followed the sidewalks, watching as cars zoomed past almost like there wasn't any speed limit.

At the corner, a group of people had gathered around the crosswalk, with one older man in a polo shirt and slacks pressing the button every three seconds.

"That's not going to make the light change any faster," an exhausted-looking woman next to him snapped. She looked in my direction. "Peyton, get over here." No, not at me. At the tiny little girl in the elaborate pink...gown.

"I'm a princess," she announced, looking up at me.

I smiled down at her. She did some sort of dance that involved hopping and a pirouette as she circled around me. She giggled and spun toward me. I took a giant step forward, bounding out of her way so she could continue her dance.

That's kind of cute, I was thinking to myself when I noticed the bus barreling down the street. Like the other cars before it, it seemed to be completely disregarding speed limits.

The little girl's dance stopped and she looked up at me. Her eyes were wrong. Hollow. "You shouldn't have come here, Braden," the princess said in a much quieter, more adult tone.

And then she pushed me so hard I went right off the sidewalk and into the street. Right in front of the oncoming bus.

Ten

There was a horn. Shouting. The sound of brakes screeching.

I didn't even think about it. I tore the glasses off my face, already twisting the magic inside me into something, anything, that would help.

An implosion of light, a thunderclap of the space between broken sound, and a force that slammed into me like a football player.

The bus wouldn't have stopped in time, the momentum was too great. I'd done basic lessons in physics, and I had a very basic idea of how things worked. But apparently using magic to rip away the momentum of a moving object wasn't a smart idea. Instead of collapsing and being totally fine, I'd caught some of that momentum and gone tumbling down the street.

People were still shouting. The hydraulics attached to the bus door released, and the driver came out yelling. Somehow I had managed to keep hold of my sunglasses, and I slid them on.

The little girl—hell, the whole family—was gone from the sidewalk where I'd seen them just a few seconds before. My palms burned from where they'd ground against the concrete in the street.

"Where'd they go?" I asked, trying and failing to stand up on my own. A woman knelt down next to me, cautioning me to wait for an ambulance.

"Jane! Jane, come on!" A man's furious call distracted me. I looked to my left. He was shouting at the woman next to me. "*You don't know who caused this.*"

Only then did the woman look up, shocked into motion. There was just a moment where she looked at me, a moment where she almost started to speak, before she stood up and started to hurry off with the man's arm tightened around hers.

What the hell? All around me, people were rushing to put some distance between themselves and the scene. Only the bus driver and a few others were waiting around, focused on the aftermath of the "accident."

The second time I tried to stand was a little better. My whole right side was throbbing, and I felt like I had gravel in my hair, but the pain wasn't significant. I'd dealt with worse.

That little girl tried to kill me.

I crossed in between the traffic and started running.

¤ ¤ ¤

I didn't stop until I'd reached the 600 block of Washington Street. I expected to see a few tiny office buildings each splitting up the block, but there was only one building here, and in looking around, it was one of the tallest in the city.

The building opened up into a sort of mud room—floor mats covered the floors, and more doors led into the actual lobby. I took a few minutes to finish brushing myself off, checking the status of my clothes, and catching my breath.

Aside from a few scrapes along my arms and legs, I wasn't seriously bleeding or anything. My jeans weren't quite so lucky, with one of the back pockets losing part of its stitching.

Someone tried to kill me. If the bus had been moving any faster, or I hadn't reacted so quickly... And then I froze.

I'd used my powers in public. Worse, I'd used the witch eyes. There was just a hint of throbbing in the back of my head, but whether it was from the power or the accident, I wasn't sure.

What if someone had seen me? What if people find out? My stomach was rumbling something fierce by the time I walked into the lobby of the building. I saw a woman exiting the elevator and asked her about Fallon—she pointed toward a sign on the wall. Fallon Law held the entire top floor of the building. Every floor below it was split between dozens of different offices and agencies, but Fallon had one all to himself.

The elevator was completely mirrored, creating reflections of myself that tunneled out into the distance. It was unsettling to see myself alone in the elevator, and yet crowded by so many mirror images. It was something surreal—like seeing one of my visions. But it was just an optical illusion.

Just for a moment, I thought I saw something move that shouldn't have. Before I could help myself, I glanced to the far right. Out of the corner of my eye, I caught a glimpse of something dark swirling behind one of my reflections. I turned, but as I moved my eyes, the darkness moved to. It wasn't something solid, like oil or shadows; it was granular, like black sand.

I shifted around, pivoting to my right and even going so far as to pull the glasses away. Whatever I had seen was gone. Bright light smacked me in the face, drawing out colors and images that weren't there a moment ago. *Rings of purple bruising from the tears I never should have trusted him angry red stains copper on the carpet must get that fixed fire bowing down in his wake all angry oranges and gas blues money green in my purse the best job I've ever had. Why doesn't he respect me as much as the others?*

Through the haze of senses, I saw my reflections. The panic in a hundred pairs of eyes, growing more fearful and unhinged the farther back they went. It was almost like each reflection was slightly different, and the ones farther back were becoming something I couldn't quite recognize.

I shoved the glasses back on my head, instantly disori-

ented with double and triple reflections that had nothing
to do with mirrors.

The elevator chimed, and the doors opened.

This is such a bad idea.

¤   ¤   ¤

"Mr. Fallon will see you now," the supermodel behind
the secretary's desk cooed. Fake hair, fake lips. Fake everything. I didn't believe that any parent would willingly
name their daughter Candy. She was a Playboy Playmate
dressed up as a secretary. This had to be some kind of joke.

Despite the note saying Lucien wanted me here at
5:00, it was almost a quarter after before he was "ready for
me." In that time, I sat and tried to pull myself together,
watching his office doors. No one entered or left. How
busy could he be?

I walked up to the double doors with their gold plat-
ing. LUCIEN FALLON, ATTORNEY AT LAW. I closed my eyes,
and tried to take a deep breath. Counted back from ten.
Anything to stop the throbbing behind my eyes. It was
getting worse.

The office walls were wood paneled and stained dark,
drawing the eye toward the full-length window that over-
looked the rest of downtown. The school was easily visible, one of the few landmarks I recognized already.

There were no law books—or anything to suggest the
man's office was in any way linked to the legal profession.
Instead, the walls were lined with tasteful art. At least, at

first glance, I thought it was tasteful. In one a woman lounged on a chair while something swarmed over her.

"Hello, Braden," Lucien said from the desk. He was wearing a charcoal suit that was identical to the one he'd worn in the diner, and a pair of tiny reading glasses. The desk itself was longer than I was tall. It made Lucien look tiny and unthreatening. "You're late." He made a show of looking at the gold watch on his wrist.

I was *late*? "Your secretary kept me out there waiting."

"Did you really come here to argue over the time?" he said, pulling the reading glasses off and putting them into some sort of black case.

I stayed near the door. "Someone tried to kill me," I blurted out. "Right down there, on the street." I pointed toward the windows, as if Lucien would be able to spot who did it.

An eyebrow raised. "Well, aren't you a precocious lad," he said. "Your life nearly snuffed out on your first real day of independence. Bravo."

I couldn't be hearing this. "Sorry?"

"You didn't think you were the only witch in Belle Dam, did you?" Lucien laughed. "My dear boy, you're in between two of the most powerful magical dynasties to cross over into the New World."

"You mean..."

He waved a hand dismissively. "The vassals don't even understand *why* they fear the Lansings and the Thorpes as much as they do. I suppose it's become something of an inherited instinct." He grew oddly wistful. "Wouldn't that be something, if people were simply *born* to fear you."

"Well, one of them tried to kill me about twenty minutes ago."

"Oh, I've no doubt," he said, with utter calm. "I suppose you're wondering who?"

I waited, somehow knowing that Lucien wanted to drag this out. It was like some sort of production to him. But this was what I'd come to Belle Dam to find out. Whoever tried to kill me was probably the same one from my vision.

"A balance has existed for far too long. After certain regrettable events that took place years ago, Jason and Catherine called a cease-fire. Catherine has been looking for a secret weapon ever since."

"A secret weapon?" And then I understood. "Me?"

Lucien nodded. "She'll make sure everything between you and her is decimated; razed to the ground. While your life is still burning, she'll stroll in, offer you her heartfelt comfort, and then make all your little dreams come true."

Trey had told me at the library that Lucien worked for Jason Thorpe. "And since you're working for the other side, it's in your best interests to stop that from happening, right? And probably recruit me for yourself?"

He looked amused. "My role in these little games is a bit more complicated than that."

"And what do they—"

"—want with a boy like you?" He shook his head.

"Don't be coy, Braden. Who is to say how powerful your gifts will make you? It could be that one day they'll proclaim legends about *you*."

"I'm not somebody's weapon, Lucien. That's crazy."

Something on his desk beeped, and then Candy-the-Strippertary echoed from the telephone, "He's coming off the elevator."

Lucien pressed another button, cutting her off. His eyes grew vacant and he glanced behind him, toward the view over the city. "He does so enjoy unraveling my schedule." A sigh, and then he spun back around, his arms extended like he was about to ask for a hug. "I've tried to tell him, countless times, that things must happen on a timetable."

"What are you talking about? Who's coming?" I glanced back at the door I'd come through and stepped further into the room. Backing away from the door.

"Feel free to tell him you're no one's weapon, Braden." Lucien glided past me, reaching for the door handle. "Although I imagine you'll have other things on your mind." I watched him pause and mouth some sort of countdown to himself. Only after he reached "one" did he move.

He pulled the door open, and a man in a solid black suit stepped through without the slightest hitch in his step. My heart caught in my throat, choking off any thought of breathing. I recognized the nearly black hair, the height, the purposeful stride.

Pieces of the puzzle were slamming into place so fast I

should have gotten whiplash. That was my uncle's hair, his height, his stride. But where Uncle John was round in the face and prone to laugh, this man's face was narrow, and he was all business. There were streaks of gray in his hair, and that suit ... Uncle John would never have sacrificed comfort for couture.

But otherwise the resemblance was unmistakable.

"That will be all, Lucien," he said, his voice reverberating through the room. Lucien dipped his head in a nod and closed the door from the outside.

Alone, I stared at the man who could only have been Jason Thorpe. Lucien's boss.

My father.

eleven

"Hello, Braden," Jason Thorpe said.

I took another step backwards, my legs smacking against Lucien's desk. *Don't throw up. Don't throw up.* Lunch was hours ago, but between the growing pulse in my head, and now the rebellion in my stomach, it was only a matter of time.

This is some sort of joke. A test. My father was in the room with me. "What are you doing here?" I whispered, as if someone was listening.

Jason kept his distance, crossing to the far side of the room and looking out the window. There was a clear shot to the door—if nothing else, I knew I could be out the door and out into the offices before he could catch up. His stuffy leather shoes couldn't keep up with tennis shoes.

The headache was growing in intensity, threatening to split my brain right down the middle. "Lucien's been treating you well? He hasn't given you any trouble?"

He was so casual, like this was any ordinary conversation. I tried to swallow, but my mouth was dust. "No, Jason. No trouble."

"I was surprised when he told me you'd be returning to Belle Dam, but I learned long ago never to doubt his counsel." He turned and strode behind the desk, taking the seat Lucien had so recently abandoned. "Have a seat, Braden."

"I'll stand." It was stupid, because my head was starting to throb so much that sitting would have been so much better. Actually, curling into a ball on the floor would have been the best, but I'd have to wait until I could get back to the hotel for that.

Jason's mouth moved upwards, proving he *was* capable of smiling, but the expression didn't look quite right. "Yes, you are headstrong, aren't you?" he murmured. Apparently it pleased him. And just as quickly his voice got sharp ... and concerned? "What's wrong?"

My legs had started shaking, the mere idea of sitting enough to throw them into rebellion. And so I sank into one of the chairs, as much as I didn't want to. Jason, the room, all of it vanished as I focused inward. It took everything in me to hold my stomach down and not sink into unconsciousness.

I couldn't even reach for the pills in my book bag. Why hadn't I taken them earlier, at the first sign of the headache? What was wrong with me?

My hands were cupped around my eyes, blocking out as much of the light as they could. I focused on my breathing, the way my uncle had taught me. When Jason laid his hands on me, like he was some sort of priest, I flinched in surprise.

His palms were on either side of my face, his fingers pressing against my temples. My face was flush, but his hands were a balming ice against my skin. At the edges of my awareness I could feel him gathering the magic around him. Slowly the ice began to seep into my skin, crackling and spreading its way inside and soothing away the pain.

It was several minutes of breathing before I realized just what was happening. It was like I zoned out for a time, and when I came back to myself, the pain was gone. Completely.

I started to lift my head, only to realize that Jason was still holding my head. He let go and rose to his feet, and I looked down at my hands. There wasn't any trace of the scrapes or scratches I'd suffered on the street.

Jason healed me? How is that even possible? Uncle John had never even mentioned magic that could heal or take away pain.

"I wouldn't get used to it," Jason announced, clearing his throat. He seemed shaken.

"How ... did you do that?"

He walked back across the room and stared down at the city. "The powers at your disposal, they have more costs than you know. You can heal the symptoms once or twice, but then immunity sets in." He looked over his shoulder— not quite at me, but at least in my direction. "Why do you think he only treated you with pills?"

I didn't like the caustic tone he had. "At least someone was there when I needed him," I said, matching it tone for tone.

Another one of those faux smiles. "Why are you here, Braden?"

"I thought you wanted me here," I said, confused at his ambivalence. "Lucien said—"

"Lucien says a great many things. I'm asking why *you* are here."

Why had I come? "Because someone was going to come for me. Catherine Lansing, Lucien says. And she was going to kill Uncle John to get to me."

I didn't miss the flare in his expression when I mentioned his brother's name. No love lost there. "Ahh." I couldn't quite decipher the emotion that flashed across Jason's face before he turned back to the window. "And she already tried to kill you once today, I heard. That was sloppy."

"Sloppy?" My body started to warm as the anger took hold. "She tried to have me killed and all you can say is that it's 'sloppy'?"

"No," he said, his tone cold. "I meant your reaction was sloppy. I'd almost be embarrassed, if I didn't remember who'd been left to train you."

He held up his left hand and passed it over the windows. The view of downtown clouded over, and sidewalks and traffic appeared. *An illusion.* One that I couldn't have come close to matching. I could veil myself from most senses; that wasn't too difficult. But to actually bend light to create something that wasn't there, like a hologram—that was infinitely more difficult than what I did.

It was the sidewalk a few blocks away, where I'd been pushed into the path of the bus. And as I watched Jason's re-creation of the event on glass windows that were now some sort of mystical television, I saw how everything must have looked to outsiders. The little girl, the push, the way I'd stumbled in front of the bus, and then the way I'd gone flying back without the bus even touching me.

He held up his hand, and the image froze. "Don't you think the spell would have been much more effective if you'd channeled *all* that energy away from you? Instead of letting it throw you around?"

I couldn't believe I was hearing this. "You're critiquing my *near-death experience*?" Asshole, thy name is Father.

"Don't be so sensitive." He dropped his hand and the illusion faded. "If I'd known you were so poorly trained, I'd have—"

"What? What would you have done?" I snapped. "You don't know anything about me."

"I know *everything* about you," he replied, his tone going colder, if that was even possible. Another wave of the hand, and our log cabin in Montana appeared in the window. The view circled the building, stopping once there was a glimpse of movement at the rear of the house. Uncle John was on the back porch, rocking in that chair he loved.

"You've been spying on us?" This was all too insane to

process. The infamous Jason Thorpe was my father. He knew exactly where I'd been all along. And he was also some sort of stalker freak slash magical badass.

"I don't know what he was thinking," Jason said. "If you can't even control your powers, how in the world are you going to eliminate her?"

"Eliminate her? I just want her to leave us alone."

"Don't be naïve," he snapped. "You can't possibly think it's that easy."

"This is crazy," I announced. "I don't know what you think I'm here for … but he's wrong. I'm not going to be some pawn in your vendetta or whatever."

"Braden!" he snapped.

"Jason!" I retorted. "God, someone tried to *kill me* and the only thing you can say is 'well, sorry kid, but your magic sucks.' You're like some kind of psycho Little League parent."

"I don't know who you think you are," he said tightly, "but that tone is unacceptable."

"Well, accept it," I said. "Or don't. But I'm so over this."

He could have stopped me as I stormed out of the office. Lucien was with the secretary behind her desk, in the midst of some private conversation as I hurried past. "Lucien!" Jason's voice was a thunderclap from the office. I saw him pick himself up and slide back to his office. The door closed behind him just a few moments before the elevator doors opened and I could finally escape.

I kept my eyes closed on the way down, only now

remembering the images I'd seen in the reflections just a little while ago. Now what was I supposed to do?

¤　¤　¤

There was something about the city now, the way people scurried from shop to shop, to their minivans, and the way they carried their grocery bags. Everyone had a motive. Everyone had picked their side, but I couldn't tell one from the other.

The town's ruled by this feud. Everything Drew had said on the bus was right. Only now one of those warlocks was my father. Was this why Lucien wanted me to come back here?

Uncle John was safe, but I still wasn't sure what I was supposed to be doing. I'd come here to keep him safe, but this Catherine Lansing was still after me.

Everything was getting more complicated.

Twelve

I could have headed straight for the hotel, but I needed to pull myself together first. A sharp wind was coming in from the west and cutting right through me. I was shivering within a block.

Washington Street opened into a residential area the farther north I went. Old Victorian offices gave way to a neighborhood of southern belles—ancient-looking houses hidden behind their veil of iron-wrought gates.

Jason Thorpe is my father. It was hard to wrap my head around that one. I thought I understood, now, why Uncle John had never talked about his hometown. Who would want to remember growing up in the midst of some sort of battle. Was that why I'd grown up away from all of this? To hide me from Catherine Lansing?

Soon the old homes gave way to newer developments. I kept going. New houses like cookie-cutter outlines of the ones near them, all looking disposable and yet fresh.

"Braden?" Trey's voice shouted through my thoughts. It had started to drizzle, I realized, glancing down at the sidewalk in front of me. I turned toward the sound and saw Trey behind the wheel of a black Ford F-150. "What are you doing?"

It was almost like the rain was attacking me, the damp spots of my T-shirt darkening from red to *massacre*. "Walking."

"Come on. I'll give you a ride," Trey said, leaning his head out the window. A moment later, I saw him grabbing things off the passenger seat, tossing them in the back.

You barely know him, I reminded myself. I didn't think I even liked him. Well, other than the fact that I liked looking at him. "I'm fine. Don't need a ride. I'm going right up here."

He turned to look straight ahead and squinted. "Only thing up there is Sather Park. C'mon. It's going to start pouring any minute."

"I'm fine," I insisted.

The truck continued crawling along at my pace. "Even runaways need to take some help now and then," Trey said.

"I don't need a ride, Trey. Go on." I waved him on. *Everything's fine here. No big deal.* Even offered him a smile.

The truck didn't speed up, though. It parked. Right there, in the middle of the street. Trey slid out of the driver's seat and strode across. "Get in the truck," he demanded.

"And if I don't?" Everything else was too much to deal with. This was something more logical. Picking a fight with him would be so easy.

"What's with you?" he exhaled. "It's raining. You're going to catch the flu."

"I told you I didn't need a ride," I replied and nodded toward the truck. "Someone's going to hit you if you don't get back in. You can't just park in the middle of the road."

"It's not like I'm taking you to a remote spot out of town to carve out your liver."

I clenched my teeth and tried to focus. Deep, even breaths. Trey wasn't responsible for what was going on. It wasn't his fault.

The rain started picking up. I could fight this all day, but Trey looked like the stubborn type. "If I get in the car, will you leave me alone?" I said finally.

"Of course." He climbed back behind the wheel, seasoning the slam of his door with a muttered, "Idiot."

It was like the sky was waiting for me to agree to really unleash. All of a sudden it went from a growing rain to a downpour. I leapt into the passenger side, slamming the door harder than I had any reason to.

"Where are you going?" Trey's voice was terse. I glanced across the front seat and saw his knuckles tightening across the steering wheel.

"Anywhere." Anywhere would be better than here. Trey threw the car into gear, and the silence inside was only highlighted by the back-and-forth of the windshield wipers and the steady patter of rain.

The silence didn't last long. "You always give someone

a hard time for trying to help you out?" Trey's eyes never left the road, but he added, "Seatbelt."

"Free rides don't come cheap," I muttered.

"You get that from a bumper sticker? Or a fortune cookie?" There was a fraction of a smile on Trey's features now, just a hint of amusement.

I watched the streetlights as they started to churn to life. "It's true. Ever since I came here, everyone has got big plans for me. Like I'm some sort of game, and they see something they want."

"So change the game," Trey said simply. "Make your own rules. You already ran away once. Couldn't be that hard to do it again, could it?"

"I can't do that," I replied automatically. Then the thought started to turn over in my head. Why couldn't I?

"Learn to live with it, then." Trey drove just slightly over the speed limit, despite the rain coming down in torrents.

"Where are we going?" I didn't recognize any of the streets we were passing.

"Nowhere just yet," Trey said comfortably. "At least for now. I could drop you off at the bus stop if you really want."

"Maybe," I said, but I knew that wasn't an option either.

"What brought you here, Braden?" Something about the way Trey kept saying my name made me want to squirm. "Why Belle Dam?"

But it wasn't like I could tell him what was going on. I shook my head.

"If you don't want to talk about it, we don't have to." Trey's voice was gentle. It was almost like I'd imagined the arrogant side of him.

I didn't realize I'd started shivering until after Trey had reached over to the console and turned the heaters on. He didn't say anything.

"I don't even know what I'm doing most of the time," I said, my voice barely audible over the sound of the heaters.

As we neared the beach, in the distance I could see the potential in the swells that suggested more chaos to come. I settled against the headrest and watched the sights of Belle Dam as they whipped past. There wasn't a lot of town left to cover, but Trey continued to drive.

We passed by the lighthouse that stuck out against the point. With the weather the way it was, and the gray sky to frame it, it looked a little more like the one in my vision, but it still wasn't exact. Were all of those visions important?

Trey turned onto a cracked, paved road near there, taking us toward the beach. I straightened in my seat, trying to figure out where we were going. For a drive in the ocean?

"I come out here sometimes, when I need to think," he explained. He pulled into a small parking lot in the shadow of the lighthouse.

"I'm not a runaway," I said suddenly. I'm not sure why I said it.

Trey nodded after a moment. "Okay."

"I mean, I'm not *just* a runaway. It's ... complicated."

He didn't look at me, just watched the waves swelling and crashing over the breakwall. The rain started picking up, slamming against the windshield. It made me sleepy.

Everything had made sense when I was running away. Get away from Uncle John. Keep him safe. Stop whatever it was that was coming for me. But everything in Belle Dam was so much more complicated. First Lucien, now my father. And the woman who was apparently after me was my new friend's mother. I couldn't control the witch eyes, and Jason seemed to think Catherine was going to kill me unless I learned how to control them.

It was like coming here had made everything worse. And I still wasn't any closer to knowing what to do.

After a while, my focus turned from watching the waves with Trey, to watching him.

He's probably straight, my mind viciously chimed in out of nowhere. Something about him put me on edge but made me feel comfortable all at the same time. Like I could talk to him if I really needed to, and he'd listen. But at the same time, he looked at me sometimes, and my stomach dropped.

"Figured me out yet?" Trey asked in the silence. I jumped, hearing his voice again after such a long silence. Reading my mind so effectively.

"Maybe," I hedged. "Depends."

"On what?"

I looked away before he caught me staring at him. "If this is just an act or something. For my benefit."

He laughed. "I could say the same for you. Haven't you ever heard that expression about not trusting a man you can't look in the eye?"

Was that a real saying? Or was he making it up? "Well, you'll have to deal. But I mean, I don't know anything about you. You could be a vegetarian for all I know. And that's just not cool."

"Fair enough," Trey admitted. "What do you want to know?"

Anything I wanted to know? "What's with the hero complex?" I didn't know where it came from, but Trey did have a tendency to interfere in my life.

"Hero complex?" Trey was quiet for a moment, and then burst into laughter. "I don't think I have one, exactly."

"Far as I can tell, you do."

The laughter didn't last long. Quickly enough, Trey sobered up, and his voice matched the seriousness of his face. "I guess you just look like you need a friend."

"I've got friends," I said curtly.

"And you don't want more?" He flashed a smile I didn't return. "I mean it can't be easy with the eye thing, but I guess—"

"Wait. 'The eye thing'? Is this some sort of pity gesture? The poor, nearly blind kid needs a helping hand?"

All the frustration and anger that had been building up suddenly had another outlet. He felt *sorry* for me?

"Let me finish," Trey was saying, as patiently as he could muster. His knuckles went white against the dark steering wheel once more.

"I think you've said enough," I huffed.

"Please don't throw a tantrum in my car. I just cleaned it out the other day. Angst is a bitch to get out of leather," Trey added, completely deadpan.

The comment caught me off guard, long enough for the rational brain to kick back in. I started to laugh.

Even Trey cracked a smile. "I realized I was kind of a dick the other day. And you looked like someone kicked your puppy. I guess I could relate."

"You go to school?"

He nodded. "The community college. I've been messing around with getting a business degree."

"Rain's letting up," I observed. The storm wasn't over; this was simply the calm setting itself upon the land. "Can you drop me off by the square? I'm staying near there."

There was a moment of indecision that hung in the air. I was waiting for him to say what was coming, and he was waiting for me to say ... something. I could see the thoughts running through Trey's head, even if I didn't know what they were, exactly.

"How old are you, Braden?"

"Seventeen. I'll be eighteen in a few months." Only

seven months until March. It was close enough for me. "What about you?"

"Nineteen." The tension was slowly melting from the cab, like it had never happened. I'd missed something. Trey turned the engine over and started driving back into the town.

"You sure you're okay? You've got someplace to go?"

I looked out the window. A few people were hurrying out of buildings toward their cars, occasionally looking toward the sky in fear. "I told you, I'm okay. I'm staying at the Belmont."

He whistled. "Not bad." I glanced at him in confusion and he went on. "The Belmont's ... kinda pricey. Tourists don't mind paying for 'atmosphere.'"

"Oh."

He shifted gears, his attention focused on the road. Instead of stopping at the square, like I'd asked him, he drove straight up to the Belmont and pulled up against the curb. "Here." Trey pulled a card out of his wallet and scribbled something on it. "If you need anything, give me a call."

"I'll be fine."

"Not in this town," Trey muttered. "Just hold on to it. In case."

"Okay." It was an insurance agent's card, and on the back was Trey's number. I slipped it in my pocket, feeling it bend around the hotel key. And then a realization struck. There was something I needed to know. "So where is the

Belle Dam anyway? I haven't seen anything like that around here, and that's what the town's named after, isn't it?"

Trey laughed. "Good luck trying to find it. They tell kids around here that it's a secret dam hidden in the woods out west. But it's actually just French. Or at least it used to be. Belle Dame. It means 'pretty lady' or something."

Time to go. I hesitated once the door was open, glancing toward Trey. But everything I could think to say sounded stupid the moment it popped into my head.

I slammed the door and hurried away.

Thirteen

Before I even walked in the door the next morning, I ran into Jade. My first instinct was panic—like she'd somehow know who my father was.

"My new best friend has taste," she noted with raised eyebrows. But if she'd learned any secrets about me, they weren't showing on her face. I released my breath and tried for a smile. Maybe today wouldn't be so bad.

I stopped long enough for her to look over my outfit. Dark jeans, a dark blue T-shirt, and a button-up.

"You act like getting dressed is hard," I said with a laugh.

Her head shifted a bit to the side. "Someone hasn't been paying attention to some of the fashion disasters roaming our halls. It's like a Shakespearean tragedy in there some mornings."

"I think you're exaggerating a little bit," I said, but then I thought of Riley in her gypsy outfit yesterday. Or maybe not. I glanced down, suddenly unsure of myself. "You're sure it looks alright?"

"Not bad," she admitted. "But go with a lighter T-shirt

next time. Too dark with the glasses and the jeans." She shook her head. "Definitely not jeans. Go with khaki. Doesn't make you look like a pseudo-goth."

"Jeans make me look like a goth?" I wondered.

The look she gave me was blank. "Of course not. Stop getting sidetracked. You're as bad as Gentry. He didn't get the fashion gene, sad to say. So it's my sisterly duty to go through his wardrobe and burn everything I hate," she said, eyes twinkling. "I mean, he wears *flannel*."

I thought back to how many flannel shirts Uncle John and I had between the two of us. "Flannel can be comfortable," I said.

Jade threw her head back and laughed. "And whoever told you that fashion was comfort?" Case in point, Jade's outfit was a black pantsuit with all sorts of gold accents. Her hair was pulled back today, everything except that shocking streak of pink, which hung down over her face.

I shrugged. "Okay, no flannel. I don't think I even have any here." I hadn't seen any in the drawers at the hotel. So maybe Lucien knew what he was doing.

Jade was still eyeing me carefully. "Actually, that shirt's still a little big. Baggy clothes won't work on you. You're too small."

"I'm not small," I laughed, looking down at myself. "They're just new, that's all. A few washes, and they'll fit fine."

"We should go shopping soon. There's a few places with some really great stuff in town." she pushed.

"Sure." We entered through the front doors, and I

glanced around as if Riley would be just standing around waiting for me to show up.

"A bunch of us are going out tonight. You should come," she said. "It'll give you a chance to meet everyone."

I nodded. "Maybe. I'm still not sure what my plans are for tonight. But if I have time, then definitely." We split up after that, each heading to a different side of the school.

It's a conflict of interest being her friend. Nothing good will come of this. I tried to shrug off the dark thoughts and focus on finding Riley in the halls. Without any luck.

"Did everyone read the first three chapters of *The Sound and the Fury*?" I flinched in English, realizing that in all the drama of the night before, I'd skipped out on homework. That meant double tonight. "Who wants to tell us what's going on?"

I hoped and prayed she wouldn't call on me. The gods of Forgotten English Homework must have been listening, because she picked a girl in the front of the class. It was much the same in Algebra, when I didn't turn in the even-numbered problems from page twenty-four.

After class, I hung back. "I'm really sorry about the homework," I admitted to the teacher, a young blonde woman whose name I couldn't remember.

"You're already a week behind everyone else," she chided lightly. *Miss Masters.* The memory came to me suddenly.

"I know. It's just with getting here the day before yesterday, and then enrolling in school first thing in the morning, I kinda spaced on it last night."

Eventually, she nodded. "I don't want this to become a habit, Braden. I realize you've got some...extra considerations, but I've got to think about the rest of the class. I can't give you special treatment every time." She closed her lesson plan and slid it into the desk. "But turn it in tomorrow, and I'll overlook it this time. After that, any late assignment will be an automatic zero. Do you understand?"

I nodded with relief. "No problem. I'm not normally a slacker, I promise."

"I hope not," she said with a smile. "Now go on, you're going to be late for your next class."

The school was a bit easier to navigate the second day. The whole experience was underwhelming. A few of Jade's friends, who'd noticed us talking the day before, went out of their way to say hi to me, which was cool.

I finally spotted Riley making her way through the halls, swimming against the tide of students swarming toward the cafeteria. I waited for the herd to pass, and then started to follow her.

She headed back toward the far corner of the school, down the hall from where Jade and I had spent lunch yesterday. I almost passed her by when I caught just the glow of a computer screen in a darkened classroom.

"Riley?" I poked my head inside.

Newspapers lined the walls closest to the ceiling, the rest of the walls taken up by whiteboard with newspaper mockups posted on it. Riley was at one of the computer stations in the middle of the room. She nearly leapt out of her chair at the sound of her name. I bit back a smile.

"What are you doing here?" she asked, craning her neck in my direction.

I took a few steps into the room, looking over the mock-ups on the wall. A back-to-school issue. "I've been looking around for you all day, but it's like you're avoiding me."

She laughed. "Not hardly. I had a dentist appointment. I just got here a little bit ago." She swiveled her chair around and looked up at me. "So what's going on?" The mix of curiosity and suspicion in her voice was hard to miss.

"I was hoping you could fill me in on some stuff around here," I said, sitting in one of the chairs next to her. "You said you were an expert in local stuff."

"Depends on what you want to know."

I sighed. What *did* I want to know? There was already too much information clawing its way around my brain as it was. "I guess I just don't understand this whole feud thing everyone keeps talking about."

She nodded, tapping a pen against her lips.

I went on. "Everyone acts like it's like . . . war, but you go outside and it's just like any other small town. I mean, if things were really that bad, why would anyone live here?"

"It's not that simple," she said, as if that would put it all in perspective. "It's politics, and it's competition, and a whole lot of other things. But it's not war. At least not anymore."

"So things used to be worse?"

She nodded. "You have to read between the lines,

because they've always controlled the media here, but it's gotten bad before. And depending on who you talk to, it was somewhere between an old Western and a horror movie."

"But then what's it like now? Because everyone talks about it, but that's all it is. Talk." I tried not to think about my close, personal encounter with a transportation vehicle.

"It's like high school," she said simply. "On the one hand, you've got Jade and her friends, right?" She held up one hand as if to demonstrate. "And on the other is everyone that doesn't fit in. Either Jade doesn't like them, or their parents work for Mr. Thorpe.

"Jason and Catherine don't actually do all that much to each other. Remember, I told you how Drew always compared them to the mob? They're like the mob bosses. They'll step in when they have to, but most of the time it's the underlings that stir up trouble. Just like Jade doesn't have time to personally ruin every single student's life. Other people do her dirty work for her."

"Jade's not like that," I protested.

Riley lifted a shoulder. "You've known her a couple days. I've known her all my life. I've gathered a lot more empirical data than you have."

I shook my head, not wanting to hear this. Jade had been nothing but sweet to me since I'd met her. "But what about her mom," I asked, trying much too hard to be casual. "What's she like?"

Riley's eyes narrowed, and I realized I'd made a mistake. Apparently nothing passed by her without getting filed away.

But instead of pressing me about why I wanted to know, she answered my question instead. "Catherine is the nicest, most charming person I've ever met," she said, unexpectedly.

"What?" That was some kind of joke, right? My heart sank, and I was picturing my encounter with Jason last night. She was *nice*?

"Catherine's a politician. She knows how to put on a front and be this classy, sophisticated soccer mom," Riley said. "But she's not really like that at all. I've seen her blow up on people before . . . she's got a temper like you wouldn't believe."

The tightening feeling started to loosen. "So she's *not* a nice person," I asked, mainly for the sake of clarification.

Riley shrugged. "I'm sure if you're Jade's new BFF she's going to be the nicest person ever. But she's not the one you should worry about, Braden. Just be careful around Jade." She put her hand on mine, the bracelets clacking down her arm. "And don't fall for her, Braden. I wouldn't want to see what she does to you, too."

"Me?" The idea of falling in love with Jade was . . . completely alien.

Riley nodded. "Just trust me. Jade's great, but she gets bored easily. Boredom brings out the Lansing side of her."

I was about to ask her what she meant by that, when her phone rang. She glanced at the screen, and then held up her hand and hurried out of the room. I waited a few minutes for her to come back, but she never did.

¤   ¤   ¤

The headache started sometime after lunch. A low throbbing behind my eyes that felt like it was trying to shove them right out of my skull. My fingertips started tingling, and I started getting cold sweats.

Going through a migraine in the building wasn't an option. I wasn't sure of the exact protocol, aside from trying to explain what I was going through to the school nurse. And that would be a waste of time. Instead, I just grabbed the stuff I knew I needed for homework, and lugged my now-too-heavy bag outside.

The hotel wasn't far from the school, realistically. Nothing was "far" from anything else in Belle Dam; the town was too small. I called Lucien to see if he could get me excused, but the receptionist wouldn't pass my call through. She probably didn't know how.

She swore they'd take care of it, though. By the time I was in my room, worrying about school was the last thing on my mind. I pulled the curtains tight over the windows, then took it a step further and threw towels on top of them. Blocking out any sense of light whatsoever. A few pills for the headache, a nap, and a shower, and I'd be okay. I hoped.

I glanced at my cell phone, pressing my lips together to stop the shaking. My first instinct was still to turn to Uncle John and expect him to bail me out. I just needed to know I'd be okay. But while I tried to think of what to say, and how to say it, I started to drift off. I was asleep before I ever even opened the phone.

Fourteen

The first thing I did when I woke up was smack my hand against the phone next to me, sweeping it off the bed and onto the floor with a clack.

Fantastic. I reached up against the nightstand for my glasses and slid them on slowly. There wasn't any trace of pain left over from earlier, just an overwhelming sluggishness trying to pull me back down into sleep.

I leaned over the side of the bed and fumbled around for the phone. The room was pitch black, so it took awhile. Muttering annoyed protests at the inconvenience, I struggled up out of the warm, comfy bed and went for the windows.

After I was done pulling down the towels and opening the curtains, sunlight streamed into the room once again. It was good to know I hadn't slept the whole day away—just the school day.

I don't know what I was expecting when I dialed our number in Montana. Would he let me go over to voicemail? Or would he pick up the receiver only to slam it down again? I expected each of these and worse, so when Uncle John answered the phone like nothing had changed, I sat there in silence.

"Braden? What's wrong?" Uncle John's voice came through crystal clear, not even a hint of static across the line.

Every ounce of tension slid out of me, and I eased back into the still-warm bed. It was so good to hear his voice. "Hey," I said. A master conversationalist, I was.

"Are you okay?"

"Why didn't you tell me about any of this?" It slipped out, along with all the hurt and confusion I was feeling.

John didn't respond right away. "Lucien told me you're in school," he said carefully. "How do you like it?"

"Someone tried to kill me yesterday, and you're asking me about *school*?"

I heard him suck in a breath. "You all right?"

"I'm fine," I snapped. "But why didn't you tell me about this? About my father, about Catherine Lansing … any of it!"

He asked me a question instead. He softened. "Why did you run, Braden? What happened?"

"Would it kill you to answer even one of my questions?" I leapt off the bed and stalked to the window.

"It could," he said, and at first I thought he was joking. And then I realized he might not be.

"Uncle John?"

I heard bedsprings squeaking as John said, "Remember we're not the only thing out there in the dark, kid. There's a lot more to the world than witches and magic." A phone rang in the background, which didn't make sense because we only *had* the one phone, and he grunted. "Remember when we talked about when it's best to use tools for your magic?"

That was another difference between casting spells with just your will, and casting them with tools. The former used a lot more power, and that power called attention to itself. Ritual spells, meanwhile, could float under the radar. "Yeah, I remember."

"You probably haven't picked up anything, have you?"

I shook my head, not even considering that he couldn't see me. So finally I added, "No."

"There's a place on Fourth Street. It's called Gregory's 'Mix. Don't be shocked at what you're going to see."

Before I could say anything else, the phone went dead. Uncle John was gone.

¤   ¤   ¤

Most occult and New Age shops had an overly bright display of everything even remotely mystical. There were friendly people behind the counter full of good intentions and pseudopsychic vibes. And there was always, always a prominent display of pentacles and runes spread out throughout the building.

Gregory's 'Mix was none of those things. In fact, as far as I could tell, it wasn't even an occult store. There weren't any voodoo dolls hanging in the window, no elaborate knives or chalices displayed in the front window. The windows were reserved for names like Alan Moore and Frank Miller. Posters for comic book characters I'd seen on television, but never read, were plastered everywhere.

I had to have the wrong place. John had to be messing with me. If it hadn't been for the tingling at the corners of my eyes, a vibration in the air that suggested old magic, I might never have gone in.

The man behind the counter wasn't as young as the store itself would suggest. Comic book stores appealed to kids, or so I thought, and I figured whoever was working would be closer to my own age. At first I thought he was Uncle John's age, somewhere in his forties, but his novelty T-shirt and messy hair suggested younger. He had a laptop opened next to him, the screen turned away from me.

"Help you?" He had light gray eyes underneath his glasses, the color of the sky after a particularly strong storm had let up.

"This is just a comic shop?" I wasn't sure how to say 'Hey, is there magical contraband hidden in another room?'

The man's expression grew guarded. "It's *my* comic shop, if that's what you're asking." *Oh, so this is Gregory.* "But you need an adult for anything you're looking for. Unless it's the new Wolverine."

Well, that wasn't the reaction I was looking for. By far. "You have anything Old World?" I asked instead. It was a term I'd heard my uncle use before, an expression that was supposed to refer to the old days when magic and monsters had still walked the earth.

The man's expression intensified even more, but ultimately he shook his head. "No adult, no access. This is not the store you're looking for."

"But you have something," I pushed. I craned my head over the iron racks that held this month's comics, to look for a door, or an entrance. Nothing I could see.

The man turned back to his laptop and started typing furiously. "Another scoop for me. Haha, beat that Legendseeker10."

"Excuse me?"

"I wasn't talking to you," Gregory said loftily. "I'm talking about the S.A.C."

He sounded so serious, and so self-important, that it was probably not a good idea to laugh. My lips definitely twitched though, a lot. The sack? I'll admit, part of me wanted to snicker. "The, uh, what?"

"Belle Dam's Supernatural Apparitions Committee," Gregory said. "Maybe you haven't figured it out yet, but there's more to this sleepy little hamlet than what you can see."

"Oh." A website about the weird in Belle Dam? This I'd have to see. "Right. Anyway, I need to get into that back room," I said, trying to turn the conversation back around. I had a feeling that if I let Gregory go, he'd ramble on for an hour about how awesome he was.

"Like the fact that I've got a witch standing in my

shop right at the moment. Most witches know better than to come here."

Sonofabitch. I whipped around, to see how many other people had heard the declaration. Seriously, was there something on my shirt? Some giant sign on my back?

But no one else in the store seemed to be paying any attention. "Don't go freaking out. I have a friend on the outside, lets me know when anyone *interesting* comes to town."

The only person who knew about me being a witch, besides Lucien and Jason, was Drew. "If you know what I can do, then you know I can handle what's back there," I pushed. The urge to do something pretty bad to Gregory was growing every time he opened his mouth.

"I haven't even Googled you yet," Gregory chuckled with surprise. "I don't know anything about you."

"Just what Drew told you about me, right?"

Gregory's eyes narrowed before he inclined his head. "What's your name, anyway?"

"Braden." I relented. Only slightly.

"Sorry, Braden. No adult, no access." Gregory turned back to his computer and didn't look up again.

I sighed in annoyance. Freaking figures. I was walking out of the shop when inspiration struck. I grabbed my phone and scrolled through the tiny handful of numbers.

"Hey, are you busy? I kinda need your help."

¤   ¤   ¤

Gregory looked up when I came back twenty minutes later, but didn't say anything. Just a slight shake of his head.

"He's with me, Gregory. It's okay. I'll take full responsibility." I turned to watch Trey follow me inside. He'd said an adult. He didn't specify how old of one.

Gregory's expression didn't waver, but he jutted his head toward the back. "Your mother know about him yet?"

Trey winced, but recovered swiftly. "Don't know what you mean. He's just a friend."

I could see the wheels in Gregory's head start turning, the way his eyes narrowed at the two of us. He opened his mouth, and I was sure he was going to say something even worse than normal stupidity. The word "witch" was going to hit the air, and Trey would never look at me the same way again.

"Well, I'm going back then if it's all settled," I said quickly, shaking my head enough that my glasses started to slide down my nose. I was rather proud of the movement, as it lacked the dramatic implications but got the job done. Freed my eyes enough that when I glanced at Gregory, I had enough time to slam the spell into place before the words slipped out of his mouth.

Gray and black and silver, shades all too different from one another for there to be any blurring. A silence spell, one that John had used with glee when I was younger. It barely required any thought at all—I'd seen the spell often enough that even without my vision, I could duplicate it.

There was nothing but blissful silence as I followed

Trey into the back room, hidden in a corner I hadn't noticed before. I pushed the glasses back up my nose, glancing over at Gregory as I did so. His mouth opened and closed several times, and then he resorted to furious typing at the keyboard as we left the room.

"You really believe in all this stuff?" Trey asked, flipping through a box of quartz crystals set up near the landing. The door had opened onto a stairway. The second floor of Gregory's 'Mix was devoted entirely to the supernatural. Books lined the walls, and it was pretty much every cliché I could have thought of. There were even authentic voodoo dolls hung up on one portion of the wall, complete with an authentic price tag: $49.95.

"Sure, I guess. Everything's got a spirit," I said lightly. "You don't have to babysit, you know. I'm fine on my own."

Trey glanced up at me from the voodoo dolls. "Sure you are," he said.

"I am," I repeated, trying to sound more stern.

"I'm not arguing," he said, holding up his hands in a classic "I surrender" pose. His smile, however, was more mischievous than anything else. It was almost like there were two different Treys—the one I met that first morning, and the one who gave me a ride home yesterday. I didn't like how quickly he could annoy me, either.

I busied myself picking up some of the essentials. Clove oil, sage, and some candles. Things that could be used in a wide variety of spells with a minimum of effort. Uncle John was clearly worried about me using too much "big magic" and attracting unwanted attention. A fair assessment, all things considered.

I added a small vial of sea salt to my collection. "So what did he mean, about your mother?" Did Trey know more than I thought?

It got so quiet that I thought Trey had left the room. He was standing on the far side of the room, looking out the window. "My mom's ... selective about who I spend my time with. She thinks I'll jeopardize my future."

"Why would hanging out with me jeopardize your future?" That was an easier explanation, at least, but it still didn't make any sense. Or did it? "Wait. Let me guess, you've got a habit of trying to pick up strays, right?"

"Something like that," he said, the tension easing between his shoulders, although he was staring hard at me.

I wish I knew what you were thinking. The staring made me uncomfortable, and I turned away, but it became hard to concentrate on anything. I thought I could still feel his eyes on the back of my neck. I started downstairs, figuring he'd follow when he was ready.

There was a girl behind the counter now, and no sign of Gregory. Or his laptop. She smiled broadly at the two of us. No, she was smiling broadly at Trey. She hadn't even noticed me.

She was the kind of girl that should do skin commercials. Or was voted Prom Queen. Or was doing skin commercials while being voted Prom Queen. Her hair was a deep chestnut, where mine was just brown, and she smiled a lot more than I probably ever did. I wanted to dislike her instantly, but no one in their right minds ever disliked this girl, I figured.

"Haven't seen you around here in a while, stranger," the girl said, tossing her hair to one side, like in a shampoo commercial.

"Hey, Kayla. You know how school is, keeps us busy." I looked up to see Trey shifting his weight from one foot to the other, looking at Kayla and then looking away.

That answers one question, I muttered to myself. At that moment, I wanted nothing more than to finish buying my stuff and get out of there.

As much as she might have rather spent her time mooning over him, Kayla added up my purchases quickly and recited the total. I handed her one of the credit cards Lucien had given me, interested to see if it actually worked.

She swiped the card in the little credit card machine and handed me one of the slips that printed out. I signed it, slid it across, and grabbed my bag of goodies. Rather than intrude on what was clearly a private conversation, I headed for the door.

I was almost a block away by the time Trey caught up with me. "Old friend?" I asked, hating the neutral sound in my voice.

"I've known Kayla all my life. She works for her uncle to help pay for school. It's just her and her mom now."

"She's pretty."

"She's gorgeous," Trey corrected.

Of course she was.

"So you get mixed up with Lucien Fallon, and then the next day you're going shopping at the Oogie Boogie store? You sure you know what you're getting into, Cyke?" There was an irreverent charm to the way he chewed on the piece of gum he'd popped in sometime between the store and catching up with me.

"Not entirely," I admitted. "'Cyke'?"

"Like Cyclops? From the X-Men?"

I knew what he was talking about, but only because I'd seen the movies. There hadn't been a lot of comic books growing up with Uncle John. "What's wrong with Braden? It's been working for me all my life."

"Everyone gets to call you Braden," he said, flashing me a wicked smile that was like a punch in the gut. "I'm the only one calling you Cyke, right?"

"You realize you're annoying, right?"

Trey's smile was brightly comfortable. "I've heard that once or twice."

I shook my head and wrapped the bag tighter around my palm. "Do you listen to yourself sometimes? Or ever? And why are you following me? You got me in, and I'm thankful, but that's it." *Stop trying to decide whether you want to annoy me or dazzle me.*

"I work down the street." Trey's humor vanished. "Besides, I like trying to figure you out."

"I'm an open book," I said flatly. "Really."

"Maybe in Latin. Or Arabic. But you're not as easy to

read as you seem to think." His eyes were thoughtful. "And you don't hate talking to me as much as you pretend."

I was sorely tempted to point out that at least I could read Latin. Trey was just one more person who thought they had me figured out. Maybe he didn't get the same memo from Drew that Gregory did, but that didn't stop him from making assumptions. "I need to go."

I didn't stop to see if Trey followed. Instead, my cell phone chimed, and I answered Jade's call.

Fifteen

I agreed to hang out with Jade and her friends, but I absolutely had to get home early enough to catch up on my homework. Second day at a real school, and it was already getting all screwed up.

An hour later, I had showered and changed. Hanging out with people my own age was a lot more intimidating than getting locked up in a binding circle. What if I said the wrong thing? Or made the wrong comment? What if they hated me?

I didn't even notice at first that she pulled up in the same car she'd had the day before. "Isn't your brother going to notice?"

She shrugged. "He loves me too much to say anything. At least that's the plan."

I chuckled and pulled open the passenger door.

"Rough day?" Jade asked. "You skipped out kinda early."

"Migraine. I went home and slept it off." For a few minutes we chatted about school. It wasn't until we skimmed past the quickly changing light that I remembered getting into a car with Jade was yet another bad decision I'd made this week.

"God, I can't wait to get out of here," she muttered at random.

I looked at her over the rim of my cup. "It's not really so bad, is it? Don't the Lansings get to walk around town and do whatever they want?"

Jade glanced at me, and I could tell she wasn't amused. "You won't understand."

"What?"

Another light turned red, but this time Jade didn't try to squeeze through at the last second. She stopped, and turned toward me. "You don't know what it's like. My mother walks around this town like she's some sort of celebrity, and everyone around her is so fake. I don't want to grow up like that."

You wouldn't understand. It was like a punch in the gut. A reminder that Jade wasn't *just* my friend, but she was also supposed to be my ... archnemesis or something.

Luckily, Jade wasn't one to bemoan her fate for too long. "So, about homecoming. I know just who you should go with." Jade darted between lanes to pass a red SUV. As we cut in front of the soccer mom driving, I heard a loud honking behind us.

I turned to look, grateful for the distraction. "I'm not interested," I said. The last thing I wanted was to get roped into going to some dance with one of Jade's girlfriends.

School dances were one of the things about high school that *didn't* interest me. The fact that I didn't have a clue how to dance only reinforced that.

"Well, I'm already planning on taking K.C., so it's only fair if we focus on your date."

I shifted in my seat, pulling myself closer to the door. Anything for a closer exit.

"If you think it's going to be a big deal, then don't worry about it. Every year a couple girls end up going together because they can't get dates. I really doubt anyone would care who your date is."

"Uhm … what?"

Jade beamed a patient smile in my direction. "Braden? Have you even *tried* looking down my shirt? Or even real- ize that it's cut low?" She was right; the white chemise she was wearing exposed a lot of skin. "So like I said, I know the perfect guy for you. Don't worry, I'll set everything up."

"I don't want to talk about this," I said quickly, before she went any further. I could feel my face getting redder and redder. Nothing had been said about having the gay talk tonight, and I was completely unprepared.

"Braden, it's not that big a deal. I mean, the fact that my new best friend keeps secrets from me is a little hurt- ful, but I'll get past it in time." She glanced over at me, but I was too busy having hot flashes and rising levels of panic to catch her teasing tone.

"I already said I don't want to talk about this. Okay? So just drop it."

The minute she pulled into parking lot, I threw the car door open and walked off. For a second I wished I smoked, so I could have an excuse to just stand out here and watch traffic pass.

¤   ¤   ¤

By the time I finally walked inside the clothing boutique Jade had gone into, I was stuck between wanting to keep freaking out and hoping Jade would forgive a little temporary insanity. No one had ever just come out and outed me like that.

"Took you long enough." Jade was standing near the door, holding a dress up against her frame. She pivoted to one side, and then the other, her eyes never leaving their spot on the mirror. "You should know I don't like to shop by myself. I buy all sorts of things I shouldn't."

"Invite someone else next time, then." Angst Boy wins again. Ashamed Boy knocked out in the first round. I winced the moment the words were out of my mouth.

Her expression was cool when she turned, her face a chiseled mask of ice. "Did I ask to be the target of your identity crisis?"

She wasn't wrong. "Sorry." Trying to cope with everything that was going on was getting to me.

"Look. Obviously I'm the last person to judge anyone. If you're not ready to talk about it, then don't. Just don't turn into that overcompensating repressed guy, okay?" There wasn't putting much past Jade. She saw things in her own way, but she definitely saw through me, too. She vanished into a dressing room and came out a few minutes later clad in her latest conceit.

"Can't we just chalk it up to a bad day, and leave it at that?" I'd much rather focus on doing things that a seventeen-year-old should be doing.

Jade's expression was pensive, her lips pressed together, her smoky eyes narrowed. "I think that depends."

"On?"

Her face relaxed, eyes now burning with humor. "Does this dress make me look fat?"

¤　　¤　　¤

An hour and far too many purchases later, Jade and I abandoned our things in her car and headed for one of the local coffee shops. "The only place that's worth it around here, unless you want to drive an hour for Starbucks," she admitted.

I already knew the coffee shop she had mentioned by reputation. Their Styrofoam cups were a mainstay all around school, as students hustled to get their morning fix before the first bell struck. Only seniors were allowed to leave campus during lunch, but that didn't stop the enterprising lower classes from trying to sneak off for some caffeine.

Jade walked around the school like she owned it. Life in the coffee shop was much the same. It was weird to walk in beside her, and see people come up to us or shout out a hello. It wasn't even like she fought her way to the top; it was just that everyone else took a step back for her. Must come with being a Lansing. Instant love and adoration.

She led me toward the back, where a group of her friends were already slouched along a number of couches. One of the girls I hadn't seen before looked up.

"The blind kid?" she said skeptically to Jade.

"You think every guy not into you is blind anyway, Laney. What's one more?" Jade said lightly.

I slowed. Hanging out with Jade was one thing, but socializing with her sycophants and hangers-on was a bit much. She lowered herself down onto the couch like a debutante.

"Scoot over, Carter, give him space," Jade said to the boy next to her. The guy, proudly clad in his letterman's jacket, shot me a dirty look but did as she asked.

"You're the guy Riley was trying to get into journalism," another girl mentioned. Her smile was uncertain, but friendly—the "I don't know if he can really see me or not" discomfort. It was familiar. I quickly learned her name was Brooke, and she was the resident brain of Jade's little coterie.

"I guess," I muttered, taking a seat next to Jade. She grinned my way and slapped her hand down on my knee.

It seemed to be enough. I stayed quiet while they gossiped about the new school year. Who had done interesting things over the summer, which teachers were already in hyperactive detention mode, and where the parties were going to be.

"I'm already looking forward to the Halloween party

Tanner's throwing. Remind me again why you're not having one, Jade?" Laney said while ripping apart the muffin in front of her. There was something wrong with the top layer of the muffin though, because that half got discarded while she picked at the rest.

"I'm so over parties this year," Jade said. "Everyone expects something bigger and better than last year. I've got enough on my plate."

"We've got homecoming coming up too," Laney replied, while the jock chimed in with, "Maybe that's one game we'll win this season."

Everyone seemed to laugh at that. As I found out, the football team was one of the few that hadn't seemed to flourish since the school had gained a benefactor in Jason Thorpe. Jade rolled her eyes at the mention of his name, quickly and deftly slipping a change of topic in front of them like some sort of sleight-of-hand magician's trick.

"Braden still has to tell us what he thinks of our fantastic school," she announced with a sly smile. "And don't forget compliments. Everyone likes them. And by everyone, I mean me."

Way to put me on the spot, Jade. "Well, my new friend Jade is pretty awesome. And has a great eye for fashion." Uhm. I wasn't sure what else to say, aside from compliments for Jade. "School's okay, I guess. It's my first, so I'm not really sure what to compare it to."

Laney snorted. "You've never been to a real school

before? So you're one of those homeschooled religious freaks?"

Before I could say anything, Jade stepped in. "Actually? If you weren't trying so hard to come across as the stereotypical bitchy cheerleader, Lane, maybe you'd notice a few things." Jade's eyes narrowed conspiratorially, and she leaned forward. "New boy's got his own Black card."

I wasn't completely out of the loop. I knew what a Black card was, and I definitely didn't have one of those. But Jade met my confusion with a slow wink and a hint of a smile.

Laney sat back, opened her mouth once, and then immediately closed it.

Brooke stepped in to save the day. "So Braden, how about that physics homework?"

¤   ¤   ¤

The next morning went by like a blur. I thought I aced the English quiz, after Jade had explained what was really going on with all the stream of consciousness we'd had to read the night before.

The next two classes were simple enough. But as I was walking outside of the history classroom, I glanced at a mirror that was framed against the wall—just to make sure my hair wasn't doing anything to antagonize me randomly. It did that sometimes.

The hair was fine, and I was starting to look more well rested since coming to Belle Dam. At least some of the tension wasn't showing on my face. Just as I was about to step away, though, I saw the shadow out of the corner of my eye. I stopped immediately, instantly jostled by a pair of girls behind me who hadn't expected a sudden obstacle to their escape.

I focused my sight out of the corner of my eye. The moment I did, the colors sharpened intensely, but not nearly as bad as when my eyes were uncovered. In the reflection, there was nothing. No shadow, just a white-faced teenager with a nearly comical look of shock across his face.

I hurried out of the room and headed down the halls. I'd seen it twice in under a week. It wasn't magic, so what was it? I'd seen countless different symbols and images in the visions, and usually knew right away what they meant. Not this. It didn't make any sense.

At the end of the hall was a classroom with the lights off. Riley had explained yesterday that the school was bigger than the students it housed. There were numerous rooms that never got used because there was really no need. I just hoped this was one of those rooms.

The minute the door was shut, my mind was already opening to all the ways to handle this.

I walked with a purpose toward the blackboard, pulling two long sticks of chalk off the tray and studying the desks as I headed for the back of the room. No good—the wood was covered in some sort of enamel. Any magic I wove through the desk would dissipate right through the chemicals. Magic liked nature. They were symbiotic.

Finally, near the back, I found an older desk where the wood was polished but untreated. Perfect.

I focused on the door, narrowing my eyes. I pictured the lines of magic weaving across the door, intangible but full of blue and gold energy. *I don't need to be in here after all,* the magic said. Over and over again, I rewove the spell, centering it on the doorknob. The more focus I put into it, the stronger the spell. "Hide me from those who seek entrance," I murmured, the words focusing the magic into a final snap that seemed to hang in the air.

The shadow tugged at my memory, an image of grain-like darkness, like black sand or obsidian shavings. Images were fairly common—a spectral butterfly that hung invisible in the air might whisper of the old altars that had once covered that ground, or a ghost might mutter about how tragically he had died. There was always something to be learned. But the shadow kept its secrets well.

I reached up, grasping my fingers around the cool plastic of the sunglasses. I could do this. It would be okay. The glasses slid free, revealing the world as it truly was.

Reams of rose petals fluttered in the air, shades of how can he not see that I'm alive evergreen spotted with disease I love my job but they think they know everything so horrid little sexed up harlots smile and console don't let them see the scarlet flames that still lingered in the air, a smoke that contained lines of magical fire.

With my eyes free I felt only a moment of unburdened relief, but everything rushed forward, a thousand voices trying to claw themselves back into life. Any place well used was always more jagged and harsh than someplace remote.

"Someone used magic in here, a long time ago," I whispered to myself. The traces were faint—whoever it was had had an incredible control. It couldn't have been a student. Even I could only manage a fraction of that skill. They hadn't wasted an ounce more power then they'd needed to.

That wasn't the point of being here, though. I had to focus on the shadow. The chalk clattered to the ground under my outstretched hand, and I pressed down on it, forcing it to snap.

I couldn't quite pull off an illusion as complicated as the one Jason had performed, but I could improvise. Between the chalk and the desktop, I had enough to bind the magic I was planning to call forth. The chalk to turn thought into vision, and the wood of the desk to make it solid, to bring it into focus.

"Forces of the earth," I whispered, "awaken and come forth." I used the words to draw the magic to me, shaping it through the elements I planned to use. The most common place to draw power for the stronger spells was from the earth. There was a wellspring there that any witch could tap into. If they just asked nicely.

I channeled the magic into the pieces of chalk, which began to dissolve in front of me. From there, I pushed it upward, weaving it through the wood desk. As the chalk swirled through the flows of the spell, they began to sparkle, turning to tiny shards of color that began to coalesce. Light grew until my memory of the elevator in Lucien's office was right there on display in front of me, an illusion drawn straight from my mind.

Using my hands, I manipulated the memory brought to life. I pushed to the left, and the image shifted further that way. Pulled my hands closer, and it focused on a smaller section of the shadow.

The image was roughly the quality of a projected screen, though it hung in midair. A dark spot, more defined than I'd realized before. It was roughly oval shaped, turned on its side. Almost like an eye.

sixteen

"All this melodrama, and me without my camera," Lucien said.

I'd waited until the school day was over, hesitant to skip and cause any more waves. None of my teachers even seemed impressed that I turned in the homework along with everyone else.

Candy wasn't at her desk when I walked off the elevator. I hadn't known where else to go—it wasn't like Jason had given me a Bat-signal to get in touch with him or anything.

Lucien gestured to one of the chairs across from him. "Have a seat. And give me a little more context on what you're talking about."

"I think Catherine's spying on me," I said, repeating the same thing I'd said the moment I walked through his door.

My father's lawyer sat on the corner of his desk and feigned interest. "And why come to me with this fascinating little tidbit? I can't exactly file a cease and desist on the megalomaniacal super-witch based on a hunch, now can I?"

I ignored his sarcasm. "I've been seeing this . . . thing. This shadow."

"Now you're seeing things," he sighed. "How fortuitous."

"Mind if you hold the sarcasm until I'm done?" I wasn't exactly snapping at him, but I tried to be a little more forceful. "I've seen it at least twice now. Once, the first time I was here, in the elevator on my way up. And then again in school today."

Lucien went still. "Fascinating," he said under his breath. "Simply fascinating."

"So I need to know anything else you know about Grace Lansing. About the witch eyes."

It had made perfect sense to me a couple of hours ago. If Catherine *was* spying on me, then the only way I'd be able to really see where and when was if I could find a way to control my powers. And since Lucien was the one who'd told me about Grace, he was the only source I knew.

"'Witch eyes'?" Lucien pulled himself up off the desk and sauntered back around his desk. "I love the name. It has a bit of poetry, don't you think?"

"Then what would you call them?"

He looked surprised, and I watched him choose his words carefully. "The stories never said Grace had a name for them. She called it her Sight. But if I had to make a guess it would be that history is filled with all sorts of 'special' eyes. The Eye of Horus. The Eye of Providence. Maybe all those stories share a common origin."

"So you think it's happened before?"

"I've seen your father do any number of impossible things," he said. "And didn't you recently survive contact with a speeding vehicle?" He shook his head, making a cluck-cluck sound with his tongue. "Who knows the breadth of powers and abilities born into this ignorant world?"

If there have been others, someone had to figure out a way to control them. "There has to be a record somewhere about her, doesn't there? I couldn't find anything in the library."

"I doubt you would." The lawyer's lips twisted. "I'm afraid that woman took her secrets to the grave. Which, unless you have some skill in raising the dead, makes her a little difficult to contact."

Summoning the dead. Uncle John had always said the dead shouldn't be disturbed, but he slipped up once and mentioned a time when he'd tried—and failed—to summon a spirit. It required an incredible talent.

I could do it, I bet. I could ask Grace how to control the visions. "How'd she die? I'm surprised there's not some big story about that, too. Belle Dam's got stories for everything else, right?" I laughed it off, but my mind was already whirling—figuring out just how I'd manage to cut a hole into the world of the dead.

"No one knows for certain," Lucien murmured. "But they built her a quaint little monument down at Angel's Respite Cemetery. It can't be missed." If he knew what I was planning, he didn't let it show. Then again, there wasn't much that Lucien did show. The man had a poker face like none other.

I wasn't sure what I should do next. But maybe Grace could give me some ideas.

"Mr. Fallon," Candy simpered as she strode into the office, stopping abruptly when she saw me. "What are *you* doing here?" she asked, in this perfectly bitchy, contemptuous tone. "What is *he* doing here? He doesn't have an appointment." This was some sort of violation in her strange little world.

"Are we done, Braden?" Lucien glanced down at his watch. "I believe I've told you all about how important my schedule is."

I rolled my eyes, grabbing my bag and throwing it over my shoulder. "Just be sure to water your skank," I said as I passed him. "She's looking a little shallow." It was a completely inappropriate thing to say, but I walked out of his office with a smile.

¤　　¤　　¤

I forced myself to finish my homework before considering plans to raise the dead.

It's not like I'm nervous, I thought a few hours later, staring up at the ceiling. Just that this was a few steps beyond the normal kinds of spells I knew. It required a proper amount of thought and deliberation.

Which was how I found myself wandering the streets of Belle Dam in search of distractions when Trey called.

It shouldn't have surprised me the way he invited himself along, and then decided we were going to a pizza parlor for dinner. Mostly because the minute I got on the phone with him, I forgot I had a brain of my own.

Half an hour later we were a few blocks from downtown, in a tiny little Mom and Pop store that was sparsely lit and uncomfortably warm when we walked in.

"It's good stuff, I promise," Trey said. "Not quite the best in town, but it's definitely a close second."

The waiter led us to one of the tables against the window, giving us a view of the street. "So where's the best?" I asked a few minutes later. When the waiter came back we ordered, compromising on half pepperoni and half extra cheese.

"Closed down a few months ago," Trey said as he turned to focus his attention out the window. I watched a muscle in his jaw start to flex. "The owners had to leave town."

I didn't press the issue. I may have been dying to know more, but two things were clear. The topic was upsetting Trey, and it definitely had something to do with the feud.

Small talk was attempted, but Trey's head had gone somewhere else. I tried to apologize for whatever it was that I'd said, but it didn't register. After that, the conversation grew more and more stilted.

Our food arrived ridiculously fast. It was like some sort of angel glanced down and realized that our table had been overinflated with Awkward Conversation. Pizza proved to be the perfect remedy.

"Quit hogging the pepperoni," Trey chided, reaching over to snag the pizza slice I'd just grabbed and pulling it back to his side of the table. He replaced it a minute later with a piece from the other half of the pizza, only cheese. Extra cheese.

"Hey, I was the one who wanted it," I protested, debating whether or not to fight him for the slice. I decided not to. "You're the weirdo who wanted only cheese."

"Yeah, well I figured you wouldn't have gone for the jalapenos or black olives."

I shrugged. "Maybe those are my favorites," I said lightly.

"Yeah, right," he smirked, letting the cheese from one slice dangle between his lips. Like he was taunting me. "So tell me about school."

Did I get signed up for the Big Brother program the minute I walked into town or something? Besides, I definitely didn't want Trey to be my big brother. "It's okay. Harder than I thought it'd be. The work's not so bad, but there's a lot."

"Any friends yet?" What was with the sudden interrogation?

"A ... a few." I needed to stop focusing on the way cheese slid around the curve of his lips, or the way his eyes twinkled when he thought he was being cute. Not to mention the way veins sprang to life in his hands when he moved too suddenly, straining against the skin. Strong hands.

"Braden?"

"Huh? What? Sorry?" I could have smacked myself in the face. My brain had reacted all at once, throwing anything out there that might be an acceptable answer.

It was wickedly hot in the pizza place, but Trey's all-too-aware expression didn't show an ounce of it. Did they not believe in air conditioning or something? I put my pizza back down, grabbing one of the napkins and scrubbing furiously at all the grease staining my fingertips.

"I said it must be pretty hard. New school, and trying to make friends." Trey's face went puzzled for a second before he pulled his cell phone out of a pocket, and I heard it buzzing. "Sorry, thought it was off."

He flipped the phone open, after giving the screen a glance. "Hey. Yeah, no I can talk. I'm not doing anything." I sat back, feeling the words like a slap. I watched as his eyes narrowed and he pushed his plate away. "How long ago," he demanded suddenly.

I thought he was talking to me for a second, and I froze. Did he know something? "Yeah, I'll be there in a little bit. Just try to keep an eye out, okay?"

He snapped the phone shut and started to scoot out of the booth. "Sorry, something came up. You'll be all right?" He didn't wait for me to answer, just pulled out his wallet and threw bills down onto the table. I don't think he even looked at them when he did it.

"Uhm, what?"

"Just . . . something I have to take care of. You're going to be alright, right?" Trey paused all of a sudden. "You remember that guy Drew, right? You haven't seen him lurking around town or anything, have you?"

"I thought you two were friends," I said automatically, although I knew there was more to the story than that.

"We went to school together," Trey said, as if that was the same thing.

"So, you're *not* friends," I pushed.

"Look, I don't have time for all this," Trey said, getting sharp. "Have you seen him or not?"

I crossed my arms, and for the thousandth time tried to figure out who Trey was. "Not," I said coolly.

He winced. Maybe he realized he was being a dick. "Look, I'll talk to you later, Braden. Stay out of trouble, okay?"

Watching him rush out of the restaurant, and sitting there with half a pizza left in front of me, I realized something else about Belle Dam. Boys suck no matter where you live.

¤   ¤   ¤

It was a half hour before midnight, and I'd packed my school bag with supplies, read my journal a few dozen times, and changed outfits at least twice. I'd finally settled on a thick sweater and a pair of jeans.

There was no one in the hotel lobby when I snuck out of the building. The lights had all been dimmed, leaving it looking somber and nearly asleep. It was almost as though everyone in the world was gone. I was the only one.

Something howled in the distance. It sounded like a wolf, but that was impossible. There weren't wolves for hundreds of miles. *Just some dog with delusions of grandeur.*

It wasn't hard to break into the cemetery. A small stone wall set it apart from the street, but it barely reached my waist. It probably did a fantastic job keeping the kindergarteners out, though. I hopped over and slid between the folds of old stone and grave moss.

Lucien had said the monument couldn't be missed. But if anyone could miss it, it would probably be me. I avoided the paths winding through the graveyard, preferring to stick more in the hidden shadows between old crypts and giant statues.

It took nearly ten minutes before I saw the Lansing name gleaming under the passing glow of nearby streetlights. Where two paths met and divided, creating a three-way intersection, there was a large stone pillar. It reminded me of the Washington Monument, and the Lansing name was etched across the front. And below that, something like a rolled piece of parchment was carved into the rock.

"Know that not every door will open to the proper key."

"The hell does that mean?" Another link to keys. Grace's fascination with them transcended death, too, apparently.

I closed my eyes and sank to my knees. It had been a long time since I'd tried anything so severe.

I pulled out the supplies I'd brought, unrolled the corded tassel into a circular shape, poured out a bottle of water over it, and sprinkled some salt over both. Using tools might help me keep control if the spell went haywire. If I'd learned anything in my seventeen years, it was the little things. Don't go ripping holes in the spirit world without some restraints.

I held my hands apart, drawing the magic forth. Quicker than expected, pressure rose from beneath me. Almost like it had been waiting for this. Below my glasses, energy spilled forth in dark greens and ambers, spectral lights that spun.

The power was rising fast. Almost too fast. I hesitated, wondering whether or not to lose the glasses. Without them, it felt like there were no limitations. I could do whatever I wanted with the magic, but everything came out too strong.

The circle I'd crafted in the ground pulsed with the energies—colors that merged and crashed apart as careless tides. It began to spill outward, spinning faster and growing larger each second.

I felt something I couldn't see, some sort of timbre in the earth. Rumbling. Approaching. I hesitated only a moment, long enough to wonder what else I'd drawn from within the ground. And then I remembered my vision, and the monsters I'd seen clawing their way out of the dirt.

The circle grew warm and there was a sound like a coyote's howl heard through a cascade of water. "Bring her forth!" I called. "Come forth, Grace Lansing!"

The lights grew faster, blending together until I couldn't see anything but light. The wind picked up, circling around me like a tornado. Any stronger and it would pluck me from the ground and hurl me into the sky. I pressed my hands against the dirt as though that would hold me here. *Just a few more minutes, just until the spell is done.*

But the energy kept pouring forth. More and more, it kept growing. The spell I was weaving bulged and strained against the edges of my circle. Underneath the tide of magic, something else was unraveling.

In a matter of seconds, the perfect spell was changing, transforming itself into something else. There wasn't time to think about it; I threw the glasses off and stared into the heart of the maelstrom.

Betrayer. Vandal. Savage darkness boiling under the sky is falling and silver defiance where there is nothing but pain and remorse like sickly green ashes touching the sky to draw the black fires from the heart.

A thousand different women screamed with a single voice as the impressions crashed down around me.

Magic that had been crystal and wind was pulling open something that had been locked away. The spell had triggered it, ripping it from slumber and unleashing it into my magic. Dark taints swirled inside, quickly spreading.

It was a trap.

Something had been hidden here, waiting for someone to try invoking the spirit of Grace Lansing. Her monument was booby trapped, and I didn't have a clue what this new spell was trying to do.

I tried holding out my arms, tried to rip each bit of shadow from the spell. But with every pull, every weed I plucked out of the whole, more grew in its place.

Something golden easily pierced the swirl of magic surrounding me, a shimmering flurry of energy that leapt in one side and out the other. A moment later, something huge shot over my head, barely missing the top of Grace Lansing's monument. I saw a glimpse of paws, and then it was gone.

The spell was growing more unstable by the second. Shards of obsidian fractured the warmth, leaving only a bone-chilling cold in its wake. "Banish it!" I screamed, the wind's fury matching my fear by picking up and ripping the words from my throat. But trying to stop this magic was like holding back the ocean.

The storm is coming. I knew with absolute conviction that the skies about Belle Dam were darkening, and the rumbling from the ground was now matched by clouds that had gone feral above me.

The spell had become something different. The fire of it burned its way through my brain, the only thing I could see. A powerful summoning, far stronger than anything that would have drawn a spirit back from the other side. I knew at once I could *never* have cast something like this.

A keyhole blazed silver-white from inside the monument, a feature I hadn't noticed before. There was only a moment to piece together what I was seeing, a fraction of a second to see the light spilling out of it.

Just before the world exploded in front of me, I heard the sound of someone's breath catch. I turned my head, nearly getting whiplash in the process. Trey was panting, standing right outside the circle. In his hand, he clutched something that glinted in the light. "Braden?" he shouted over the rushing winds.

I met his eyes, realizing how futile it was to keep fighting. The magic was overwhelming me. I whimpered once. Something exploded out of the sky above us, lightning that struck the monument in front of me. The last thing I remembered was how strange it felt to fly.

SEVENTEEN

When I came to, I realized that the warmth beneath me was vaguely human-shaped. I groaned, feeling pain in all four extremities. Nothing felt broken, and migraines hurt worse than this. I shifted myself to the right, eventually rolling off and onto the ground. The coolness of grass and dirt helped me get my bearings.

The cemetery was quiet, except for the sound of muttering. It took me almost a minute to confirm that it wasn't coming from me. It was coming from the human shape I'd landed on. Trey.

I struggled to my feet, wobbling once I was vertical again. The magic had dissipated, leaving an impressive residue over the cemetery—dozens of feet in diameter. I could taste the darkness in it, something that smelled like spoiled meat and burning. There were traces of my own personal magic all over it, like a flashing signature scrawled over everything. It was already soaking into the graves, the grass, and everything.

"Next time, tell me to duck," Trey said groggily.

I stumbled toward Grace's monument, scanning the ground for my glasses. Nowhere. They were gone. Then I realized something was wrong.

Normally I'd be hunched over with the visions by now. But not this time. I saw the same as always, everything sharper than it normally was. There was no pain. Knowledge was ... fluid. I could pick and choose what I wanted to see. My eyes trailed up the base of the monument, and I gasped.

The lightning had struck Grace's monument. The top half was just *gone,* smashed into bits of rubble. It looked like glass that someone had smashed a fist through. Deep gouges and cracks lined the rest of the monument.

And there was the keyhole, the one I'd seen glowing before the spell had finished. It wasn't metallic, like I'd thought originally, but something carved into the stone. The lines of it were still smooth and sharp, something that had been done recently, and not something that had been weathering in the graveyard for a hundred years. A keyhole that had faced downwards, but was now turned on its side. A door unlocked.

I reached out and pressed my fingers against it. The stone was warm, almost hot.

Images in rose light flashed before my eyes. One after another, I watched a line of men and women who'd stood at this very spot, staring at the monument. With each one, their clothes and hair shifted, a slideshow traveling back in time. And then I saw the veiled figure, kneeling down in front, the fiery glow of magic around her. She was the one who had cast the spell. All the way back in the beginning, when the ground had just been turned over, and grass hadn't had a chance to grow.

I started to laugh. For the first time, the visions were under my control. Even knowing I'd walked into some sort of trap couldn't compete.

"Where'd it go? The wolf!" Trey was standing now. "What in the hell were you doing?" I froze in place, fear lodged in my chest. *Why was he here? Why now?*

I opened my mouth to say ... I didn't know what I was going to say.

"Braden, what were you doing here?" Trey grabbed my shoulder, his fingers digging into the skin. "Tell me!"

Fortunately for me, the coyote called out again. Trey had called it a wolf. I remembered a brief flash as something flew over me, something with four legs.

Trey switched his grip and shoved me around. There was a haunted, predatory look to his eyes. In the darkness, he looked harder. More a cage fighter than a college student.

All it would take is one look at my eyes, and everything would be different. But Trey wasn't looking at me just yet; his eyes were drawn to the monument.

"Jesus," Trey whispered. "Braden, what did you d—"

Our eyes met, and I saw through him. Trey unraveled in front of me, layers upon layers that peeled away like petals falling off a rose. I saw how deep loyalty ran within him, silver and gold threads that kept all the other parts together. I saw reflections and memories against diamond walls, decayed flowers that had been trampled underfoot, and icy winds of sarcasm that surrounded the core, the dark parts even he couldn't see.

Somewhere deep inside, far deeper than I was now, there were glimpses of charcoals that could only spark but not flame.

"You have the Widow's eyes." His shocked tone pulled me away from the visions.

I dropped my eyes and looked away. There, on the ground in front of me, were my sunglasses. I started to kneel down, intending to put them back on, but Trey surprised me again. Getting there first, he snatched them up, trying to look me in the eyes again. "I . . ." Nothing else came out of my mouth. Shivering, I heard the low moaning that took to the air as night wind swept through the city.

"I don't understand." Trey's voice was soft. "They're supposed to be a legend. But you have it, don't you. The Widow's Sight." He pressed the glasses into my hand. "I don't understand," he said again.

"Neither do I," I whispered.

"Braden . . ." Before anything else could be said, a snarling interrupted.

A pack of *things* dug their paws into the ground behind us. They were taller than dogs, and held all the proper proportions, but they were like someone's nightmare of what a monstrous dog was. Dark fur ranged from black to red to gray, mottled over their entire bodies. In places, the fur was more like spines, with long distinguished barbs.

Their eyes held some sort of intelligence, but it was the insides that were the most disturbing. Animals had a nature, a survival instinct. These creatures didn't want to survive so much as they wanted to kill.

I began to gather the magic around me, purely in defense, and the leader stepped forward, jaws parting. That's when I knew what they were. "Hellhounds," I breathed.

The legends said that a witch had bound dark spirits into a pack of dogs, creating a monster that exuded violence, but could be easily controlled with magic. At least until the hounds had started mating, giving birth to a species that was even more savage than their parents. They also had a resistance to magic, and the ability to sense and track magical energy.

The moral of the story was be careful what you conjure, and be absolutely sure you can put it down when you're done. Hellhounds, even just one, were lethal to the unprepared witch.

Four of them stared us down, huffing dark breaths into the night.

Trey stepped in front of me, his arm stretched out to one side. *He thinks he can protect me?* I wanted to laugh. The hounds would rip through both of us like wet paper, and devour what was left.

"Run," I said, my voice shaking. Trey didn't move. I grabbed his arm.

"Trey! Now!" I tugged at him.

"Stay behind me," Trey ordered. "I'll hold them off." He pulled a wicked-looking knife out of his back pocket.

"No you won't." I drew on the leftover magic from the spell, pulling it back to me. "Now's not the time, alpha dog."

I held out my right hand. I felt the threads of magic slipping out of my fingers, and I traced runes into the air. "*Vas*," I called out, summoning up the only Sanskrit word I could remember. *Stay.* "Stop!" The words caught blue fire, coloring in the runes I'd traced. Spells of binding; locks; chaining the air together.

The hellhounds snarled. The leader took another step forward, its red eyes narrowing. The moment my voice died, it leapt forward and slammed into thin air. I flinched. The fiery runes rippled but they held. For now. It might buy us a few minutes. I yanked on Trey's arm again, this time feeling it give way beneath me.

"C'mon Braden, run!" Trey shouted, twisting out of my grip and replacing it with his fingers on my wrist.

"*Now* we run?" I didn't have time for anything else. If the hellhounds were half as powerful as the stories, we were so screwed. They'd picked up my scent by now. And they would hunt for as long as there was darkness. As soon as the sun came up, they'd have to rest. So I only had to keep us alive for six hours. No pressure.

Trey led our escape through the graveyard. His legs were a lot longer than mine, making it hard to keep up.

The snarling of the hounds grew louder. I prayed fervently that they hadn't broken through already.

At the gates, Trey stopped. A howling sound, warmer than the cold snarls of the hellhounds, came from the center of the graveyard. Trey's head whipped around, his face taut with anger.

Trey wasn't looking at me. He was looking back toward Grace's monument. I glanced over his shoulder and saw something silver shimmering in the night. From this distance, I couldn't see anything more, but it looked like a wolf. Standing with the hellhounds.

"They're going to keep chasing us," I said, holding on to his arm to keep myself up. "They'll come for me." We jumped the stone wall and stopped in the street.

"Hellhounds?" he asked, and I nodded. "We have to keep them away from the town." If we could lead them away from the city, the odds of someone getting hurt went down. Other than us.

I looked in both directions, before pointing north. "This way."

"Sather Park's up there." Trey nodded, his tone grim. "Come on."

We took off running again, Trey's hand still wrapped firmly around my wrist. We passed the last two city blocks at the north edge of town and kept pushing forward. After a block, I yanked my hand free. "Hold on!" I had to know more. I closed my eyes, daring to only take a second to calm myself. When I opened them again, I turned back the way we'd come.

My visions were still there, still as strong as ever. I saw a trail of heat that showed our path and followed it back. I pushed out, somehow stepping out of my body and following the trail back. All the way into the cemetery where my magic still hung strong.

There was a silver wolf, smaller than the hellhounds, fighting two of them. A third was already on the ground, bleeding out dark magic and heart's blood. There was no sign of the fourth. I looked closer, seeing brimstone and smoke that told me the fourth had gone the long way around. It had bolted for the other side of the cemetery, where the wall wouldn't hold. And now it was trying to outrun us.

There was a piercing howl from the silver wolf. As I watched, the silver wolf growled, its snout shrinking but its legs thickening. Not silver, but mercury. Liquid, fluid, never staying constant.

Something started buzzing in my ear, but I shrugged it off. I breathed out, whispering trails of heat and smell from the cemetery that circled around each other. Trails that led away from the town, and left off where they began. Trails I hoped would confuse the wolves, and buy more time.

Trying to draw my vision back—to stop seeing the cemetery and start seeing the road again—was harder than I expected. The more I tried to pull away, the more the details of the wolf and the hellhounds drew me in. The mercury was scented with spikes of flame, rage this time and not magic. I couldn't look away.

And then there was pressure on the sides of my head. I blinked, the vision dissolving and Trey reappearing. His hands were pressed on my head, and he was shouting.

"...Got to run!" he was shouting, his eyes hard. "Braden, focus!"

"Here now." I swallowed, tasting something gross in my mouth. Trey's eyes were searching, trying to make eye contact again. "Come on," I said. "I only bought us a couple minutes. The leader's circling around, hoping to cut us off."

Trey nodded sharply. "Let's go."

We continued down the street as the concrete grew cracked and uneven. I looked down, and saw that someone had stood right here, eagerly waiting to be picked up. A troubled family home, coffee-colored violence.

I shook my head. If only it was like this all the time! The world was alive around me. Information just hung there, waiting for me to pluck it out instead of having it all forced inside. Unable to forget.

"Braden, come on!" Trey shouted. He was nearly twenty feet ahead already. Without his grip on me, he'd run at his own pace.

We fled into the city park. Swings and pavilions were spaced out evenly for summer outings, but in the middle of the night, it all looked sinister. Trey seemed confident as he led the way; then again, he had lived in Belle Dam a hell of a lot longer than I had.

We were in the woods before I even realized it, and I stumbled the moment my foot contacted a tree branch. I sailed down a hill, only to be caught by Trey before I hit the ground. He stumbled back, setting me down.

He caught me? "Be more careful," Trey whispered. I heard the howling of the hellhound closing in. The leader had caught up with us.

There was no way we could run in the woods now. A predator would pick us out easily. Unless… I looked up. "Trey, do you trust me?"

He looked startled, looking back. It was obvious he'd been trying to figure out the best path to take. "Why?"

We were at the bottom of a hill, surrounded by trees. A pair of oak trees hung to one side, grown so close to one another that over the years their barks had merged. There was a charred crack on one side where lightning had struck.

"Come on," I said as I dragged Trey toward the tree. I pushed him into the charred hollow and pressed myself in on top of him. This close, it felt like we fit so perfectly together. His chest heaved, and his arms circled around me.

"Look into my eyes," I demanded. I lifted my head, staring into Trey's blue-green eyes. Trey looked surprised but went with it.

I'd never tried to hide something as large as two people, and definitely not from something as dangerous as a hellhound. I just hoped I could pull it off.

"Don't say anything," I whispered. Trey only nodded.

The connection between us was strengthened by the eye contact and the touch.

As I drew the magic forth, I pictured it clearly in my mind. It swirled around us in waves, and each one peeled away another layer. First, the sight of us, blending the sides of the tree together until there was only one larger tree. Then our scent; the sound of our hearts and ragged breathing; the path we'd taken. On top of all of it, I soothed away the traces of magic in me, and the memory of the spell I was still casting.

When it was done, I saw it in my mind as a perfect oak, tall and strong and filled with life.

I pulled back the vision and looked into Trey's eyes. There was no fear in them, nothing but rabid fascination. His eyes revealed all the questions he wanted to ask. Questions he'd come up with later. And then they widened.

At the top of the hill, the hellhound burst forth. It leapt down the embankment that I'd sailed over. Don't move, I mouthed to Trey, who nodded.

The hellhound was understandably confused. Slowly, I craned my neck to see. Our trail had ended at the top of the hill, just at the crest of the woods. Then it vanished without a trace.

I gritted my teeth, holding the magic tightly in place. If I let it go, let the magic wrinkle or flutter in place, the hound would see through it.

I tried to breathe slowly, easing each breath out with exaggerated force. It was a struggle to hold the magic in place and ignore the way our bodies were molded together. Trey was some sort of furnace, his skin burning against mine. Even though we couldn't move, I wasn't sure I wanted to.

The hellhound whined, scratching its paws on the ground. My breath caught in my throat. When it bounded out into the forest, I sighed with relief.

How long? Trey mouthed. I shrugged. We waited there for silent minutes, staring at each other.

There was no hardness in his face now, I realized. No anger. The way Trey changed moods, it was hard to get a really good read on him. My stomach was threatening revolution, flip-flopping all over the place. Being this close to *Trey.* But there wasn't a choice right now, at least until we were sure the hound was gone.

His eyelashes are so long. The absurdity of the thought at a time like this almost made me laugh out loud.

The howling sound grew faint. It was trying to call the others. Where was the silver wolf now? Was it still in the cemetery, or was it hunting the last hellhound?

"I think it's gone," I said, releasing the spell. It hovered there still. The more we moved, the more ripples would appear in the magic, and in the image that the spell projected.

There was no need to stand so close, but moving away wasn't an option. Trey was staring at me. I couldn't move. His face softened, his lips just barely parting and revealing a glimmer of white underneath. The widening of his eyes, the dilation. The crease between them showing his concentration.

I've got to get out of here. The thought came at me rapidly, a fierce need to put as much distance as I could between the two of us. Trey's breath was warm against my skin, tingling the tiny hairs above my lip.

I was hallucinating. I'd hit my head earlier. That was the only explanation. Any moment now Trey was going to shove me down with a yell. I would lie there and take it. This was all a giant mistake. But I couldn't stop myself.

There was nothing but the two of us standing there. Trey whispered my name, somewhere between a gasp and a groan. The fire smoldered and burst into an inferno when Trey lowered his head, and our lips brushed.

eighteen

The kiss started out incredibly gentle, just a meeting of random lips in the night. I shifted my head to the side, not daring to move my hands from their desperate clutching of the bark behind Trey.

Don't let this be a dream. He pulled me closer. I closed my eyes, losing it in the feel of Trey around me, the taste of him on my lips.

It took some time to realize that the kiss had ended. Suddenly, my mouth was warm—hot—and then just as quickly it was cold again. I opened my eyes and saw Trey, humor streaking through his eyes.

"That was unexpected," Trey said, cocking his head to the side.

"Yes." My brain wasn't functioning right. In the thick of terror, I handled myself just fine. But a brief kiss, and everything turned to pudding.

Trey leaned his head back against the tree bark. "Man, Jade is never going to get over this," he said, laughing.

Wait. Something fired warning bells in my head, but I

was still too confused to see it. "Jade?" My mind was drawing a blank.

"My little sister. She's always telling me to go out and find someone. That my mother's never going to stop pushing at me until I get serious with someone."

Jade was his sister. One part of my brain tried to calmly state this fact, while a whole other section was screaming Jade *Lansing* over and over again. The fire in my veins was quickly smothered with ice. I pulled away from the tree, from Trey's warmth.

"Jade's your sister. Jade *Lansing*." I struggled to keep an even tone, to not let anything slip. Even though I knew better, I was still hoping he'd come back with, "No, my sister is Jade Edwards."

"Yeah?" Trey shrugged.

"No, Jade's brother is *Gentry*." I felt a sudden rush of surprise and satisfaction. I'd outwitted him with only the powers of logic.

"For which I can never thank my mother enough," Trey said. "Thus the more socially acceptable nickname of Trey."

Oh god. Trey's mother was . . .

And my father was . . .

This couldn't happen. It *wasn't* happening. I shook my head, looking up at him. "It's not funny," I insisted. "You're not Jade's brother."

"You're still getting used to the Lansing thing, aren't you?" Trey said, sounding sympathetic. "Relax, it's not *that* big a deal. We don't actually eat babies or lord ourselves over the peasants. Don't believe the hype."

It was laughable. In fact, the whole thing was so absurd I almost started laughing. "This is just my luck," I muttered, pulling away from Trey. The moment was most definitely over.

"Are you okay, Braden? You're looking a little green."

"I'm fine," I said. "But we need to get out of here before the hellhound comes back." And I still had to figure out a way to keep it busy until dawn.

We climbed back up the path out of the woods and into the park. It was quiet at first, both of us realizing that if we kept talking, the hellhound might hear us. But when we were passing the swing sets, Trey broke the silence.

"So is it gone?"

"I don't know yet," I muttered, wincing with every step. It wasn't the magic I'd cast that was taking its toll on me. It was trying to stop the hellhound-summoning spell. Everything on the inside that wasn't muscle ached. "It'll search until morning."

Trey was unusually quiet. "And the other ones? The ones that didn't follow us?"

"They're dead." I'd seen the bodies. "The wolf thing, the one that leapt over me? It attacked them." That was another question, one I couldn't file away until later like the rest. "What was it?"

Trey shook his head. "Not one of the good guys," he said grimly.

"It took on a pack of hellhounds and ripped them to shreds. It wasn't *just* a wolf."

Trey slammed his fist into the side of a tree without warning. "Just trust me," he snapped. "That thing's just as much of a threat as they are."

The short tone struck harder than I would have thought. I winced, wrapping my arms around me. Rather than deal with him, or whatever mood swing he was currently undergoing, I repeated what I'd done earlier, and stepped out of myself.

The hellhound had traced our scents backwards, and then followed the fake traces I'd laid out earlier, until it had suddenly gone off path. I pushed my vision up, coming out above the trees and trying to track where the hound had gone next. I could only get a feel for the one that had come after us: the leader. There weren't any other traces of darkness roaming the city that I could see.

The leader's the only one left? I played a metaphysical round of follow the leader and tracked it deep along the coastline to the west. It was pursuing something. Hunting it. But what had managed to hold its attention for this long when there was a witch to eat? The wolf? *What the hell was that thing?*

Just before I was about to head back to myself, there was movement on the far end of the park. Two guys in black were climbing out of a Jeep.

" ...heading into the park now. You're sure he's there?"

The man's voice was oddly distorted. Like it had been recorded, then played over the telephone.

I pulled myself back into my body, more easily this time around. Trey hadn't moved. "We have company," I announced quietly.

He just nodded, pulling the knife back out of his pocket. "It's circling back around?"

"Worse. It's two guys. I think they're looking for me."

Trey's neck craned toward me. "Why would you think they're after you?" It occurred to me that this was turning into some kind of bad joke. Catherine's goons, her son, and I walk into a bar.

I don't walk back out.

"Just the way my life works," I said.

Next to one of the pavilions was a brick building that housed the restrooms. We crept up against the closest wall, staying to the shadows.

It wasn't long before a branch snapped close to where we were hiding. "They said to check the woods," one of the men said. "He might be hiding out, waiting for us to overlook him."

Trey tensed, but I inched closer to him, covering my hand with his. Then I took a deep breath and tried to tap into what little energy I had left.

The sound of one branch breaking had been loud, but the sound of hundreds breaking in the forest was like rapid gunfire. They snapped, they cracked, and they split apart all at once, and we'd be lucky if the entire city didn't wake after the cacophony it created.

Within seconds, the men in black had taken off for the woods, probably thinking they'd have an easy time of it. I winced: I just wanted a few branches to start breaking, not knock down half the forest.

I went to signal Trey that everything was okay and we should get out of there... but my legs stopped working. I started to fall, but he scooped me up. "Braden," he whispered, his voice harsh. "Keep it together. Just a few more minutes."

There wasn't any other option. I had to do this. It took all my concentration, but I managed to keep my legs working. We hurried from Sather Park and back toward town. Along the way, I managed to catch Trey up to speed with the hellhound, and the lack of its minion hellhounds.

I was seriously dragging before we even made it back to the cemetery. That's how we saw the marks in the first place.

"What the hell is that?" I whispered thickly. One of the streetlights was illuminating part of the concrete street, and the normally light stone had several dark markings across its surface.

Trey went to take a closer look while I propped myself up against the side of a building. He jogged back a second later. "Track marks," he said. "Charred right into the stone."

"From the hound?" I shook my head a moment later. Stupid question. "So it burns its prints into the ground?"

He lifted his arms and shrugged. "You're more of the expert here than I am, kiddo. So what's the next step? We track it down? You said the others are dead, right?"

"I think so," I said. "But the only way to know for sure is to go back and check the cemetery."

"And the wolf-thing killed them?" he pressed.

"You're more the expert there than I am." I repeated his words back at him. "And don't call me kiddo."

He started to smile, and then he was there, wrapping his arm around me as we started walking again. On any other night, his arm over my shoulders and mine around his waist would have me scarlet-faced and unable to speak. But I was too exhausted for embarrassment.

I had to watch my feet as I walked, to make sure I kept putting one in front of the other. Trey was talking, but listening required more energy than I had at the moment. We had turned and walked up into the entryway before I even realized we'd reached the hotel.

The idea that my bed was only a few minutes away sent new energy coursing through me. I could manage a few more minutes. I disentangled myself from Trey, who was looking down at me with the most annoying, amused expression.

He started to say something, but I interrupted. "So your mom ... she knows about you?"

I knew there were more important questions I could be asking, but it was the only one I could think of at the moment.

"She ... won't be joining PFLAG anytime soon," Trey said wryly, "but she's learning to cope. What about you?"

I thought back to Uncle John. "Uhm ... the same. My uncle thinks it's a phase or something, and when I'm 'an adult,'" I even did finger quotes, "it'll all be different." He never expressed hatred or disgust about gay people, but Uncle John definitely had trouble understanding that I was gay.

There was another long pause, and then Trey said, "So you're a witch. Like my mom."

"Looks like," I said, but inside I was cringing.

"And Lucien Fallon knows who you are," Trey said slowly. Pieces were coming together too fast, and I was just waiting for him to put the last few together. Waiting for him to realize, and for the yelling to begin.

He grabbed my arm, and I flinched. *I'm sorry, I didn't know he was my father! I swear.* Apologies and excuses started flowing through my head until Trey said, "He's trying to use you, Braden. Don't you see? Fallon works for Jason Thorpe ... and they'd both kill to have you on their side."

My heart, which was burning and beating a thousand miles a minute, suddenly froze and went silent. "Wh-what?" I croaked.

Trey leaned into me, our faces inches apart. "Remember, I told you how Fallon works for Jason Thorpe? That must be why he got your uncle to bring you here." He was looking at me, but his eyes were unfocused. "That's what happened, right? Lucien had something to do with your moving here?"

I only hesitated for a second before I nodded. "Uh huh." My heart started beating again, and something sour started to rise in my stomach, but I didn't care. *He doesn't know. Everything's still okay.*

Liar. I swallowed my disgust and tried to return his smile. "Look, I already know that I can't trust Lucien," I said to him. "I'm not blind."

His eyes immediately met mine, as if he was double-checking just to make sure. "My mom can help you, Braden—"

"No!" I shook my head. "I'm not getting involved in any of that." It was my conversation with Lucien all over again.

"Don't be stupid," he said, sounding annoyed. "My mom can keep you safe. Who knows what Jason will try to do to you if he thinks you're not going to side with him."

And who knows what your mom will do? Besides try to kill me again. "Your mom and Thorpe have their own issues. I'm not a part of that." My voice took on a pleading tone as I said, "And neither are you. It's not our fight, Trey."

It was apparently the wrong thing to say. Trey let go of my arm so fast he nearly shoved me back, and his jaw clenched. "You don't have any idea of what you're getting into, do you? Well, it may not be your fight, but I'd do anything for my family."

I turned toward the door, closing my eyes. It took several deep breaths before I could speak without fearing my voice would crack. "I need to rest," I said over my shoulder.

Trey didn't say anything, and I went inside. By the time I turned back, he was already gone.

¤   ¤   ¤

Sometime during the night, I'd almost strangled myself with the Egyptian cotton sheets. I dreamt the same dream, over and over again. A hunt. A creature on four legs, sometimes two, canvassed the perimeter of the city. Lucien was there, whispering something in a language I didn't understand. Sometimes his hands were covering my eyes, and sometimes not.

I don't know how long I slept, but it was still light outside when I cracked my eyes open. After the spell, I hadn't needed the glasses. Something had gone wrong, or really really right. For the first time, I could see like any normal person. Even if I still saw more than any person should.

But the images that greeted me were blistering colors and shapes that chiseled at my thoughts. The pain started almost immediately, a night's worth of freedom exacting its revenge. Someone was drilling nails through my brain, out my eyes, and through every square inch of my body.

It was sheer luck my pills were on the nightstand. My hands shook as I tried to get the pills out. The usual dosage was two, but as bad as it was, I planned to take four.

At least a dozen pills spilled out the side of my hand

and onto the ground. I swallowed the ones I did have dry, the taste of them sticking in my throat. Then I fell back on the bed, so exhausted I could barely stay awake, and in so much pain I thought I'd never sleep again. It felt like days before I passed out again, slipping underneath the radar of the migraine.

Nineteen

The next thing I knew, my cell phone was humming on the nightstand. The sheets underneath me were slick with sweat, and while I was a little achy, I actually felt a lot better.

Brunch? Jade's name was prominently displayed on the caller ID.

Brunch? I typed back. Maybe Jade had skipped school too. Going back to sleep had done wonders; I barely felt the after-effects of the migraine.

Rich kid meal. You have gossip. 11?

She'd heard already, about Trey. I sighed. Avoiding Jade didn't work, that much I'd learned on my own. *School?*

Saturday. U sleep thru Friday?

Oh. Shit. My first week of school, and I'd missed a day and a half. Out of a possible four. That wasn't good. I hadn't even called Lucien to let him know. While I was thinking, Jade sent another text: *11:30?* I sent a positive reply, and climbed out of bed.

It was several minutes before Jade sent a text letting

me know where to meet her, time I spent in the bathroom trying to coax life back into my rough-looking face.

Jade was already pacing at the door of the bagel place when I finally made it outside. I was so hungry, I almost stopped off for something to eat on the way. But I didn't want to keep Jade waiting.

The moment she saw me, a light went off. "You've been sneaky," she said instead of a greeting.

I shrugged my shoulders, looking away. "I'm always sneaky. Haven't you figured it out yet?"

"Just say I was right, and we'll call it even," Jade said flippantly, holding the door open for me. "After you give me the details."

"You were right?" I shook my head. The words tasted strange on my lips. "I don't think I can say that. Not in good conscience. Why were you right?"

Jade's annoyance manifested itself with a brutal flick to the back of my ear. "I told you days ago I knew the perfect person for you. You didn't want to hear about it, remember?"

"I'm not talking about this," I said, hoping to avoid the topic of Trey and me.

Jade led me to a table where there was already an assortment of muffins, coffee, and little strawberry-colored pastries. "Of course you are. You think because it's my brother that I'm not going to get the dish?"

"Ooh, coffee," I said, sliding into a chair.

Jade pulled the cup out from in front of me and settled

it on her side of the table. "Sorry, no changing the subject. Breakfast is contingent on gossip. The currency is non-negotiable."

"Breakfast? I thought this was brunch?" Jade waved a hand away at the question, so I pressed on. "What'd I miss yesterday at school?"

Jade picked up a piece of biscotti. The hard-crusted bread was like a ruler in her hands. In a few moments, she'd probably start rapping my knuckles with it. "How'd you and my brother meet?"

I snatched up a bagel before she could say anything. Ripping a giant piece off, I stuffed it in my mouth. It gave me a few seconds of much-needed time to think. "We kinda ran into each other. He's got this hero complex. It's kind of annoying."

"You have no idea," Jade laughed. She scooted the coffee a little closer to me. "He thinks he's the only one that can save Belle Dam from a fate worse than death." I almost choked on the bagel, thinking she was serious, before I saw her roll her eyes. "So, how long before he asked you out?"

"He didn't." After a long moment and Jade's surprised stare, I finally shrugged. "We just hung out a few times. He's kinda stalkerish."

Jade shook her head and exhaled upwards, causing her bangs to raise slightly. "That boy gives me such a headache sometimes. I don't care what he is, there's a proper way to date." Her eyes lit up with sudden insight. "Braden, you're dating an older guy. Good for you!"

"I'm not dating anyone," I said irritably. "We were just…hanging out and then we kissed." It wasn't a total lie.

"Trust me, I know better than anyone else how Gentry can get under your skin."

I straightened up, relaxing the muscles in my face, in my best Stepford Wife impression. "Hello, my name is Gentry, and I'm *so* very important."

Jade giggled, covering her mouth with the back of her hand. "Someone tried calling him Jenny once, and Trey sucker-punched the kid underneath the monkey bars. My mother was in a *fury* when she found out." When the laughter died out, her expression sobered. "So what happened?"

"I told you—"

"That you don't want to talk about it. Remember how I always get my way? If you're not going to own up to your little tryst, I'll find out from him. I'm sure he'll have a lot of juicy dirt for me."

I could feel my face starting to grow hot, and I grabbed the ice water in front of me. "It's not like that."

"Like what? Like my brother finally found somebody that interests him? You may not know him very well, but this is a pretty big deal for him."

"So you don't care that he's gay?"

Jade gave me a strange look. It was a mix of pity and understanding, but I wasn't sure where it was coming from. "Of course not. He's my big brother. As long as he's not taking guys away from me, then we've got no problem. He's who he is. That's all that matters. He's still the same brother that used to roll his eyes when I invited him to high tea."

The image of Trey sitting at a tea party was too much, and I started laughing again. Hanging out with Jade was good for relaxing, remembering what it felt like to be normal. I didn't want to lose this.

"Is it because of your family?" she asked quietly.

It was an innocent question, but it still struck me like a slap. It was stupid to even talk about any of this—with Jade of all people—because things were so much more complicated than anyone else knew.

"I don't know," I said, even though I did. "Maybe. It's just not something I can think about right now."

"You should talk to him. He's been almost human the last few days."

"He's usually something else?"

Jade was pensive, using a fork to push around pieces of her bagel. *Who ate a bagel with a fork?*

"Aside from one very small part of his life, he's not the most independent person I know. One of us had to have been adopted. The way my mother looks at me sometimes, I know it's not him."

"Maybe I'll talk to him," I offered.

Jade nodded, her lips slowly curving into a smug smile. "I knew you would." She glanced toward the door. My stomach ran cold.

She didn't. She wouldn't have. "He's not … on his way here now, is he?" I asked weakly.

To her benefit, Jade had the decency to look uncomfortable as she shifted in her seat. "I might have said you were meeting me for brunch," she said.

That wasn't so bad. I wanted to breathe easy, but something in the way she was sitting suggested more. "And?"

"And that you wanted to talk to him about the other night." She looked away. "And that you were pretty upset."

"Jade!" I pushed out my chair and stood up. "He's coming here?"

"Well, I don't know if he's actually coming, but he seemed interested." Jade glanced at the door again and I turned, half fearfully. But it wasn't Trey walking inside. It was a pair of young girls I barely recognized.

Jade bit down on her lower lip and shrugged it off. "Anyway. He'll be here soon. You should probably call him."

¤ ¤ ¤

"Thanks for meeting me," Trey said. The sky was overcast, leaving the park looking darker than it should have. I had found him sitting on top of a picnic table in one of the pavilions, dressed in a dark gray shirt and jeans.

"Sure." What else could I say? Even before approaching, I could feel the tension rising. After last night—*the other night* my mind was quick to correct—everything was only getting more confused in my brain. Losing a day wasn't helping any. "Did anything happen last night?" That was my main concern—that losing an entire day meant the hound would have really hurt someone.

"No," he said, his eyes narrowed. "I kept driving around town, but there was no sign of it."

Trey didn't say anything for a moment. He was studying a little boy on the swings across from us. The boy's mother was settled under one of the trees, watching him with a casual eye. Anyone that passed might have thought the book in her lap was more appealing, but I saw the way her eyes barely ever connected with the page. Her attention was on her child.

"Why'd you do it?" I knew it was a loaded question, but I asked it anyway. I hadn't had a lot of down time to think about the kiss, but finding out that Trey was Catherine's son had made me nervous.

"What really brought you to Belle Dam?" Trey countered.

I fumbled, closing my mouth before something wrong slipped out. *Focus, Braden.* I shoved my hands in my pockets. "I told you already," I said. Trey cut me off.

"The truth."

This serious, somber Trey was disquieting. It wasn't helping the tension either, which seemed to swell even more.

"It's complicated."

"It's always complicated," he said. He reached out, grabbing my hand. "But I can't help you until you tell me what's going on."

"You recognized it that night, didn't you. You said I had the Widow's eyes. Grace's?" I waited for his hesitant nod. "The things I see are like some sort of beautiful monstrosity.

I can pick out shades of green in a forest that only wolves see. But put me in a room where someone was murdered, and I soak up every ounce of violence there was. I can't control it most of the time."

"And you saw something?"

I nodded, but couldn't elaborate. I wasn't sure how much to tell him.

"Your uncle never came to Belle Dam, did he?" It wasn't really a question.

"No," I said, looking down at the ground between us. "I think something would have happened to him, if I'd stayed."

"Something bad?"

"He would have died," I said, sounding more assured.

I could feel the pressure of his thumb slowly rubbing in a circle on my hand. He stepped off the picnic table.

"Someone would have killed him? Like with magic?"

"Yes. Or with something they summoned with magic." I shook my head. "How much do you know about it? The magic."

He was quiet for a moment. "Enough. I know what it is, and what it can do. My mother never taught us much about it, but I picked it up by hanging around her. I don't have the gift like she does. Like you do," he added. "But I've seen enough of it to recognize it."

I didn't have anything to say after that, so I pulled away and then hugged myself. He reached out, tilting my chin up, and stared at me. "I kissed you because I wanted to," he said, lowering his mouth to mine. It was a short, nearly chaste kiss, which Trey followed up with some sweet nothings. "What are we doing about that thing? You're going to try and kill it, right?"

We? "Kinda have to," I said, my voice barely above a whisper. I just wasn't sure what that would entail. Or even how to go about it. "That thing's nearly immune to magic."

"Not entirely. You held it back at the cemetery, and you managed to hide us from it." His lips pressed against my neck. "Did I say thank you for that?"

"I have to go," I said weakly. Leaving was not even close to what I wanted to do, though. "I need to do some research before tonight."

"Then I'll come with you," Trey said.

On one hand, that thrilled me to no end. On the other, I knew it was a fine line I was dancing along. I'd keep lying to Trey, as long as I could, to keep my secret from him. I couldn't stay away from him either, as much as I kept telling myself I should.

What if this was the only chance I got? I didn't want to blow it.

Twenty

Our first stop was Gregory's. The comic shop was about as busy as I remembered it, but this time there wasn't anyone manning the front counter.

"He's probably upstairs playing on his website," Trey murmured.

We headed through the back and up the stairs. Sure enough, Gregory was ensconced at a small table near the windows looking out over the street. "Back already?" He swiveled around in his chair, facing us.

"Do you have a copy of *Montserrat's Grimoire*?" I asked, stepping forward. It was the book that had the legend of the hellhound in it, and from what I knew from Uncle John, it was also a fairly common tome in magical circles.

Gregory's eyes lit up, and without giving an answer he swiveled around and started typing. He didn't look thrilled to see me. No surprise there.

"Hey, he asked you a question." Trey was getting angry.

"Yes, yes, I heard the first time. My hearing is quite exceptional, as a matter of fact." Gregory's fingers slowed as he typed and talked at the same time. "Two reports of a spectral dog roaming the outskirts of town. I don't believe in coincidence."

So whatever the wolf was, it hadn't managed to kill the last hellhound. Part of me had hoped it would be that easy, that the wolf would have killed all of them. But the leader was smart—I'd seen that firsthand.

Trey looked at me quizzically, not understanding the connection. I sighed and explained. "Montserrat collected myths and legends from the magical world. The legend about the hellhound is one of his particularly notable entries." Gregory knew that too, apparently. I made a mental note to pay more attention when I was here—Gregory didn't just sell the books, he clearly knew his way around the supernatural.

"So what's he doing?" Trey mouthed silently at me.

My new sunglasses were starting to slide, so I pushed them back up my face. "He's using that as confirmation, posting to his Internet buddies."

"It's an Internet *forum*," Gregory sniped. "One that knew you were in town only a few hours later, so I wouldn't deride it too much."

"Right," Trey drawled.

God only knows how long Gregory was going to be busy confirming the sightings of the mysterious doglike creatures from last night. It reminded me that I'd lost a day, and anything could have happened in the meantime. "No one was hurt last night, right?"

Gregory favored us with a brief glance. "Lucky for you." He only glanced at Trey for a second, but the look he gave me was longer. And a little afraid, I thought.

I didn't like the way he always acted like he knew so much. He was just some comic book shop owner. "Do you have the book or not?"

"Look on the shelves. You might want to take the fresh meat home to meet your Mother, Gentry. She was here bright and early yesterday, thanks to that little display in the cemetery. Your new witch friend stirred up quite the little magical CGI. She's in a bit of a tizzy."

"I already planned on introducing him," Trey said slowly.

"See that you do. Won't look good, Catherine waltzing around town when *he's* right under her nose."

"What's that supposed to mean?" My heart was suddenly racing. The last thing I needed was another bus incident.

"Belle Dam has a bit of a reputation. Witches don't come here. Almost ever," Trey murmured.

"Most take a wide berth to avoid us. This area's been claimed since it was founded," Gregory said, his eyes flickering toward Trey.

"There's no room for outsiders," Trey continued. "That's the impression they're given. A few have tried challenging that fact over the years, but not anymore."

"Why?" I directed my attention to the store owner.

Gregory turned a sly glance at Trey. "Your little friend doesn't know what happened, does he?"

The muscles in Trey's jaw flexed. "C'mon Braden, let's find your book."

I was liking the situation even less. "Tell me now."

Trey sighed. "Jason hired an outsider, a few years ago. The terms of their cease-fire stopped my mother from interfering directly. So she hired someone as well. It stirred up a lot of chaos."

"And the witches?"

Trey looked away again. "They died."

"Don't know that I'd call it dying, exactly," Gregory said, his voice thoughtful. "No one ever saw them again. Hard to say what happened to them."

"Fantastic," I said, throwing my hands in the air. "And you get mad at me for not wanting to get involved with them?"

Trey turned toward me then, his face flushed. "That won't happen to you. I'll make sure of it."

I waved him off and started investigating the stacks for myself. Gregory hadn't given me a straight answer about the book one way or the other, but if it was here, I'd find it.

"Do you want some help?" Trey asked. He was hovering near Gregory on the far side of the room. Either giving me space, or quietly chewing Gregory a new ass. It didn't make a difference to me either way.

Already, I'd found a couple of new texts. Different books than ones I'd seen before. "I don't need help," I said absently. "I'm fine."

Trey snorted. The lighting in the store sucked, and though I tried squinting to get a better look, it was near impossible to read some or all of the titles. I wasn't asking him for help. No way. "Got it," I said, plucking the notebook from the shelves. It was partly a grimoire of spells, and partly a description of everything the witch had encountered in the supernatural world. And it was the only thing I'd ever seen on hellhounds.

"That's it?" Trey asked, as I crossed the room.

I nodded. "There's a few others I wanted to pick up. Spells I'd never seen before. But I wouldn't know how useful they are until I'd ripped through them all anyway."

"Sounds like Jason," Gregory wheezed with a shake of the head. My head shot up, and Gregory stared me down. *He doesn't know anything*, I kept repeating to myself. "Never was much of a fan. He used to say the same things when he came in here. Thankfully, I banned his ass years ago. Catherine, on the other hand, now there's a looker."

"That's my mother," Trey reminded him quietly, an edge to his voice.

"Wasn't always your mother, was she?" Gregory's tone was all conversation now. "I'll put it on your tab, Gentry. I figure he'll be on the payroll soon enough anyway."

They were talking about me like I wasn't there. "Don't think you know me. You don't have a clue." I wasn't a weapon. I wouldn't get sucked in.

Since Gregory wasn't charging us, I took the *Grimoire* and hit the stairs. The owner's voice chimed in behind me.

"Might want to be careful, Gentry. Don't think the leash will fit this one."

"Are we going to talk about this?"

They hire witches to fight for them. They'd done it at least once before, and they killed each other. There wasn't a whole lot to talk about. "Aren't you going to show me the recruitment package?" I said in an even tone. "I probably have some cavities, so the dental insurance better be killer."

Trey jogged in front of me, crossing his arms. "If you're going to ask me what happened, then just ask. Don't play stupid with me. You're not."

"So tell me what happened, then. Was Gregory exaggerating?"

He sighed, running a hand through his hair. "It wasn't as scandalous as he makes it sound."

I narrowed my eyes. "So, your mother and her archnemesis *didn't* hire out a pair of mercenaries who apparently blew themselves up?"

"My mother hired her like any other employee. The girl just turned up on our doorstep—what was she supposed to do?"

"Makes perfect sense to me," I snapped.

"She said they weren't strong, either of them. Nothing to worry about." He swallowed, his eyes far away. "Something happened. No one's sure what. By the time anyone knew there was trouble, a storm had blown in off the coast. It knocked out the power, and smashed into the city. When she sent people out in the morning to find out what happened, there wasn't anything left."

"Maybe they got smart and booked it out of town?"

Trey shook his head. "Too easy. Carmen's contract with my mother was mystical. She knew where Carmen was all the time. She was just gone."

"They blew each other up? Is that what you think?" I posed the question, and then answered it before he could. "You do, don't you? But if your mother said they weren't that strong, they couldn't have. I don't even know if I could blow someone up."

Trey looked troubled, though he didn't say anything. I saw the tension furrowing between his eyebrows, and the way his jaw flexed and unflexed.

"Why come here in the first place, then? Money? If Jason's so powerful, wouldn't your mom have known better?"

"She didn't go looking," Trey said. "Carmen came to her. The same way I think the other one came to Jason."

I thought that over for a second. "Like someone sent them in this direction. You think there was some sort of plot involved?" I saw Trey's nod, and knew we were on the same page. For once.

"My turn to run an errand." Trey glanced at his watch. "It won't take long. You mind?"

I shook my head and Trey squeezed my hand. "It'll be fine," he tried to assure me. Too bad it wasn't working.

The trip through town wasn't far. In fact, it was only a couple blocks before I saw the high school looming out in front of us. How much did I miss yesterday? How much trouble was I in? I glanced at Trey, but the truck never slowed until we were past the high school.

Trey parked in the street in front of a small restaurant. The name was simple. Cay's. Floor-to-ceiling windows gave an immediate view of the interior, which seemed to be done in a lot of green and gold.

"You're taking me out to lunch?" I laughed.

Trey shrugged, hopping out of the car. As we walked inside, I noticed the hours of operation were for late afternoon and evening only. We were still several hours early to get a table.

Besides the gold and green, the only other colors evident were the dark-stained oak tables and chairs, and splashes of white lighting fixtures for ambiance. The layout was complex, with wooden booths arranged chaotically to create smaller nooks and crannies. There were few straight lines in the whole restaurant; everything was turned on an angle and shifted out of the way. Something about the design was familiar.

I closed my eyes while Trey chatted with what I presumed was the manager. He was behind the bar with a clipboard. While he was busy, I tried to figure out what was bugging me about the design.

I pictured the restaurant as far as I could see it. Stripped away the tables, the chairs, and pictured the lines. Everything was split up, the lines broken and twisted across the entire room. It was almost like someone was trying to break up ... wait. Was it that simple, that the restaurant was designed to break up any magical acts in the area?

It was possible, as far as I could tell. Magical architecture was never something that interested me, the way that the flood of magic could conform to geometry. Something like this took way too long to plan and execute for me.

Trey came back a few minutes later, while I was still looking around curiously. "It'll only take a minute," he said, resting an arm on my shoulder. "My mom needed to see me."

It was like my body went numb all at once. Bad idea, bad bad idea. "I'll just wait outside then." I tried for casual. It wasn't as embarrassing as fear. This was not a meet-the-parents kind of situation.

"Don't worry about it so much." Trey grinned, rubbing my shoulder. "She's going to love you."

"That's what I'm afraid of." A part of me was dying to find out a little more about Catherine Lansing. I just wasn't willing to actually die to find out.

He leaned his head down, and all conscious thought left as our lips met. The kiss didn't even have a chance to deepen before an annoyed huff and a glacial voice chimed in.

"When you're done molesting the townie, I need to speak with you, Gentry. If it's not *too* much trouble."

I pulled away quickly at the sound, my body going from numb to painfully freezing cold. In front of us was a tall woman, with Trey's blonde hair and Jade's classic beauty. Dressed in white and gold, she looked every bit as powerful as people in town claimed.

Catherine didn't even look my way; her eyes were for Trey alone. The snub was clear and to the point. She thought I was just some local, so I wasn't worth her attention.

Realizing that actually made the situation easier. *She doesn't know who I am.* My lungs began to work again, and the rushing in my ears died down. Underneath the sheer terror, there were still epic levels of panic, though.

This was her: the woman who would have killed Uncle John—and had already tried to kill me once.

I didn't want to kill her, the way everyone else seemed to want. But I had to stop her somehow. Not to mention, I had to keep Trey from finding out who I was for as long as possible.

Whoever said teenagers had it easy didn't really think that one through.

Twenty-One

"This is Braden." Trey's tone was calm, maybe even a bit forceful. I wasn't the only one who'd noticed the frosty reception.

"I don't need to know his name, Gentry," his mother chided, her voice somehow managing to get even colder.

"I think you do," Trey replied, matching her ice for ice.

I dug my fingers into his hand, but he didn't react. And worse, he kept talking. "Braden and his uncle just moved here," he said. "Lucien Fallon led him to some sort of trap in the cemetery the other night. Gregory mentioned you paid him a visit, so you obviously know about it."

"You work quickly, son." A moment of surprise turned to approval in her eyes. She nodded to Trey, eyebrows rising. "I wanted a look at the new witchling in town, and you bring him to my door." She turned to me then, extending her hand. "You weren't quite what I was expecting, were you? I've heard interesting things about you and your work. Braden, was it?"

I glanced sideways at Trey, but his focus was on his

mother and not on me. I couldn't believe he'd done this to me, brought me here and basically told her all about me.

"Braden Michaels." I didn't bother trying to shake her hand. I was trying not to tremble. This woman had changed my life, and now she was acting like she didn't have any idea what she'd done.

Catherine tapped a finger against her lips, slowly withdrawing her hand though she continued to watch me with curiosity. "Interesting," she mused. "I apologize. My son is not one to be so indiscrete. I should have had more faith in him."

Something's not right here. This wasn't the way I expected our first encounter to happen. My gut was telling me that this wasn't a woman who'd put out some sort of hit on me only a few days ago.

"Obviously I was on top of things, Mother." My head whipped around. He made it sound like I was just some pet project he'd been working on. Keeping tabs on the witch. "I only found out a few nights ago."

Catherine was too busy watching me now to even look at her son. It was more than enough to make me shift on my feet, looking anywhere but into her ice blue eyes. "Yet you know how important it is that some things not be put off, my dear."

Trey nodded his head quickly. "Of course. But I think the extenuating circumstances alter things slightly."

"Mrs. Lansing," I said, raising my voice. "I don't know what it is you think you want with me, but I'm not interested. I'm not here to get in the middle of some family problem."

"Yet you're involved with my son," she pointed out. "By that simple fact, you're already in the middle. Or have I mistaken things?" She was enjoying this. Like the spider watching the fly struggle on the web.

"You haven't," Trey said. "But I'm not going to let Jason get his hands on Braden. Besides, Thorpe can't offer him anything that would make him turn against me."

"Do you always wear sunglasses indoors, Braden?" she asked mildly. "I would have thought your family would have explained the etiquette behind such decisions. Much like wearing hats indoors."

"He has an eye condition," Trey answered automatically. I was surprised at the lie. Trey knew the truth. "I think Jade called it photophobia. Right?" He prodded me with his fingers, avoiding eye contact.

"I was born with it." On the other hand, I lied more smoothly. I'd had enough practice. "There's not really much I can do with it. No treatment, no drugs really do much for me. Just heavy-duty sunglasses."

"I see." Catherine seemed to buy it. I hoped she did. A sudden memory of Grace Lansing, and she might start asking questions I couldn't answer. The woman didn't get where she was by being stupid. It was only a matter of time.

"If there's nothing else, I should get Braden home. He's got some homework to catch up on." Trey was already slipping his hand into mine, a sign of solidarity between the two of us. "And I have an exam on Tuesday to prepare for."

"Hmm." Catherine didn't look entirely mollified, and I was sure she knew something. "Bring him to the house tomorrow night. We'll have a dinner party." I could see the calculation in her eyes; I just didn't know what it was leading to. A show of support to her son? I didn't think so.

If I thought he would argue, I was in for a losing battle. "Of course," Trey said, steering me toward the door. But my mind was spinning. Dinner? With the entire Lansing family? A full meal where they could poke and prod at me, trying to uncover my secrets? Worse, they'd be expecting answers about our relationship and, in Jade's case, details.

Somehow, things had gone from bad to worse.

¤   ¤   ¤

"I lied to my mother." Trey's voice was filled with shock. The restaurant wasn't far from the hotel, but even the few minutes of driving were impossible to fill with idle chatter. Or serious conversation. I squirmed in my seat, unable to find a good position while Trey's tapping the steering wheel only got more erratic the further we got.

"I lied to her about you. She wouldn't have understood," he went on to say. "She gets ... paranoid, sometimes."

"What would she do? Try and have me killed?" The sarcasm was lost on him, though, but it reminded me of the weird vibe I'd gotten in the restaurant. If Catherine hadn't been the one trying to kill me, then who? Jason?

"She'd see you as a threat. She's very big on the Lansing ideal. That power is our legacy, and what you can do ... she'd see it as some sort of threat. At least until I can explain it to her."

"How do you know about it, anyway? I thought it was just some old legend not many people had heard of?"

Trey nodded. "Not many do. But my dad's always been fascinated by the Lansing family, and the legends associated with them. He's not like my mom, but he knows what she can do. He probably knows more about the Lansings than anyone else in Belle Dam, my mom included."

He dropped me off a few minutes later, and I nearly leapt from the truck in order to put some distance on everything that had happened so far. Catherine knew about me now. Trey had acted like I was some sort of assignment. And I didn't have any idea who was really out to get me.

¤   ¤   ¤

"C'mon John, call me back." I was sitting in my room, staring at the cell phone I'd set carefully on the bed. After Trey dropped me off, I'd spent time reading through the grimoire, but nothing in there was any help.

I'd called Uncle John three times almost fifteen minutes ago, and still nothing. He hadn't picked up, but the voice mail hadn't clicked on either.

Trey and I were meeting up later; I still wasn't sure

why. He seemed to think I'd need help in dealing with the hellhound. When really, I was thinking he would just be in danger. The whole thing was just too much to worry about. So I focused on the hellhound. I ran through different ideas—spells I could try to slow the thing down. I'd never heard of anyone successfully stopping a hellhound—usually, when they accomplished whatever they set out to do, they went back where they came from. The grimoire confirmed it.

My phone lit up, and I exhaled in relief. It was about time.

"I need to know everything you know about hellhounds." No time for hellos.

"Why? What's happened? Is there a hound after you?" John's voice went instantly alert. "Did Catherine find out who you are?"

I explained the situation as quickly as I could—about the cemetery, and summoning Grace, and what happened next.

"What were you thinking?" he snapped when I was done. "You know better than to go trying something like that."

"Well, maybe if someone would tell me something instead of playing games with me, I wouldn't have had to."

John started muttering. I don't think he was even talking to me. "This was all a mistake. He's in over his head."

"John! I need to know anything you know. These things are going to kill people if they don't find me."

"Give them a target," he said abruptly. "If you're the

one who summoned them, they'll have to listen. Otherwise they're going to come after you instead."

I must not have heard him correctly. There had to be some mistake. Sending them after someone else was like signing their death warrant. I couldn't order someone's death! "You're crazy! I'm not sending them after someone else!"

"You can't stop a hellhound with magic, Braden. No one can. And unless you've got a creature just as deadly in your back pocket, you can't kill it with violence. You either give it a target, or you wait for the spell to dissipate naturally and pray for the best."

"Well, how long's that going to take?" I demanded.

He sighed. "Hellhounds aren't like the big powers. They don't *have* a lot of power, so the spell could hold them here for … weeks? Months? Unless you can give them a target, and let them do what they're supposed to."

"Well, that's not happening." My voice was flat.

"Where do you think you are?" I could picture the way the veins in his forehead were flaring up and his skin was turning that blotchy red color, like tomatoes that had gone bad. "Belle Dam's not a happy place. No one's going to pat you on the head for being a good little witch. They'll be measuring you to find the best place to stick the knife. Haven't you been paying attention?"

"You're insane. I'm *not* killing someone. And when the hell did you become so bloodthirsty?"

"When I grew up. You can't do this by yourself. You're going to make too many mistakes. I've got … "

"You've got what? Listen." I tried to calm my voice, to speak with confidence. "If there's a way to stop them, I'll figure it out."

"No. You're not strong enough for this. They're going to chew you up. I'm going to have to … " He sounded like he was struggling with his words, stumbling over them. What was going on with him?

The phone went dead with a shriek of noise worse than nails on a chalkboard. I flinched, throwing it down onto the bed.

John didn't know anything either. So I was going to have to figure this out on my own. I dropped down onto the bed and stared at the ceiling. Hours till dark. Hours to find the perfect solution.

No worries.

Gulp.

Twenty-Two

There was nothing in the book that helped me out at all. I even read through it two more times just in case something would pop out. I did find a section that talked about legends outside a Scottish village where witches had seen creatures in the forest, but the townspeople summarily denied anything. Montserrat thought the town was under a *geas*—a magic that creates walls and chasms in the mind to keep certain information from being revealed. It made me think about Uncle John.

Eventually the sun began to set and I started to get ready.

When I called Trey, he told me to wait for him inside until he got there. The assertive tone immediately made my lip curl. I still wasn't sure how I felt about Trey's ambush, or the way he was drafting me into the Lansings whether I wanted to go along or not. I had to fix things, get them back on track before everything got too out of control.

"Hide inside like a scared little bitch," I said to myself, pretending to be him as I headed outside. "Don't worry,

I'll fight the big bad monster with my perfectly gelled hair and charming smile. Just do as you're told."

That annoying, rational part of me kept trying to inter-ject. Things like *Trey's just worried you'll get hurt* and *He just wants to help*. But it wasn't helping, and I wasn't going to get hurt. It was going to take a lot more than a hellhound to stop me.

"Should have guessed you wouldn't listen," Trey chimed in to my inner monologue, in front of me so suddenly that I jumped. The inner rage I was working myself into flick-ered at the shock. I must have really been out of it.

"I'm not a little kid," I said, bending down to tie the shoelace that had come undone.

"What are you doing, Braden?" The exasperation in Trey's voice made it clear that he wasn't referring to the shoes. "I thought you were going to wait inside. It isn't safe to be standing out here, with that thing out there."

"I was," I snapped. "Then I remembered that I'm not the one that needs protecting. Sorry, Dad."

As I straightened, Trey stepped forward and invaded my personal space. "I'm definitely not your father," he whis-pered, his warmth stirring against the cold surrounding me.

"I thought we had work to do. God's holy mission or whatever." I tried to hold on to the anger, the annoyance, anything but the flutters in my stomach.

Trey wrapped his arms across my shoulders, drawing closer. "You're okay. And that's a start."

You shouldn't be doing this. It's wrong. "We need to

go back to the cemetery." My voice was shaky. "Where it started." But try as I might, all I could focus on was the little bit of light glinting off the tip of Trey's lower lip, the curve of his cheek and the dark lashes shining above his eyes.

"Who says romance is dead," Trey said, his eyes dancing in the streetlights. "Some days, I think you have a death wish," he continued. "Doing stuff like this, wandering around when there's something out there that wants you dead."

"You don't know the half of it," I replied automatically. The hellhound was the least of my problems, the smallest part of a much bigger problem.

"You'll tell me," Trey was confident. "When you're ready."

We decided to walk to Angel's Respite, figuring that if the hellhound was already roaming around, we'd have a better chance of seeing it. There wasn't much small talk along the way. I kept my distance, hands shoved in my pockets. I was still trying to come up with a workable plan, although I had the feeling I'd end up winging it as usual.

The entrance to the cemetery stretched in front of us. One of the streetlights had gone out sometime after we'd left the other night, and masked much of the park from our eyes.

"How long before this thing turns up?" Trey asked.

The hellhound would track us down eventually, but there was no telling how long it would take. With the migraines back as usual, I couldn't track the hellhound like I had the other night. And in the meantime, the hell-hound could be anywhere. Terrorizing anyone.

"They can smell magic the same way I can smell your cologne," I said, trying to think of something. Some sort of plan.

"Maybe we should have told my mother," Trey said, sounding uncertain for the first time.

I could just picture the ways in which Catherine Lansing would approach the situation. "Sure. And after Jason Thorpe was found mauled to death, what then?"

"Then why summon it in the first place. That's what you were doing in the cemetery, right?"

I wanted to explain that it was an accident, some bizarre trap set in place to be triggered if someone came trying to summon Grace's ghost. But Trey wasn't done yet.

"You weren't planning to send them out on anyone, were you? I mean, I'd like to believe it was just some sort of accident, but the way you're acting..." Trey's voice trailed off, but the doubt and accusation were clear.

There wasn't time for this. "If you're going to ask if I was sending them after your mother, then just do it," I said, sinking down to rest on top of one of the gravestones. Maybe it was sacrilegious, but I'd already brought evil into the world.

"Did you?"

Once it was out there, the question hung between us like some sort of scarlet accusation. A monster that magic couldn't stop, bred to seek out and destroy anyone that had even a sliver of the power in them.

"Braden?" Trey had gone still. I looked up to find myself the victim of an intense scrutiny.

Even if I'd wanted to, the idea had never crept into my head. Something else had interfered, a trap hidden in the ground that had infected my spell like a parasite. But that was starting to give me an idea. A way to undo what happened.

"Of course not," I said slowly, carefully choosing my words. "You can leave. Everything will be fine now." *No one knew how to kill a hellhound, but had anyone ever tried infecting one?*

Trey took a step closer, leaving his face shrouded by the darkness. "What are you talking about?"

I went to the monument for Grace Lansing. Behind me, Trey's voice got loud. "I'm not going anywhere."

The night had grown cool already. My thermal hoodie wasn't going to protect against the chill for very long. I could smell a fire burning somewhere in the distance. I closed my eyes. Maybe it was fair to call this suicide: drawing out the spectral monster that adapts and grows immune to magic—while having nothing in the arsenal *except* magic.

I held my hands out, palms down, and focused on the magic. *Come forth*, I thought, feeling the power slowly rising like a tide. I hadn't taken my glasses off. I'd hoped to wait until the magic was in full swing. Maybe that was the trick—if I overextended my powers, I could short-circuit the visions.

"Braden!" In the middle of feeling out the spell, Trey's voice ripped through my concentration. I tried to smooth away my focus, to ignore him.

Big mistake. Something shoved me from behind, sending me slamming into Grace's monument. The jagged edge at the top hit me right in the stomach, knocking the air out of me in a rush.

I was spun around just as quickly as I was shoved in the first place. Everything around me was spinning, but this wasn't some drunken escapade. There was a blur in front of me, a man in a red sweatshirt moving faster than he should have. He grabbed the front of my shirt, acrid breath in my face.

"Not again," he growled, shunting me upward like I weighed nothing at all. The tips of his knuckles smacked into my Adam's apple and I started coughing instantly.

All in a matter of seconds. I recovered quicker than I'd have expected, shock making everything sharpen itself too fast. A red sweatshirt with "Arizona" etched across the front. Dark hair that had been shaved close to the scalp since the last time I'd seen him. A blazing anger that seemed to make even his eyes glow red.

"Drew?" I was still coughing. But now the pressure was focused on the tension of my sweatshirt as it pulled against the back of my neck, and underneath my arms.

"You let those things out. No more." He was a big fan of the growling, threatening alpha male.

"No, you… you don't get it," I tried to explain. He lifted me higher. My shirt was pulling tight around my neck, chafing the skin. I tried extending my feet, to touch solid ground again, but I was too far up. I could barely breathe.

Then I heard a sound right off every cop show I'd ever watched.

"Put him down, Drew." Trey's voice was cold. I saw a glint of silver against black, heard the cocking of the hammer. I was too busy trying to grab onto Drew's shirt to really understand what was happening.

All of a sudden, the pressure on my neck released and I fell to the ground. Coughing again, and trying to draw in as much oxygen as I could.

"Oh, have you been looking for me, Gentry?" Drew went on smoothly, as though a moment ago he hadn't assaulted me. "Next time, leave a message."

"Wha-what are you doing with a gun, Trey?" I wheezed. It was getting easier to breathe, but I thought for sure my Adam's apple had become an innie in the process.

"You're not going to shoot me." Drew seemed oddly confident in that, his back still to Trey and his eyes locked on mine.

Trey snorted. "You tried to kill my sister. I promised my mother I'd take care of the problem."

He'd tried to kill Jade? Riley had said that there had

been an incident that got Drew kicked out of school. She hadn't mentioned it involved attempted murder, though. No wonder the school expelled him. All things considered, it didn't sound all that crazy, since he'd just assaulted me a few seconds ago.

"No." Drew was full of composure and calm. "Your sister claimed I tried to kill her. There's a difference." His eyes focused on me in a narrowed slant. "I tried to warn you. Went and got mixed up in their lies, didn't you?" He shook his head in mock pity.

"Don't talk to him," Trey ordered. "Just back away."

I had to do something. "Put the gun—"

"How long after I got expelled was it before Mommy reinstated Jade's allowance?" Drew cut me off, glancing over his shoulder. He took a step backwards, doing what Trey'd told him to do.

"Put the gun down, Trey," I demanded.

"He just attacked you. Don't be stupid, Braden," Trey snapped.

"You let him make you the new little pawn?" Drew asked, sneering. "Too much to hope you'd actually stand up to them, huh?"

"Shut up," I said, my voice shaking. "Just shut up."

"'Cry havoc, and let slip the dogs of war,'" Drew laughed.

"You're quoting Shakespeare while I have a gun pointed at you?" I could see the grimace on Drew's face lengthen as Trey pushed the gun further into his neck. "Back up, Braden. I don't want you getting hurt."

"You were the wolf," I said, looking up at Drew. How was that even...I shook myself. Now was not the time to worry about all of that. I looked over at Trey. "I can handle myself."

"A lovers' spat. How gay," Drew said with a smirk.

I reacted before Trey could open his mouth. I threw my hand out, instinctively throwing magic that twisted into azure lines. They smacked into Drew and hurtled him backwards. He wasn't exactly airborne, but his heels skidded past two rows of graves before he tumbled into an angel statue. Perfect. The angel's arms flowed downwards, a look of lament on her face. I wrapped the spell around him, tying it tight.

I turned to Trey. "Put. It. Down." It was almost like they wanted me to forget the reason we were here.

He hesitated for a moment, but eventually he uncocked the gun and slid it back into the waistband of his jeans. "You don't know what kind of mistake you're making, Braden. He's dangerous."

"Stand back." I pulled the glasses off, bracing for the pain. It was pointless. The moment I did it, everything crashed forward with the force of a highway collision. It blindsided me the way it always did.

Nothing will ever be the same my soul feels murky blue darkness drowning from the inside left us too soon violent red so glad you're in the ground bitch shadows once dwelt here a color that could survive the light shades of yellow in a better place. A woman with a veil stands before me, her eyes glowing through the lace design.

True power locked away, keys that cannot feel. All that was torn lies fallow here. It is not death but is still dying. Silver and red and heavenly blue, tales I am told, she says to me under cover of darkness, magic in greens and browns hides in plain sight a place of absence, where something does not dwell where it should.

My mind started to clear as they passed, too quick to grasp them all. Only snowflakes in the storm. I forgot about Trey and Drew, pushed everything to the furthest corner of my mind.

The hellhound's trail was still visible to me, full of dark fire and burning shadows. I held out my arms again, turning my palms to the ground. The energy hadn't returned to sleep. There was still magic in the air. All it would take was a little nudge.

I placed my palms against the ground. The magic came surging forth, free of restraints and totally wild. It began to spiral, colors of the rainbow becoming crystalline and dark at the same time. Every shade that existed in nature, and many that couldn't be seen by the naked eye. And for a moment, they bowed before me.

It was like there was some sort of underground spring full of magic. The more I drew up, the more power came rushing out. I'd never felt anything quite like it—drawing magic out of the air was one thing, but this was like drawing up an ocean.

I didn't try to channel it into any sort of spell, I just continued pulling it forth. The energy began to spin around me, creating a vortex.

Somewhere deep below me, I felt things unraveling. Not more booby traps. This was something else. It felt like bolts in a door, being thrown in succession.

The hellhounds could smell magic, attuned to it from the very start. What I was doing was the equivalent of a thousand signal flares, all leading to this spot.

Time passed; I wasn't sure how much. My focus was on the cyclone around me, watching it spin so fast it fed itself. The force of it all drew more power from the ground, which in turn made it circle faster.

Braden! His warning pressed against my skin. I heard growling. The plan had worked. So far. Then again, I didn't have much to go on after this.

I ascended through the maelstrom and looked down upon the town. Belle Dam was laid out before me in an organized series of lines and lights, each of them twinkling against the darkness that swirled around the town. The lines reminded me of the restaurant. Magical architecture.

And then I saw the darkness. At first I thought it was some sort of shroud, a spell of darkness and rot. It was something alien, beautiful but full of *wrong*. It drew on the unnatural the way magic drew upon nature.

I'd never seen anything like this before. Though I tried

desperately to file it away somehow and understand it, that wasn't in the cards. This wasn't magic at all. The shape of it came into focus as black settled into different shades of gray. An oval shape emerged. An eye.

Except this one covered the entire town.

The moment the realization hit, I was dropped to the ground. The wellspring of magic was still pouring forth. The growling was getting louder. The hellhound pushing its way through the magic. I felt something else throw itself against the magic, only to be cast aside as flotsam.

In my absence my legs had started cramping and rigor mortis plagued my arms. Sweat was pouring down my face, covering my body with an icy sheen. Everything was heightened beyond control. As the wind pushed its way through each individual blade of grass, I heard explosions as they collided against each other.

I struggled to my feet, trying to keep focus.

The hound snarled again, its muzzle finally breaking through the circle around me. The power was starting to falter, growing unstable at the intrusion at its side. "C'mon, just another minute," I pleaded to the torrent, as though it could hear me. I just needed to buy myself a little more time.

I widened my eyes, seeing the fractures and ripples created by the hound as it tried to force its way inside the circle. The energy was growing more unstable, like a spinning top that was about to fall over. I tried to strengthen it, force the magic to spin faster. Ever faster.

Once the majority of the hound was inside the circle, I focused on the spell that had summoned it. The hound was linked to the spot it had been summoned from. In this case, right here in the cemetery. The summoning spell had infected my magic two nights ago. Now I was going to do the same thing in reverse.

I felt the strands of magic that had given the hound a home in this world, and I tugged at them. At the same time, I pulled at the hurricane, tying the two together— infusing the power of the magic with the spell that had summoned the hound. It was like plugging a toaster directly into a nuclear power plant.

The more I pushed and pulled, the slower the hellhound advanced. Uncertain what was happening, the hound began to whine, scratching at the ground with its paws. The magic churned into it, and back out the other side.

Each time the magic cycled, it tore away a little more at what made the darkness inside the hound real. Finally, like a balloon that had undergone too much strain, the hellhound popped. It exploded into shreds of magical power, quickly sucked up into the hurricane.

I did it. I'd just made history. No one had ever killed a hellhound before. All that was left was to disperse the flood of magic around me. I was starting to get lightheaded.

"I release everything," I shouted, clapping my hands together in one final motion. My dismissal closed the floodgates immediately. The magic circled only a few more times, but with no more magic drawn from the ground, it spiraled out into the atmosphere.

There was only a moment to see Trey's eyes widen as what remained of the magic exploded into ozone and concussive sound, no longer constrained to the simple circle. Like a tornado that touched down and then vanished, it evaporated, taking the remains of the hellhound with it. It had worked.

"That was cool," I said, a moment before everything went dark.

Twenty-Three

There was only a brief sense of something cool and silken, deep amidst the dreams. I walked the streets of Belle Dam, but a city that was poised to be built, not one that had been old and stable for over a century. The air was crisper here, cool and inviting and full of promises and possibilities.

The energy in the town was electric, as faceless people wandered the streets in a hurry. Huge trees lined the main avenues of packed dirt and cobblestone sidewalks. Where the high school should have been was a grassy field, devoid of flowers or trees of any kind.

It was a clear morning, and I could see all the way to the coast to the north. The water glinted against my eyes, charmed by the morning sunlight.

"The door is the key," someone murmured from behind me. When I turned to find the speaker, there was nothing but empty street. Instantly, Belle Dam gave way to a forest path, wilted and broken as if by some powerful storm. The trees slanted on all sides, branches cracked and shattered by lightning. There was a smell of smoke in the air, the smell of charred and blackened meat.

"The door is the key," the voice whispered again. I spun back around, hoping to see the city once more. But there was just another path, this one branching in two directions. At the crossroads, Lucien Fallon stood in an old-fashioned suit and top hat.

"The door is the key?" I asked, my voice scratchy and rough.

Lucien tipped his head to the side to consider it. His hand raised, he tilted the top hat forward.

"Irrelevant." Lucien shrouded his eyes with the brim of the top hat and lifted a cane I hadn't noticed before.

"I don't understa—" In a moment, the forest in front of me exploded into lights and sounds and memories. Visions that passed by so quickly I couldn't see them. The wind whooshed past my ears, and as I smacked into the tree trunk nearby, I fell out of the dream.

¤   ¤   ¤

"Mmph." I stretched in the bed, feeling the strain the previous night had carried out on my body. The room was incredibly bright, even to my closed eyes. I fumbled against the bedside table. My sunglasses were where I always left them, and I slipped them on automatically. The effort took what little energy I'd had, and I fell back. The top of my forehead throbbed, like horns were threatening to burst out of my skin.

It took some time for the fog in my brain to ease. Somehow, I'd gotten home. Trey must have brought me here. Across the room, someone cleared their throat. At first my heart jumped, thinking Trey must have stayed and waited with me. Then he spoke.

"You're pushing yourself too hard."

I recognized Jason's voice immediately.

"What are you doing here?" I whispered. Déjà vu struck me until I flashed back to the first time I'd seen Jason and asked the same question.

"I'll order breakfast," Jason said. I couldn't tell if my words had any effect. It was like business as usual.

"I need to get dressed," I muttered. I untangled myself from the sheets, which had become wrapped around me like a full-body noose, slick with sweat and cold. It was a wasted effort. I could barely get the sheets off of me, let alone accomplish the monumental task of getting out of bed. Every shift of my body made my brain jiggle free and loose in my skull, flashing lines of fire and barbed wire.

Jason walked over toward the bed, holding a dark blue coffee cup in his hands. "Drink this, Braden. It'll ease the pain." He held the cup out. I wouldn't have reached for it, but my throat was completely arid. My hand shook so much that Jason knelt upon the bed, pushing it down.

"Relax. Let me." He moved the cup closer to my mouth, his free hand smoothing back the locks of hair curling with sweat against my forehead. Jason's hands were smooth and cold, and I flinched. A mortician's hands, not some powerful witch mobster. I sniffed hesitantly, the scent of vanilla and lavender wafting from the cup. The cup pressed against my lips and my mouth opened automatically, swallowing down the sweet liquid. He could be drugging me right now, but anything was better than the putrid sleep taste on my tongue.

He flourished his hand at the wrist, revealing two of my migraine pills like it was some sort of magician's big reveal. "Swallow these," he said, lifting the cup again.

After another few slow sips, Jason pulled the cup away. "Not too fast now," he cautioned. "You'll make yourself sick."

"Why are you here? What happened to Trey?" I asked.

"Shh. Go back to sleep," Jason whispered, his hand still resting on my scalp. "When you wake up, you'll feel more like yourself."

I wanted to argue, to push and struggle until I could focus on what was really going on. But the warmth of Jason's elixir soaked into me, relaxing everything with a comforting heat, paving the way to real rest.

The next time I awoke, the sun was much further along in the sky. I stretched automatically, feeling muscles that should have screamed moving languidly. Had I lost another day?

Jason sat in the same chair as the first time I'd woken up. He had a cup of coffee in front of him and was watching the skyline. Finding something of myself in the man was hard. His hair was black and gray, mine was a flat brown. His was fine, where mine had a tendency to curl.

Plus, he was a total dick last time he dropped in for a visit.

"You've certainly been making waves since you came here, haven't you," Jason mused. He looked up from the view, watching me with something that looked like concern. There were rumples in his suit, ones I hadn't noticed earlier.

I still wasn't sure what to think. "So this is a father/son pep talk? Eat all your vegetables and join my arcane mafia and you get ice cream?"

"Don't be snide," he said quietly. He gestured for me to take a seat at the table across from him. "Braden..." He looked away. "You can hate me for a great many things, but sending you away isn't one of them. You had to be protected. Catherine wouldn't have stopped. She'd have come for you too."

"What do you mean, 'too'?"

"Catherine's magic is insidious. Powerful in a much different way than yours or mine. She's mastered disciplines that our families thought lost generations ago. We knew you were a special child even before you were born. Your mother, the most vivacious person I'd ever met, saw things as you grew inside her. A darkness she thought was killing the town."

"What does this have to do with Catherine?"

"The final weeks of her pregnancy, those visions turned darker, drawing your mother down with them. The doctor thought she was suffering from depression. A few days after you were born, she took her own life."

"Then it was suicide." As much as I was trying to stay stoic, it was hard.

Jason shook his head. "If I'd had your sight, maybe I would have noticed earlier. But I couldn't see, and you were still a baby. A newborn baby that cried every time his mother came into the room." He was quiet for a moment. "Your eyes didn't hurt you then. Maybe they were weaker. But magic killed my wife. And Catherine was responsible."

"But you don't know that for sure. Like you said, you can't see the things I can." It made me wonder how much he really knew about my visions.

"I know," his voice was immediate and hard. "Just because I can't see it doesn't mean I couldn't feel it. The air buzzed with it. It couldn't have been anything but magic. It was *her*."

As hard as I wanted to be, as tough as I wanted to act, as soon as Jason started talking about my mother, everything started crumbling. "Why?" I whispered.

"The feud? Or your mother?" Jason's tone was gentle. Who was this man?

"All of it. Why keep it up?"

Jason closed his eyes, clasping his hands around the coffee mug. "Because I'm not the one who's supposed to end it. You are." His eyes opened and then immediately narrowed. "You'd know all of this already, if Jonathan had done his job right.

"Jonathan was supposed to tell you everything, Braden. It was never my intention to leave you in the dark. Then, when you were strong enough, you could stand up to Catherine if you needed to."

That's not right. "He told me he couldn't. That there was some sort of... binding on him. What's that word? The thing that means a promise you can't break?"

"A *geas*." Jason looked at me. "If he told you he was under some sort of vow of silence, I can assure you my brother was lying. Avoiding his responsibilities has always been his prime concern in life."

That didn't sound like the Jonathan I knew at all. "He raised me and took care of me all my life. That's a huge responsibility." *Even if he was lying, he would have slipped up at least once. But Uncle John had never said anything about his past. Or mine. And he struggled with the little he could tell me.*

He dipped his head in acknowledgement. "Fair enough. And for which I'm grateful. But now you're home."

"So what now? You've got your secret weapon, and you want me to go blow out her tires or something?"

"Ending the feud will require a little more effort than that."

"I won't." I imitated the Lansings' icy tone as best I could.

"Braden, she'll kill you," Jason snapped. "She won't hesitate. As soon as she thinks you're a threat, that's it."

"And I'm sure she's telling her kids the same thing," I said. "Both of you, keeping up this stupid feud. People would get hurt. *I* could get hurt. But you don't care about any of that. You just want to win."

"Son, that's not what's happening," Jason tried to say, but I kept going.

My vision started skewing toward shades of red. I felt the magic drawing itself from the air around me, responding to the feel of my anger. "Don't ever call me that," I said quietly. "I don't know you. And I'm not sure I want to."

"You're being petulant," Jason said finally, after several deep breaths. "You think I don't understand why you're angry? This was the only way I could protect you."

"Bull. If the all-powerful Jason Thorpe couldn't protect me, then no one could," I snapped. Pointing to the door, I forced it open with magic. "You know the way out."

A thin trace of humor shifted his face, an expression I didn't think occurred very often. "You have my temper, don't you?"

"I think I told you to leave." The evenness in my voice was scaring me.

"Lucien didn't mention you would be quite so difficult."

"Yeah well, Lucien forgets to mention a lot of things," I snapped. I'd dreamt of him last night, the only person in the strange alternate Belle Dam. "How long's he worked for you?" I hadn't forgotten the research I'd done on him, and the way his age didn't seem to match up with his background.

Jason's gaze sharpened. "My staff are not your concern," he said, instantly confirming that I was onto something.

"Really? Because he's got to be pushing at least fifty by now, right? I mean, you are, aren't you?"

"Why this sudden fascination with him, Braden? I thought there were more pressing concerns. You cannot allow your focus to waver. Catherine is the target, son."

"I told you to stop calling me that!"

His lips thinned. "You've had a free hand too long, Braden. I'm still your father, and I'll do what I think is best."

"If you don't leave now—" *If they wanted me to be a weapon, they got one.* "—then I'll make you."

But Jason was not to be intimidated. "You are my son," Jason said quietly. "And some boundaries need to be established."

Power slammed into me, and the worst case of vertigo I'd ever had was pulling me in every direction. The floor grew uneven, and I could barely stay standing. Even though I couldn't see it, I could feel the effects of the magic, a force Jason directed so casually. "What are you doing?" I whispered.

Jason's voice sounded deeper than it should have, a horror movie monster with access to a synthesizer. "Making sure you understand me."

Twenty-four

"Don't strain yourself, Jason." I grasped the edge of the bed for stability. The vertigo sensation was only growing worse, hurtling through some imaginary chasm I couldn't see.

"I'm your father, Braden." His voice sounded even darker now, rumbling across the room like some sort of demon.

With my free hand, I struggled to reach my face. But there was a disconnect between my mind and my body, and I couldn't quite reach it. The more I moved, the more intense the nausea in my stomach. I started gagging as my stomach threatened revolution, but I kept trying. Finally, my fingers slipped onto the glasses, and I ripped them off. My vision sharpened instantly.

Silver violet rose pink scarlet amber forever and ever she never meant anything to you can't trust gray embers burnt out sparks of thank god I needed this forest green relief and rest and burning trails of magic.

Through the haze of a thousand lives, I saw it. The spell was a sickly green, the color of pine needles suffering before death. They formed chains that stretched across the room. I could just barely see over the top of the bed, where they trailed right toward their source. For once, I tried to focus on the impressions sweeping through me, anything to avoid the effects of the spell.

"You're not stronger than me." It was hard to even choke out the words. I pushed against the chains, forcing them to unravel in front of me. Power surged inside of me, a strength I'd somehow drawn out of the emotions smothering the room. I took it in, and turned it into magic.

It was slow at first, one link at a time wavering under my concentration. And then all at once, the spell snapped, the chains ripped apart and hurtled toward Jason. Immediately the nausea faded, like it had never been there. I pulled myself up from the side of the bed.

"Very good," Jason said, sipping at the cup of coffee.

"I don't want to hurt you." Part of me didn't, at least.

"You won't." Jason settled the cup back on the table, and then stood up. "You have an incredible gift, Braden. But you don't intimidate me."

I hesitated. Everything was just getting too confusing. First Jason was a jerk, and now he was some sort of concerned alpha-parent. I'd come to keep Uncle John safe, but once I got here everyone wanted me to actually kill someone. Someone else had once had my powers, but hadn't left anything to help me learn control.

Jason's tone was grave. "You're already winded. I've barely gotten started." He indicated the distance between us. "Could you stop me, if I continued? Or if I'd bound those glasses to your skin? You don't know the first thing of what you can do. I can teach you strength. I can give you that control. You have to fight through the pain.

"I want you to live. To grow strong, and be the son I know you can be. I won't lose you to her." Jason's voice was suddenly savage. "I don't dare."

"Do you hear yourself?" I snapped. "You don't know a thing about me. What was my first word? What did I ask for at Christmas when I was six? God, what's my favorite book?" I waved my hand in a circular motion, drawing the magic out through the fingers. "I'm just a project to you. A strategy."

Maybe Jason saw what was coming before it happened. His eyes narrowed, and I saw the magic he'd started drawing to him.

I'd drawn much, much more than he had, and I pushed it out all at once. It ripped through Jason's spell before it had time to gain a form, and shoved him back down into the chair. "At least Catherine was a bitch to my face."

I threw on a shirt and a pair of jeans. My phone and keys were on the nightstand by my bed, and I scooped them up as I moved for the door. Jason hadn't recovered by the time I slammed the door behind me. And he didn't appear before the elevator doors closed around me.

I sank to the cold tile floor of the elevator, and watched the floor numbers gradually descend.

¤　　¤　　¤

I'd managed to pull myself back onto my feet by the time the elevator reached the lobby. I wasn't nauseous anymore, but it was almost like the memory of feeling that way was enough to start the process all over again.

The guy at the desk eyed me as I headed out the front doors, but I soon forgot about him. I focused on my phone, and scrolling down the pitiful address book to call home.

"What's wrong?" John demanded immediately.

I hesitated. A part of me wanted to drop to the ground and lose it, expecting that he'd come in and fix everything. But that wasn't who I was anymore.

"What do you know about Lucien? I mean, really know?"

Silence from the other end, and although I heard his breath catch a few times, he never actually started to speak.

"You can't tell me anything either?" I closed my eyes and looked up toward the sky. Absolutely perfect.

Finally, after several more moments of some sort of struggle, Uncle John managed to spit out, "What's happening?"

What was happening? I still wasn't sure. Something about Lucien was bothering me, but I didn't know enough to know what it was. "Something's wrong. I don't know, I had this dream about him last night that was all strange. And he's told me one thing, but he's telling Jason something else. And I think he was telling you something, too. Wasn't he?"

More silence. It's impossible to actually hear someone go red in the face, but I almost thought I could.

That's when the inspiration struck me. "You can't tell me the truth," I said slowly. "But you can lie, can't you?"

John didn't say anything, and I wondered if I was completely off base. But I had to try. He inhaled, and I waited. "It doesn't work like that," he said finally, the words leaked in a rush.

"Catherine doesn't have any clue who I am," I said, lowering my voice. I'd walked over to the town square, and was sitting at one of the benches facing the fountain. The square was deserted on a Sunday morning, but I didn't want to take any chances. "But someone's definitely been after me since I've gotten to town. They're having me followed, and I think they're using magic," I said, thinking back to the weird shadow images I'd been seeing.

"When I was growing up, and my brother and I would fight," Uncle John said, "he'd never wait around if I pissed him off. He'd beat me bloody, but he was always up front about it. And when it was over, all was forgiven."

The story came out of nowhere, and I almost questioned him in confusion. But then I stopped myself. Uncle John wasn't allowed to tell me anything useful, but maybe he wasn't completely helpless.

"So if it was Jason trying to scare me," I said slowly, trying to put the pieces together, "you think he'd be more up front about it?"

I waited for silence. Expected silence. Silence would

have confirmed my theory. "I haven't said anything," John said immediately.

Crap. Did that mean I was wrong? Or that I was right, and the question had edged too close to whatever was wrong with him?

"Braden," he said, sounding more upset, "I can't help you with this. Not now. You just have to trust in yourself. Remember where you come from, and what you know."

On my own. I sat with that for a minute. What I needed was help. And information. I knew exactly where to turn.

¤   ¤   ¤

"Braden? What's the matter?" Riley hurried across the square, accompanied by her own personal armband percussions. "You're freaking me out."

I'd curled up on the side of the fountain. I needed to tell someone. I couldn't stand the lies anymore, and everything they were doing to me. Anything, just so I could figure it all out in my head. "Everything's gone to hell."

"If this was any other town," Riley's voice was dubious, "I'd think you were being metaphorical. But since it's not, just one question. What did Jade do now?"

"Jason Thorpe is my father." The moment I said the words, it felt like everyone else in the square turned to look at me. But I was too ashamed to look up and meet their eyes. I dropped my head back down.

"Your ... wait ... your ... " Riley sputtered. Her eyes were wide, and she grabbed at me.

"Father," I supplied. "Dad. Parent. Paternal relation. Genetic donor."

It took the normally hyper girl a minute to process. I could relate. I was still struggling. "You talked to him?"

I lifted my head. "He showed up this morning like we were best friends."

"But Jason doesn't have any kids. Just a son that..." Riley trailed off, as she put the pieces together.

I didn't need to see her face to know what she was thinking. "Yeah, apparently I got snuck out of town to hide me from Catherine and everything going on here."

"Does anyone else know?"

I shook my head. "Just Jason. And his lawyer, too. And now you."

Riley leaned back. "God," she breathed. "It's kinda cool, though. Don't you think? Jason's got loads of money, and you can pretty much do what you want." She grimaced. "You don't need to be Jade's pet project anymore."

"I'm not." Riley's issue with Jade was none of my business. "She's my friend."

Her skin flushed, and she looked away. "I'm just saying."

I'd hurt her feelings. "Sorry, but it's not like that." I sighed, looking up toward the sky. "I just had to tell someone."

"Why is it such a big deal?"

"I just need to figure some stuff out. Maybe why they're both so amped up about the other one."

"Like why the feud's such a big deal?" Riley asked,

and I nodded. "Always has been. But if you're looking for answers about it, I know a guy. He runs a comic book shop, and knows more about the weird stuff in town than even I do."

Of course it would come back to Gregory. "Yeah, we've met."

Riley closed her mouth and nodded. She had the strangest look on her face, a mix of surprise and shock. I wasn't sure what it meant. "Come on, it's only a couple blocks."

Gregory's was closed when we got there. The lights in the building were on, and according to the sign they should have been open, but the door was still locked. Weird.

"There's something you should know," Riley said, but I wasn't really listening. I had a feeling that Gregory was inside, and that the door had only gotten locked once he saw us crossing the street.

"Door's just stuck," I muttered, hoping it was convincing. Unlocking a door was pretty simple if it was a normal lock. Lucky for me, this was. The plate surrounding the keyhole was the color of tarnished gold, complete with a number of scratches where the key had dragged against metal. Just as long as Riley didn't realize I was doing magic, I'd be okay.

"Braden? Are you listening to me?"

I grunted something noncommittal, my attention more on the lock than on Riley. I closed my eyes, imagining the hole filling with a silver and gold spell that formed itself into a key.

"You know, you're not even listening to me, and I'm trying to tell you something important here," Riley announced. But I missed the urgency in her voice. I was focused more on waiting for the click.

"Just hold on a minute," I muttered. There it was, the click. I reached out to touch the doorknob, hesitating for a moment. I wasn't sure why, but all of a sudden breaking in didn't seem like such a good idea. Gregory seemed to be close to Trey. I had a feeling my visit would be the topic of a very interesting phone call very soon.

"You're on the Internet!" Riley blurted out, just as the door swung open under my hand.

If I'd thought the day's surprises were going to end with my father's appearance that morning, then I was sorely mistaken. "What?"

"I was going to tell you," Riley insisted, reaching out to tug on my sleeve. "See, there's this website about Belle Dam—"

"The SAC something or other," I interrupted.

Riley flinched, dropping her hand. "Uhm, right. How'd you know about that?" Since she couldn't see my eyes, I had to trust that pressing my lips together would get the point across. "Right, anyway. I mean, not *you* you. But this really pretentious guy named Myth Man posted about this boy witch who'd come to town. I didn't even know they *made* boy witches, but Myth Man seemed insistent. Then you showed up at school and I got curious, right before he followed it up by saying the witch always wore glasses."

So Riley thought I'd be her best friend, and she'd learn a little something about witches. "So that's why you're hanging around." Riley'd been playing me too. Everyone in this damn town had an agenda.

"No!" She looked near to tears. I realized then that I had almost been yelling. "I just thought I could prove him wrong, that's all. It's crazy, right? A boy witch?"

"Why'd you wait until now to tell me?"

Riley looked down, her hair spilling into her eyes. "I was going to, but I figured if I did, you'd think I was faking being your friend. Or that I just wanted something from you."

Gregory had told me about the site before, but I hadn't thought I'd be on it. "What else is on there about me?"

Riley shook her head. "Nothing, I swear. It just said a new witch showed up in town the night before Labor Day, and it seemed like he wasn't involved with either side."

"So you think I'm a witch? Just because some jerk posted a rumor about me?"

Her forehead crinkled. "It's just this board where people get together and talk about the weird stuff. And there's a whole section for talking about the people that can do things."

"Like Catherine Lansing."

She nodded. "Who told you about it?" It was the

reporter in her. Now that I knew her better, I could hear the shift in her voice, the way her words took on an edge.

I shrugged. "Who else? The man behind the curtain." I pushed the door open. Gregory had some explaining to do.

Except that he didn't seem to be anywhere in the shop. I gestured for Riley to follow me toward the stairs, but the sound of voices coming from a different room stopped me.

"Now's not the time to play loyal lapdog," a younger, deeper voice was saying.

"You don't have any idea what Catherine can do when she's pissed off. She's like Dark Phoenix and Emma Frost combined," said the other sulkier, wavering voice.

"If it wasn't for the kid, that thing would be roaming around the town right now, stirring it all up again. The last thing Jason needs is to come back and see Catherine just itching for a fight."

"Jason's too scared of her, he won't do anything." The voice was whining now. I walked back toward the other room, seeing Drew pacing the way I knew he would be, and Gregory sitting in a computer chair, his head in his hands.

"Someone want to tell me what's going on?" I walked into the room and stared at both of them.

"Planning committee for your execution," Drew announced without missing a beat. "How about we skip the catering and just get everyone Happy Meals?"

Twenty-five

"Drew, what are you doing here?" Riley pushed past me, her neck craned backwards to look at him. "And what do you mean, execution?"

Gregory looked like he was about to jump out of his chair. Or piss his pants. Hopefully, not both at the same time.

Drew's blasé attitude didn't last long. He actually looked mollified for a second.

"You just stay away from me." Gregory looked more nervous than I'd ever seen him before. Gone was the arrogant comic book owner. Something had happened.

"He's been sucking off your girlfriend's son, Greg. I'd think you'd be happy to see him." Drew's discomfort didn't last for long. His arrogance put Trey to shame.

I looked at him in shock. "What the hell did I do to you?"

"She's not my girlfriend," Gregory muttered, but no one was listening.

"Hey, you're the one that's working for the lawyer,"

Drew said with disdain. "Not my fault you've got shitty taste in guys."

"I'm not working for Lucien Fallon. He's my uncle's lawyer."

The look he gave me was patronizing, and just like that, I realized, *He knows who I am.* "You should talk to my buddy Greg. He's got you all twisted up, focusing on the wrong bad guy. Or girl, I should say."

Riley stomped her foot on the ground. "I'm talking to you, Drew. What are you doing here? I thought you said it wasn't safe for you to be in town."

I turned to her. "Riley, take him somewhere and hash this out. I need to talk to Gregory."

Gregory's eyes went wider, and he tried shuffling his chair backwards. Like distance was really going to make a difference. All it did was make him look like some cracked-out chicken kicking his legs out.

"I told you to stay out of this, Riley," Drew growled. Lucky for me, he took the hint and stalked out of the room. Even luckier, Riley started chasing *him* around like a dog looking for a bone. I could hear her voice getting louder and sharper the further they got, until the door chimed, signaling they'd gone outside.

But there was still tension in the room, and a shop owner who still looked terrified. Why? I hadn't really done anything *that* bad to him. Something had to have happened since yesterday. Something had made him terrified of me. Drew?

"If you start casting spells on me again, Catherine's going to be really mad," Gregory started saying, but I held up my hand and he cut off.

"Listen," I said gently, "I need information. And everyone in town knows that you're the go-to guy if anything is happening here, right?"

The calming tone must have worked, because some of the stiffness left his posture. "R-right. I mean, I don't like to toot my own horn, y'know. But it's true."

"That's what I've been hearing all over town," I assured him. "But we don't have time for that. I need to know everything you've got on Lucien Fallon."

¤ ¤ ¤

Half an hour later, Gregory came sauntering back into the room. Riley and Drew had never come back, and I'd spent my time paging through some of the more esoteric grimoires on the shelf.

"One of the city's most interesting anomalies," Gregory announced, a stack of computer papers in his hands. "There isn't a lot out there," he warned. "Just a lot of speculation."

"But there's something," I pressed. "So he's definitely off somehow."

"Well, I'm guessing you don't care about how many secretaries he goes through?" I shook my head. "It's strange, though. Hiring so many local girls. You wouldn't think the turnover would be as high as it is."

"So he's got a thing for young girls. Gross, but that doesn't help me."

Gregory huffed, plucking a sheet from the stack and dropping the rest into the garbage can. "That's fine," he mumbled. "Only spent three weeks cross-referencing hair color to height."

"Greg, he's supposed to be in his forties or fifties," I announced impatiently. "But he looks like he could be attending his ten-year high school reunion. There has to be something there, right?"

"Here, look." He dropped the sheet in front of me, a picture of Lucien that could have been taken yesterday. "Key Festival, circa 2006." Another sheet got dropped, this one in black and white. "Key Festival circa 1906." And finally one more, the quality on this one a lot worse. "And a painting from 1853. Right around the time Belle Dam was founded."

I lined the three pages next to each other. The two photographs were taken from almost the same angle, facing the town square. In one it was a haphazard mob, but my father and Lucien were clearly noticeable on the courthouse steps. In the second, a group was posed together. Off to one side, in a top hat like the one in my dream, was Lucien.

I squinted at the painting, which had apparently been scanned from a picture of the painting, then printed up, ruining most of the quality. There was a large distortion in the middle, splitting the group in two. On one side were a group of men, but on the other side I immediately recognized Lucien and a woman in white. "Wait a second. Is that...?"

Gregory nodded. "Grace Lansing. The Widow herself. They just folded the original in half, hoping no one would ever notice those two were missing. The founding fathers of Belle Dam, gathering together for the first time."

Lucien hadn't changed a bit in one hundred and fifty years. Even the hair styles in all three were nearly the same. Short and slicked back. "So why doesn't anyone notice? If this guy's been walking around Belle Dam for over a hundred years and never gets any older, then someone had to catch on."

"Why would they?" Gregory pulled the pictures back into his stack. "In case you haven't noticed, people in Belle Dam try to remain as ignorant of the truth as possible. Why do you think no one's ever tried burning a Lansing at the stake?"

He rolled his eyes and continued. "As far as they were concerned, Lucien Fallon, or Lucas Fallon as he was in the '50s, worked in town for a decade or two and then supposedly left for New York. When he came back pretending to be his own son, no one batted an eyelash. Everyone thinks his family's been working for the Thorpes for generations. But this time around, Lucien didn't disappear after showing up."

"So how's he do it? Some kind of spell?" My head was already buzzing with ideas. Magic was possible, but how would he have sustained the effect? Hypnotizing the entire town permanently would take a lot of juice. An impractical amount of juice.

Then I remembered the shadow eye—both the visions I'd seen and that dark blanket of energy curled atop the town like a tourniquet. Was that what it really was? Some giant spell over the town? Stretched so tight over everything that I couldn't see it for what it was?

"Probably." Gregory shrugged. "Or there's something else going on. Maybe he's cursed, forced to live out his life over hundreds of years trying to right the wrongs done to him in search of atonement. Or he could be of a race of immortal men and women who must fight to the death."

He didn't have any idea how ridiculous he was sounding. "What about the downtime? Any idea what Lucien's doing when he's not in Belle Dam?" I asked, but Gregory immediately shook his head. "He's got to be doing something, right?"

"Sleeping? That's what I'd do, if I could live forever. Take a nap for a few of the boring years. Like the seventies, or the boy band era, y'know?"

Think, Braden. Figure out what he is, and maybe that'll help figure out how he did it.

I'd seen him in daylight, so he wasn't some sort of vampire. Courted fey were immortal, but I'd spoken to Lucien, and he was too ... sane to be one of them. Plus they preferred chaos to order, and Lucien was all about his timetables.

Demons didn't have the power to just… hang out. They could be summoned, but they were too strong to stay here. Gravity dragged them back to where they came from. Anything else was too powerful to even care about this dimension.

"Besides, he's not the most interesting part of that legend," Gregory went on. "You know the stories about Grace, right?"

"More than you think," I muttered.

"Highly doubt that," he sniffed. "She's our very own Dumbledore. Until she vanished, never to be seen again."

"I know all this. Tell me something I don't know."

"Well, did you know that Grace was the one that picked this spot?" He waited pointedly while I didn't say anything. "Grace wanted the town built here, and so it was. She picked the location, and while the public records don't give her the proper credit, they do frequently mention her sketching ability."

"So she could draw?"

Gregory smiled. "I wouldn't imagine you could understand. She was an artist. Some may say an architect. It's notable that right from the start, Belle Dam was organized in a way most other towns were not."

"Meaning?"

"Meaning that the popular theory among people in the know," Gregory puffed out his chest, "is that Grace designed the town. The layout, the mix of residential and commercial areas, the local parks. Belle Dam's been the same size it's always been."

Grace designed the town. My mind flashed back to the image of Belle Dam from above, ebbing and weaving with energy. "How is it no one knows about this?"

"There's a ... separate archive for sensitive information," he said slowly. "Certain information would only stir up trouble in town."

"So you're censoring the info that's out there," I reasoned out. "Trying to keep the Lansings happy?"

"It's not like that."

I crossed my arms in front of me. "Really? Because everyone else in town's picked a side. Why not you, too? But you *are* going to give me everything you have."

His face was turning a deeper red. "I don't work for you. Besides, this is why things need to be carefully monitored. Or something like Carmen would happen again."

"Who's Carmen?" The name was familiar, but there was so much I'd picked up since coming to Belle Dam, it was hard to remember where I'd heard it.

"She worked for me, too. I mean, Catherine employed her," he said, almost dismissively. "Brought her to town and all, but she wasn't just here to do witch stuff. She worked here in the shop."

Of course. The two witches who'd come to Belle Dam in hopes of a freelancing job or something. One had gone to Jason, the other to Catherine. And now both were dead.

"What happened to them?"

Gregory shook his head. "No one's really sure. Drew was too young then, and Catherine wouldn't, or couldn't, tell me what happened. But it must have been pretty bad. She was in some kind of fury. Said that the town had gone nuclear the night before. Whatever that meant."

I wondered. Witches could sense magic, like a tingling on the skin. Nowhere near as well as I could, but they could feel a tremor when powerful spells were being worked. For Catherine to say it was "nuclear" meant it was some serious magic. "She came here the other day, right? After the spell I cast?"

Gregory nodded. "She was concerned." I saw the connection finally trigger, and his eyes lit up. "I thought summoning things was powerful stuff. So you're thinking she should have been more concerned?"

I shook my head. "No. I think she was just concerned enough." Which was really making me worry. If what I'd done had amounted to a grenade explosion, then what happened to Carmen and the other one would have been a nuclear bomb. How would second-rate witches have raised that kind of power? And if they hadn't, then who had?

"Can—can I interview you for the site?" Gregory asked with hesitation. Like I would really waste the time to blast him across the room for it or something.

"Trust me, if things don't get better, you're not going to want to." And it was true. If the truth got out, then half the people in town were going to wash their hands of me. Trey, Jade, and Gregory for starters.

"Do you have any idea what kind of megapocalypse we'd have if things really heated up?"

"Mega..." I wasn't sure how to respond to that.

"Belle Dam history is full of genocide. They've just got really good press." Gregory started typing away on the laptop. A few minutes later, he swiveled it around to face me. "The last big struggle was in the twenties. The Armstrongs were siding with August Thorpe at the time. Jason's grandfather." On the screen was an image of a newspaper clipping. *Floods Swallow Town.*

There was a picture in the yellowed clip, an image of the Belle Dam docks nearly submerged. I said the only thing I could in that situation. "Oh."

So if it got bad, then we were talking major damage. Not just to me, but to everyone in town. Until then, I needed Gregory. Him and Riley both. "Listen, I need you to start pulling out anything even marginally related to the feud. Anything that you've taken off that website."

"But what about Catherine?" He seemed shocked. The idea of going against her was nearly blasphemy.

"Greg? If you help me?" I struggled for some description he would understand. "You'd be like Jimmy Olson jumping in to save Superman before the world ends. You'd be doing everyone in town a favor. They'd owe you." My geek-fu was sadly lacking. It was the best I could come up with.

I could see the idea taking root in his head. Slowly, the

gears started turning, and he got behind the idea. "So I'd be a hero."

"And then some," I agreed. "There's a really good chance something bad is going to happen in the next day or two. Just be careful."

The idea of being a hero was new to Greg. He was staring off into the distance, the lines of his forehead thick as he lost himself in thought. I took the opportunity to start heading out, taking the pictures with me.

When I got outside, Riley wasn't there. I'd figured she and Drew would have stuck close, waiting for me, but no. *Leave me alone to figure out my next move. Perfect.*

I started heading for the library, not even sure if it was open on Sundays. I'd barely started to cross the street before my cell phone rang. I left it in my pocket until I crossed, then finally slid it out.

Trey's cell. Should I pick up? The last time we'd really talked, he'd had a gun on someone. Not entirely without reason, but that wasn't the point. I wasn't sure what to do with that new facet of his personality. If he could pull a gun on Drew, then he could certainly do the same to me. Or worse.

"Hello?" Like it or not, I still wanted to hear his voice.

"I didn't think you were going to pick up," he admitted after a moment of static.

"I wasn't sure I was going to. You pulled a gun on someone," I said slowly.

There was a draw of breath on the other end of the

line. "Braden, you don't understand what you got involved in. I tried to warn you."

"Yeah, you did. And I didn't listen." Somehow, that didn't make it any better. "But you went out there with me hoping he'd show up, didn't you? You knew he'd come back."

"You're feeling better? You were out of it last night."

That's right. Trey must have taken me home. I didn't remember anything after the cemetery. "Better now. What do you want, Trey?"

"Dinner. A chance to talk. And, remember? My mother's expecting you."

That was all I needed. Having Catherine breathing down my neck while I was trying to figure out what was going on with Lucien wasn't the best idea. Then again, maybe I could learn something if I went to dinner with them.

There wasn't much Catherine could throw at me that I couldn't stop. But the encounter with Jason had just stressed something I hadn't thought of before. Endurance. Jason had it, and if Catherine was even close to as strong as he was, then she could probably outlast me in a fight.

"You still there?"

"Today's not a good day. There's a lot of stuff going on," I said, trying to find some way out of it. *Our parents want each other dead, you hate my father, and your mother's going to try to kill me when she realizes what I see.*

There was a sigh on the other end of the line. "Maybe

you're not understanding me. When she invited you to dinner, she wasn't leaving you an option to cancel. There's enough going on out there without her thinking you're going to fall under Jason's spell."

I laughed. Couldn't help it—that was funny. Falling under another witch's spell. Trey wasn't laughing, of course. "Why? This isn't the meet-the-boyfriend dinner. We'll do it another time." Like never, if I could help it.

"Where are you at?" Trey's voice was full of curiosity, as a car horn blared behind me.

"Somewhere in town." At some point in the conversation, I'd stopped paying attention to directions, and now nothing really looked familiar. "I told you, I've got a lot on my plate. I already missed a day of school, and I can't get behind."

Trey wasn't buying it. "I'll come pick you up," he assured me. "She'll calm down once she's had a chance to get to know you, I promise."

I debated. More research, or a chance to learn more about the Lansings firsthand?

"Fine, whatever. Let me just figure out where I am first."

¤   ¤   ¤

There wasn't any talking on the drive. It was an unspoken rule from the moment I stepped inside. Trey barely looked at me, just pulled up to the curb and waited.

Maybe I could use the time with Catherine to find out more about Grace. A family anecdote, or some sort of ghost story that had been passed down. I glanced at Trey, and saw the way the muscles in his jaw were clenching and then releasing. Clench. Release. Maybe talking to him right now wasn't such a good idea.

We nearly drove out of town, heading the way I'd come in from the bus station. Trees lined one side of the road, thick and green and barely touched by the onset of fall. There was only a hint of red to the leaves, almost as if they'd decided that this year they wouldn't bow down before the cold season.

"She'll think you're trying to play both sides. Jason's back in town, so she doesn't have the luxury to ignore it. Everything's been quiet since he tried to kill my dad, but something like this would start it all over again."

It wasn't so much his words as the sound of his voice that surprised me. I'd gotten used to the silence during the ride. We were turning down into a long and elegant driveway with little brick markers leading the way. "I thought it stopped after whatever happened to Carmen?"

Trey shook his head. "Jason really didn't do anything that time. Nothing that could really violate their truce. But Mom never got over the first time he tried to kill my dad."

"Is that why you hate him? Jason?" I asked gently.

He didn't say anything, but I saw the jaw flex again. Hesitating, I reached out for his hand, clutched around the stick. The skin was cool, a dampness I didn't expect. Trey was always so in control, always comfortable taking the lead.

"You're just not thinking clearly," he went on, as though nothing had happened. "She'll take care of you. I will too. Jason wouldn't touch you after that. Besides," he added, with a semblance of humor streaking through his eyes, "you can take care of yourself. Can't you?"

All he wanted was to take care of me. I knew that. He knew Drew was a threat, and that's why he'd pulled the gun. Something wrenched itself in my stomach. Someone finally cared about me, and I didn't deserve it.

The path of trees cleared. We were there.

Twenty-Six

Even knowing the size and prowess of the Lansing name, I was stunned to see the house. The mansion. It was every bit as elegant as I should have expected from someone like Catherine, a brownstone complex that was full of large windows and gardens everywhere.

It was one part English manor and one part Gothic Revival, which somehow made perfect sense. The Lansing house was far enough away from town that you could almost forget it was within the city limits. It was exactly the sort of place you'd expect one of the founding families to live—isolated from the locals, and yet completely majestic.

Trey slowed the car as we pulled around the circular end of the drive. Everything I saw, from the hint of rose gardens off to one side to the sculptured ferns and bushes, suggested someone with exquisite taste had gone to town all over the property. It wasn't over the top; in fact, if anything, it was understated compared to the house.

Thick auburn stones made up the bulk of the manse— not quite a mansion, but something far grander than a house. The building gently sloped off to the sides, hints of expanded wings in the back with a much lighter, newer-looking stone.

"You ready for this?" Trey was all cool and calm once more, unaffected by our conversation.

Was I? "Sure," I said, sounding a lot more positive than I actually felt. Keeping secrets in town was one thing, but walking right into the Lansing home and lying to Catherine's face was something else entirely.

Part of me felt like the longer I was around Catherine, the faster my secrets would come spilling out. Like all she had to do was look at me, and she'd know.

"There's still an hour or so until dinner," Trey said after a glance down at his watch. "C'mon, let me show you the house."

I wiped my hands against my jeans, trying to stave off the dampness as he led me through the foyer.

Trey saw the movement, and he smiled. "No reason to be nervous. She already likes you."

"Only because I'm a witch. She doesn't know me."

"She will," was all he said.

I expected to walk into a museum, but the interior of the house surprised me. Everything was done in shades of creams and whites, but everything was functional instead of standoffish the way I'd assumed. Despite the colors, everything felt warm and used.

"C'mon, I'll show you the kitchen."

He led me through the back of the living room, down

a hallway, and through a formal dining room that was already set with four plates. My stomach turned again, seeing double. But I wasn't having some sort of vision problem—there really were two spoons and two forks on opposite sides of the place settings. I was totally out of my element.

Everything I'd seen so far was a mixture of taste and restraint. I didn't need to be told that Catherine had decorated everything herself; I could almost see her walking through the house, pulling the decorations back just a little bit.

But what about the secrets, I wondered. *All the places that she doesn't want the public to see.* I half-expected Trey to point out the bricked-up wing of the house where they'd chained their enemies, or the rooms that Catherine had devoted to her dark magic.

"Braden?" I looked up to see that Trey had left me far behind. Or I'd slowed on my way down the hall. "What's wrong?"

I shook my head, glancing down a darkened hallway to my left. *Victims trapped in guest rooms. Conditioned. Manipulated. And why is the house so quiet? Don't they have servants?* "I'm ... I'm fine," I finally managed, tearing my gaze away. Trey was giving me a look, but I ducked my head and stepped into the kitchen.

Massive. All the appliances were stainless steel, the countertops were dark marble, and everything else was white. White cabinets, flooring, a white chandelier over the islands in the center of the room. And as much as I'd have liked to imagine Catherine hanging people from the hooks in the ceiling, the only thing they actually held were copper pots.

It was also empty. No sign of the meal we were supposed to be eating soon, or anyone to prepare it.

"So what do you think?" Trey asked, leaning against one of the island counters.

I think maybe this is a trap. My stomach was crawling. "It's … interesting."

His eyes locked on mine. "That's it?"

"What do you expect?"

He shrugged, and looked away. "Most people act a little more impressed."

"You want me to ooh and ahh?"

He looked annoyed, which I didn't understand. "Forget it."

I wasn't sure what I'd done to piss him off.

"Sometimes, you're so—" He cut himself off, shaking his head.

"What?"

"Forget it." He opened the refrigerator door and rooted around inside. After a moment he emerged with a pair of bottled waters. He tossed one to me, which I managed to catch without dropping. Hurray for Team Braden on that one.

"Hey, I didn't even want to do this today," I said. "So

if I did something to piss you off, you might as well say something."

The look I got in reaction was incredulous. "Do you have any idea how much of a risk my mother's taking? And you're so ungrateful. She's doing this to *help* you, and you act like you can't even be bothered."

Now it was my turn for surprise. I wanted to laugh, but didn't. "This doesn't have anything to do with helping me. Or helping *you*, for that matter. This is all about collecting the new piece on the chess board."

Surprising both of us, Catherine's voice cut through the budding argument and stopped my irritation cold. "And how's Braden enjoying his tour of the house, Gentry?" She swept into the room in demure silver cashmere and jeans. Her hair was pulled up, leaving her looking not a day past thirty, let alone mother to two teenagers. She reminded me of the stories of the faerie Ice Queen I'd heard when I was younger.

Trey glanced my way, his expression unreadable. "I think he's a little underwhelmed."

"Have you taken him through the library yet? He might find something there to whet his appetite," she said casually, as if she just invited everyone in to peruse her books. "Or maybe he'd like to see the trophy room?"

"You have a trophy room?" I blurted out without thinking. Catherine's amused chuckle was all it took for my face to flush.

"It's really just a room to collect some important

memorabilia," Catherine said, her voice warm. She was really freaking me out with the Happy Homemaker thing. "Some of my sister's early art is in there. And Gentry has a few swimming trophies in there too, don't you, dear?"

Trey nodded. It was still hard for me to picture him as a Gentry. The name fit, but it was still strange. "Our Aunt Alex lives in New York," he explained for my benefit. "You'll probably like her work. She uses a lot of light and color."

I almost choked on my water at that, and the way Trey's gaze was homed in on me. "I didn't realize you had any brothers or sisters, Mrs. Lansing," I said, trying to recover some semblance of control over myself.

"Catherine, Braden. Call me Catherine. I insist." The request hardened her voice, suggesting I wouldn't like it if I didn't listen this time. "Especially if we're going to be working together soon."

"Sorry, of course, Catherine." I twisted the cap back onto the water, and then kept twisting, feeling the grooves of the plastic top pulling at my skin. "I don't know what Trey's told you, but I … can't be involved in whatever it is you're involved in."

The two of them shared a look before Catherine turned another beaming smile in my direction. "No one's asking you to do anything you don't believe in, Braden."

Trey was right there to chime in after her. Almost like they'd planned this. "But you don't have any idea what

Jason Thorpe will do to you. I told you he's a monster, Braden. I wasn't exaggerating."

"Jason isn't the one who tried to kill me," I said, watching Catherine.

I expected some sort of shock, a stumble or a flicker in her eyes that would admit that she knew what I was talking about. But there was only a moment where she absorbed the words, turning fully to me. Studying me, almost like it was the first time.

"Braden!" Trey's face was instantly scarlet.

Catherine held up a hand, warding him off. "And someone's convinced you ... ahh, I see." Her lips pursed out, and for a second it looked like she was going to smile. "Someone tried to kill you? You're sure?"

I nodded. "I'm sure."

She moved past her son and opened the refrigerator. She pulled out a tray full of small, golden pastries with some sort of white and gold cream on top. "I almost forgot. It's a new recipe I'm thinking of introducing at the restaurant."

"Mom, I didn't—"

"It's fine, Gentry," she murmured. The plate was set on the island between us, Catherine and me. "Braden's right to be suspicious." She leaned on the counter, eyes locked with mine. "But you already know I wasn't responsible, don't you?"

"No. I don't know. Maybe."

I couldn't look away from her eyes. It was like I was

locked in place. "You snuck in under my nose, influenced my children, and flaunted your gifts for all to see. But if I'd wanted you out of my way, Braden, I have had two days to rectify that situation."

"Mom…" Trey's voice was a warning.

"Just making sure Braden understands I'm not the monster he seems to think," she said, as if we were talking about anything other than murder. "Although I have a good idea who's been planting these nasty little ideas in your head."

She knows. My heart wasn't content to leap into my throat: it slammed against my ribs, snapped my chest in half, punched a hole through my stomach, and nearly—

"You boys should try some of these. I made a fresh batch last night." With a sly smile in my direction, she added, "They're just sinful."

My hand had reached out and grabbed at one of the delicacies while I was still in the midst of my panic state. I couldn't help myself; my fingers moved without my control.

Catherine didn't seem to notice; her smile was simple indulgence. "You know better than that, don't you, my boy? I would never ruin a useful tool before I had a chance to test it out. Although keeping you out of Jason's grasp does make a certain amount of sense as well."

My lips parted, the doughy dessert starting to melt the second it touched my tongue, leaving behind only a sweet explosion of icing. The taste shocked me out of whatever fugue state I'd been in.

I glanced at Trey. He had turned to face one of the windows, his head shaking. A queasiness started to unravel in my stomach. I forced myself not to look at Catherine again—it was something in her eyes that kept me from looking away. Something wasn't right here. Something had gone very wrong.

"What brought you to Belle Dam, Braden? My son mentioned your family was going through some sort of separation?"

The words came out almost automatically. I didn't even realize I'd spoken until after I was done. "I lived with my uncle, but he was in trouble. I had to get away from him."

That wasn't what I'd meant to say. My eyes widened slightly, thankfully hidden from Catherine's expectant look.

"That's enough, Mother." Trey's voice was firm as he turned away from the window and came to stand by me. "Besides, you have a visitor."

"Braden and I are just getting to know one another," she replied smoothly, resting her perfectly manicured nails against the marble countertop. "Aren't we, Braden?"

"Yes, ma'am. I mean, Catherine," I blurted. What was wrong with me?

I looked to Trey, but he was staring at his mother. What was I missing?

Catherine wasn't about to be told what to do by her child. "You're not trying to hurt my son, are you, Braden? This isn't some game to snare yourself a Lansing, is it?"

"I'm trying not to. It's the last thing I want," I said,

again without thinking. It was like the filter between my mouth and my brain was gone, and everything that was coming out was…

She couldn't have. I would have known if Catherine had used magic against me, felt it brush against my skin or something. The nausea in my stomach was getting worse, threatening to unleash contents in my stomach that weren't even there.

"Come along, Catherine. We have business to attend to, and I have to be back in the city before dark." Lucien swept into the room, clad in a tailored blue suit.

Catherine and Lucien were working together screamed through my head. Followed immediately by *he's going to tell her about me.* I spun around, but Trey was blocking my way like a wall of steel. I tried pushing my way past him, but he wasn't going anywhere. I could see the tension tightening the lines on his face, and knew he wasn't any happier to see Lucien than I was.

"Have you met Braden yet, Lucien? Braden Michaels, isn't it?" Catherine swept her gaze between the two of us.

Lucien's expression was inscrutable. "Your son finds himself a beau, and you invite him over for a playdate. How very modern of you."

Catherine's hollow chuckle reverberated through the room. "You should know that *my* family has always been very accepting of our own. All the more reason for you to reconsider."

Reconsider what? I pressed my lips together, afraid of what might come out.

"A pity Jason missed out on this one," Catherine murmured, a hint of feral satisfaction settling across her face. "He'll be quite the talented apprentice, won't you?"

She looked at me, and my tongue loosened itself once more. "My uncle never thought so. He said the magic came too easily to me, and it made me lazy. Not like him." My mouth opened to continue, a fact I realized with horror, and I bit down as hard as I could.

Fire lanced through my tongue, betrayed by the nearby teeth. The throbbing heat that burned my mouth stopped whatever else I had been about to say. It gave me the opportunity I needed. I shoved at Trey, trying to make him relent.

He grabbed my arm, the muscles in his jaws flexing. "I'm taking Braden out to see the gardens. He's starting to look a little green." He didn't wait for Catherine or Lucien to acknowledge us, but pulled me to the French doors leading outside.

Fresh air helped. The turmoil in my stomach was rising higher in my throat now, preparing a passageway for everything to come back up. I almost wanted to laugh. My stomach wanted to betray me too, but there was nothing there to unleash.

I leaned over one of the stone railings, gasping in huge breaths of air. This was the second time today I'd felt nauseous, and I wasn't enjoying it.

"I don't know why she meets with him. He's a snake." Trey's voice was grim behind me.

I couldn't focus on that. I had to spend all my energy keeping my stomach in line. It was wasted effort.

I heaved, and heaved, and heaved some more. The pastries had decomposed into something grayish and clumpy as I threw them up. Right into one of the bushes.

I couldn't see Trey, only the bush in front of me. The constant heaving made my glasses start to slip down, and I closed my eyes. With each successive attempt to purge everything inside of me, my eyes opened just a slit.

The pile of goo that had been in my stomach a minute before glowed with gold fire. Catherine had used magic on me after all.

Twenty-Seven

"What are you hiding from me, Braden?" Trey's tone was gentle, but there was an unmistakable demand to his words.

It was a spell. My mind started unraveling it, seeing the strands of silver and gold that had been hidden inside the food. How had she managed to do that? And why hadn't I seen it coming?

You never eat the food when you come to a witch's house. Even fairy tales tell you that. Everything started falling into place. Jason had told me that Catherine had found a way to channel her power in a new way. It wasn't in the food itself, but somehow woven into the crafting of it—an ingredient that wasn't apparent in the final product.

It was some sort of truth spell. The magic was subtle, even in its current state. More Jason's style than mine.

I had to know that the effects had worn off, to know that it was safe to open my mouth again. "I'm really a girl," I muttered, my tongue shrieking with every motion.

When I looked up, I could see the shock in Trey's eyes. "What?" His face had gone white, and if I wasn't currently vomiting up my nonexistent breakfast, I might have laughed.

"It isn't working anymore," I went on. "Save your breath. And your questions."

My gag reflex started to diminish, and I rested my head against the cool marble stone and practiced my breathing. My body was already starting to recover now that the magic was gone from inside of it.

"What are you talking about?"

Had he known? Why else ask me that question? "That was the point of dinner, wasn't it? Give Braden the magical roofie and watch him spill his guts. See if he's got any deep, dark secrets your mother can exploit, right?"

"You're talking crazy. You're just not feeling well, that's all." Someone had flipped a switch, and now Trey was all gentleness and smooth edges. Just trying to make sure I was okay. I wasn't.

"I can't believe I thought this was a good idea," I raged. "She basically threatened me, and you don't even see it."

"Hey!" He grabbed the fabric over my shoulder and used it to yank me back up. "She wanted to get to know you. The least you could do is show a little respect."

I struggled to get myself out of his grip, but the fact was that he was bigger than me. "Did you miss what happened in there? She tried to put a spell on me." I shook myself. "No wait, she actually *did* put a spell on me."

Trey was breathing hard, his eyes narrowed down as he glared at me. "Was she wrong? My mother's not an idiot, Braden. You show up out of nowhere, start looking into Grace, and she's not supposed to be suspicious? She's worried you might be a threat."

"Of course I'm a threat, you idiot." I lashed out, striking him with an ineffective fist. He didn't let go, and didn't even budge. "It's not like you've been honest the whole way through either, Mr. Lansing."

If I'd thought he couldn't get any more angry, I was sadly mistaken. His eyes burned like a gas flame as he pulled me forward. "This isn't some stupid high school game. Jason's always looking for a way to hurt my family. And he'll hurt you if you don't give him what he wants."

People in Belle Dam had issues with personal space. "And what happens when she finds out what I can really do?" It was too bad the nausea was passing, because I would have really liked to purge myself all over his shoes.

Trey didn't seem to care. He just kept pulling me closer, until we were nose to forehead. "What the hell's the matter with you?" he breathed. "We're just trying to protect you. Jason needs to be stopped. You know he does."

He was never going to see the truth. Catherine had raised the perfect little soldier. "Listen to yourself. You're talking about violence." Inspiration struck me. "People could get hurt. The last time there was a war between the Lansings and the Thorpes, they flooded the town! What, the serfs and vassals aren't special like us so they don't matter?"

It was the wrong thing to say. Trey shoved me back, finally releasing me. I stumbled, barely catching myself on the railing. "Of course you wouldn't understand," he seethed. "You're just a kid."

Just a kid? Trey didn't have a clue what my life was actually like. Just being some spoiled kid would have been a blessing. I almost told him everything, right at that moment, until something drew my attention to a far corner of the house.

The house was shaped like a backward "L" from what I could see, and the rear part of the house looked much different from the rest. New siding had been put up, but it was clearly part of a much older structure. Above the house, a railing circled the roof. A widow's walk. Standing against the edge, a finger pressed to where her mouth should be, a veiled woman with glittering eyes was looking down on me.

I reached up, not to pull off my glasses, but to make sure they were still there. The woman was transparent; I could see the old bricks of the cupola through her midsection. But I could see her, even through the glasses.

She didn't speak out loud, but I could hear her just the same. *Be silent*, she said. *Don't act.* This was the woman I'd glimpsed in the vision last night in the cemetery. Seeing her again was like an anchor, allowing the details to be dredged up. In all the confusion of dark magic, attacks, and adrenaline, I'd forgotten about her. *True power locked away, keys that cannot be held or felt or seen. Torn into death, from one world to the next.*

I wanted to protest, to explain that I didn't understand. But Trey was still standing behind me, and I couldn't just start talking to myself. I knew without question that he wouldn't see the veiled woman. Grace.

I turned back to him. "You're right." I kept my voice quiet and low. "I don't want any of this." I walked past the railing and into the garden, following the side of the house back toward the front.

"Where are you going?" he shouted, still rooted in place on the patio.

I shrugged and kept moving. I'd been about to tell Trey the truth about everything—why I was here, and about Jason. Grace had warned me to stop. What I couldn't figure out was, why?

¤　　¤　　¤

Jade was just getting out of Trey's car when I reached the front of the house.

"What's wrong?" she said cautiously, hesitating with the car door. Whether to shut it and move on, or get back in.

"I'm a threat to your mother's evil empire, and your brother and I are fighting again." My words were short and succinct, a rapid-fire summary of the afternoon.

Her lips thinned, and she nodded across the car. "Get in. I'll give you a ride back into town."

Jade was the only one of them I actually trusted. Maybe because with her, what you saw was what you got. A few minutes later, we were pushing the speed limit in silence. "What's my mother's issue with you now?" she finally asked, once we were back in the safe haven of commercial property.

I stared out the window, watching the yellow lines at the side of the road dip left and right as we accelerated. "Well, aside from the dinner party from hell, she kinda…threatened me, I guess." I stopped. "Well, she didn't *actually* threaten me, but you kinda had to be there." I still didn't know how much Jade knew about Catherine's lifestyle, and getting into the magic stuff was way too much to handle right now.

"Oh, I'm sure she was threatening you," Jade said, like it was an ordinary occurrence. "That's her style. Most kids have a father cleaning a shotgun to scare the boys off. We got my mother and her dinner parties."

"She was meeting with Lucien Fallon," I added. "So the interrogation got cut shor—Jade, watch the road!"

In the middle of my sentence, Jade had whirled on me. Her shock was matched only by my fear of the oncoming traffic we were drifting into.

She focused back on the street, and turned the wheel so we slid back into our own lane. Angry horns trailed in our wake. "She was meeting with him? Again?"

This wasn't the first time? "I don't know. I guess. He said he had to get back to town, though."

"Lucien's their intermediary or something." Jade's tone was grim. "He shows up so she doesn't have to deal with Jason."

"They seemed a little more friendly than that," I said, thinking back to the exchange. "And I think she was offering him a job."

Jade's hands tightened around the wheel like her brother's. "Did you know he hit on me when I was a freshman? Got all pervy and kept talking about all the things he could show me."

"He's slime," I agreed. How many girls had he hit on over the years? It was extremely gross to think about. "It's disgusting. He should stick to girls his own age, y'know?" I said it halfheartedly, secretly wondering how old he really was. Were there even girls his own age? He had to be over a hundred.

She pulled into a parking spot in front of the hotel. "One of his secretaries was on the cheerleading squad a few years ago. Had a full ride to college and six months later, she walked away from it. She moved to Seattle to live with her aunt or something." Jade pursed her lips. "I think I heard she was waitressing now. Just dropped out of school entirely."

After working with Lucien for only a few months? "Does that happen to all of them? I heard someone say that none of them last long."

"I dunno. Maybe. Most of the girls that go to work

for him don't know any better. They just see a hot, single guy that's willing to pay them crazy money."

I thought about that after I got out of the car. What was Lucien's obsession with young girls? Aside from the obvious, of course. Was there something more to it? Or was he just a pervert?

¤   ¤   ¤

There was no sign of Jason when I got back to the hotel room, but maid service had been busy. Everything was neat and orderly—they'd even gone so far as to fold the clothes I'd left strewn over the bed. Or maybe Jason had done it. How long had he stayed here after I'd left?

I ordered a hamburger from room service, and took a shower while I waited. Later, a much cleaner and fuller me curled up under the covers of the bed. Night was just starting to approach, but so much had happened today. I figured I could sleep for a few hours, and then get back up and try and make some headway on both schoolwork and the Lucien issue.

Catching up on schoolwork didn't take nearly as long as I thought it would. Half the things I had to finish up were in subjects I'd already gone through with John. I gave up about halfway through the math homework though. When I couldn't even manage to finish the easy problems, I knew it was a lost cause.

There also wasn't anything to find out on the Lucien front. Everything I'd seen on the Net was the sum total of what was out there. I was still feeling anxious and nervous about the things that had happened today. Being set up by Trey, accosted by Catherine, and then having Lucien stroll in like it was no big deal.

I'd never get back to sleep this way, unless I seriously tired myself out. John used to run, back when I was younger, but I'd never taken up the hobby. But now, it seemed like a great idea. It only took a few minutes to change into something warmer and slip on a pair of tennis shoes.

There was only one car on the road when I finally got outside and crossed the street. It turned the same way I was heading, passing me by and allowing me only a momentary glimpse of the dark metallic color as it passed under a streetlight.

I started running so I wouldn't have to think. About Lucien, the feud, Grace, any of it. I crossed block after block, expecting any minute would be the one where I'd lose steam and need to stop. But I didn't. I kept going, taking turns at random. Eventually, I ended up turning back toward the docks on the north side of town, far past Sather Park.

A block down from me, a car turned to the left. Black chrome. I slowed my jog, feeling a moment of concern. Part of me wanted to shrug it off; it could have been anyone. Belle Dam wasn't that big of a town, and if I'd learned anything, it was that it paid to be paranoid.

Instead of continuing down the sidewalk, I crossed into the small car dealership next to me and watched. Sure enough, I could see a glimmer of red brake lights where the car had paused. Just out of sight from the street.

Someone's following me. I pulled the silver necklace from out of my shirt and rubbed it between my thumb and finger.

"Hide me from their sight," I murmured, releasing only a trickle of magic. Since I planned to run, it wouldn't work very well this time. But it was better than nothing.

I turned back the way I'd come and zigzagged along streets. I stuck to the shadows, running through darkened parking lots and run-down yards.

My footsteps echoed all around me, louder and more distinct than they'd been when I was running for the fun of it. *They're still out there.*

I was almost back to the hotel, but from here to there the streetlights blazed. I'd gotten turned around with all the running, and was coming back from a different direction. There wasn't a cover of darkness to hide behind.

I stopped running, but the echo didn't stop around me.

"You run like a girl." Drew jumped out of the shadows and shoved me into a row of bushes.

Twenty-eight

"Stay down," he grunted, keeping his dirt-crusted hand clenched over my mouth. The black car, some kind of foreign model, sped down the street in front of us. It circled around in front of the hotel and pulled up across the street. Right where it had been when I'd first seen it.

"Someone's curious about what you're up to," Drew said, releasing me. I had tiny little branches shoved in all sorts of hard-to-reach places.

"Who is that?" I eyed the car and tried to remember if I'd seen one like it at the Lansings'.

"Don't know, don't care. Maybe Boyfriend thinks you're screwing around on him."

"Funny how you're the one who keeps putting your hands on me," I said as I dragged myself out of the bushes. I focused on the magic around me, drawing it closer. Just in case; I wouldn't be caught off guard again.

Drew made a clicking sound with his tongue, flashing his eyes at me. "You don't back down, do you?"

He was just a stupid jock, I reminded myself. Lecturing him about homophobia was a waste of time. "Why were you following me?" I demanded instead.

"Riley seems to think you're in some trouble. She didn't say as much, but she wants me to keep an eye out."

"You attacked me last night!" What was Riley thinking? "What do you care anyway?"

Drew shrugged. "I don't. But if it'll piss Gentry off, then why the hell not?" He sniffed at the air, his face screwing up in disgust. "You stink. Cut it out with the mumbo jumbo bullshit."

"*You smell like fire.*" He'd said as much on the bus. "You can really smell it?"

He rolled his eyes. "Do I need to be all silver and four-legged for you to figure it out?"

"You're not a witch," I said with only a little certainty. I'd never looked that deeply at him, but changing shape wasn't something a normal witch could do unless… "You're a werewolf?"

"You sure you're not some sort of moron?" Drew pointed to a corner of the yard we were near, where two fences met. "I'm not a werewolf. Or did you forget there wasn't a full moon out the other night?"

He was right. "Then what are you?"

He pulled out a cell phone and flipped it open. "You think the only thing lurking around town is a couple of witches? Don't be naïve. All sorts of things will line up for the right amount of money. Ask Gentry. If he'll tell you the truth."

Of course I knew there was more to the supernatural than just witches and warlocks. John used to tell me bedtime stories of things that really existed. I don't think creativity was really his strong suit—most of my bedtime stories were true accounts of one nasty or another.

But I'd also never met anything like Drew was talking about.

Drew wasn't content to let me work it out for myself. "I'm a Shifter. As in shape. Mostly animals, but sometimes other things if I really push myself."

The only thing I knew about shapeshifting was that there was always something that gave them away. "Your eyes glow when you're about to change, don't they? I saw them the other night."

Drew nodded. "Maybe you're not all fluff up there." He leaned up against the wooden fence and tilted his head to the sky. "That's why they killed my dad. We won't be tamed."

"Why are you telling me this now?" If I thought Trey was hard to figure out, then Drew was nearly impossible.

"So you'll watch yourself. Trey thinks I'm out to get him. He's not entirely wrong. But he's a waste of time. He wasn't any more involved than I was. Cathy and Jay think I'm going to just run along and let them have their war, which you seem to be the poster boy for lately."

"I'm not. I've told them I don't want any part."

He glanced at me with hooded eyes. "When's that

ever stopped them before? If they say you're in—you're in. Unless you're planning to take them both on."

And that's when I knew. I didn't matter either. He was feeling me out, to see if I'd help him. "Isn't that what you're trying to do?" He could probably snap me in half, but I'd thrown him around a little bit, too. I wasn't entirely helpless.

"Someone has to step up," he replied. "I take it that means you're going to keep pretending you don't have to pick a side?"

I shook my head. "I'm here for my own reasons. But I don't think it has anything to do with either one of them, or their feud. Or you."

He shrugged. "You're just another tool to them. They'll use you no matter what you want. They can't help themselves."

"You know anything about some big spell they've got working over the town?"

He stared at me with a blank expression. "A what?"

"Some sort of spell," I repeated. "It's like this giant blanket of shadow pulled across the whole town." There was no moment of recognition or understanding in his eyes, and my voice went flat. "Never mind. You don't have any idea what I'm talking about."

There had to be someone who knew where the shadows I kept seeing had come from. Or why they kept taking the form of an eye. I didn't know why that was important, just that it was.

Drew couldn't help me, but he wasn't my enemy either. At least not yet. I gave him one last look, shook my head, and walked out of the yard.

The black car was dark when I walked past, tinted windows preventing me from seeing inside. I knew they were there, though. And I think they knew I did.

Dawn was still many hours away. I could go back to bed, and try and be ready for school in the morning. The mornings here had been extraordinarily cold for September, a fact that popped into my head as I hit the door.

I glanced back at my stalker and narrowed my eyes. I pictured the motions in my mind, traced them over and over again.

With the early morning frost, or even a decent fogging if they left the car running, they would understand. Letters traced on the glass that wouldn't appear until I was deeply asleep.

I See You.

¤ ¤ ¤

It was Monday again. A week ago, I'd arrived on a bus. Now I was being pulled in a million different directions.

I left for school early, so by the time Jade called to see if I needed a ride, I was already bumming around the front plaza. "I'll see you at lunch or something," I promised. I wanted to find Riley first, and talk to her about what was going on.

She'd spoken to Drew on my behalf, and told him to keep an eye on me. What was that about?

While I waited for her rattling bracelets, I hesitated with my phone still in hand. It couldn't hurt anything, I reasoned.

I dialed my uncle and held my breath. The phone rang and rang, but neither he nor the answering machine ever picked up.

Almost as soon as I flipped it shut my ringtone went off, and I saw "Jason's Cell" appear in the little screen. I certainly hadn't programmed his number into my phone. *But he had hours alone while you were sleeping yesterday to mess with it.* "What?" I demanded, already irritated.

"Stop antagonizing the boys, Braden." Jason's voice was cool across the phone with just a hint of distraction. I heard random sounds and static in the background, and quickly figured out he was in a car somewhere.

"The boys?"

I heard him sigh. My fingers tightened around the plastic phone. He sounded just like John. "They're only there to make sure you're safe. You seem bound and determined to uncover every viper's nest in town, don't you?"

"The car? It's yours?" I'd assumed it had something to do with Catherine. "Wait, you hired me security? Are you kidding?"

"They're only there to keep an eye out for you. Stop upsetting them."

So they'd seen my little display after all. My smile widened. "If that's all it takes to freak them out, then I'd start looking for a refund."

Jason didn't say anything. I waited, checking the phone twice to see if the call had dropped, but he was still there. Just not saying anything.

"I need to talk to you," I said, finally.

There was only a moment's pause. "I have meetings all morning. Lunch. One o'clock. I'll have Lucien call the school and make the arrangements."

"Fine. Goodbye, Jason." I hung up the phone before he could say anything back.

By the time the first bell rang, I still hadn't seen or heard Riley approaching anywhere. Before I knew it, it was time for lunch, and I still hadn't run into her. Someone dropped off a note from the office, directing me to meet my guardian at the tiny restaurant across the street.

I left the school and saw a small black car parked in the street, a different model than the one I'd seen the night before. This one didn't have the same tinted windows.

"I'm sorry, we're closed for a private party," the manager interjected as I stepped inside.

"He's with me, Frank." Jason stood in a corner of the room, staring out the window. He glanced over his shoulder at me, and I was hit again with how much he and Uncle John looked alike.

Frank disappeared into the back, and we were left alone. "You rented out the whole place?" Never mind the fact that it wasn't very big; even still, that seemed extreme.

"It seemed appropriate. Now what is this all about, Braden?"

I fell into one of the larger booths near Jason and leaned up against the wall with my knees in front of me. "You know something's going to happen, don't you." It wasn't a question, but a realization. Jason knew a lot more than I did, of that I had no doubt. "That's why you've got people watching me."

Jason turned away from the window, and I saw the cup of coffee held between his hands. He sat across from me, upright where I was slouched. "I thought I'd see something of myself in you. My hair, or maybe my nose. But I look at you, and all I can see is her."

I heard the musing softness to his words, and understood something else about my father. "My mother?" He nodded once, almost a sharp jerk of his neck. Whatever else had made him this way, he'd loved her. The regret was there, in his voice and on his face.

"What was she like?" I thirsted for it. Needed to know more. About both of them.

"She was from a family like ours. And like ours, they'd lost their hold on the magic many years ago. Lucien introduced us, when I was just a little older than you are now. By then, things with Catherine had already started to crumble, and when I saw her..." He trailed off, looking back to the window.

Things with Catherine? "You and Jade's mom?"

Jason shook his head. "Never anything like that,"

he said with a wave of his hand. "I thought, once, that I could love her. But even when things were on better terms, everything was always a struggle. Who was superior, who had more control, and who could achieve more."

I didn't care about their history. I wanted to know more about the woman that had died after giving birth to me. "You said before, that she saw things. My mother. Before she died."

He hesitated, choosing his words carefully. "She felt a darkness... something she thought pursued her. She saw things that sounded like any other nightmare." He looked out the window, as though he couldn't look at me while he talked. "Your mother had the magic in her blood, but she had never managed anything but parlor tricks. I had no reason to suspect..."

"Suspect what?" I didn't trust myself to say anything more than a few short words. But I had to know more.

"That maybe she'd tapped into your gift, Braden. And she saw that Catherine was going to kill her."

"She saw the future? That didn't come from me." With only one exception, I'd never seen what *would* happen. I only ever saw what *was* happening, or what *had* happened.

"Maybe not yet. But with the right training, who knows what you could do with your gift? We only know the smallest fraction of what your visions entail."

"Wait... what do you know about the witch eyes?"

He startled, glancing over at me for the first time. Almost as soon as he did, he'd reached into a pocket and put on his own pair of sunglasses. If I had to bet, I'd say it had something to do with the reddening of his eyes. "Witch eyes? Is that what you call them?"

I shrugged. "We had to call them something."

"Yes, well, Lucien and I have spent the last few years researching everything we could find on Grace Lansing, but I'm afraid there hasn't been much we could learn. Grace never gave her visions a proper name, and wrote down even less about them. But we were talking about your mother."

I nodded. Lucien had mentioned some of this before. "So Catherine killed her, thinking it would kill both of us?"

"Yes."

"And then you went after Catherine's husband. A partner for a partner?"

He didn't respond, but neither one of us needed him to. I knew the truth. "You tried to kill him," I whispered, shaking my head.

"I was a different man then. We, your uncle and I, were raised to believe we were greater than the rest. That their lives meant nothing." He glanced down at his hands. I saw a golden band still circling his finger. "Now it's different."

"So what changed your mind?"

"Almost ten years ago... you would have been seven or eight... I hired a girl. A tiny little witch, wanting to make her mark on the world. I'd lost the chance to train you, but this was almost like my second chance. A student I could teach."

"What was her name?"

"Adele. A few weeks later Catherine had her own witchling under her wing." Jason's hands tightened around the cup. "Things escalated. When they died, we made a truce. I would stop coming after Catherine, and she would do the same."

Jason waited while Frank, the manager, exited the kitchen, bearing a tray of various subs that he set down between us. After checking to see if we needed anything, he vanished into the back once more. "Catherine's been planning something for a long time."

I shook my head in surprise. "And you think Lucien hasn't been?" He couldn't be that blind. "Did you know he's some kind of immortal? Gregory has pictures of Lucien that go back a hundred years. And he's the same age he is now."

"The same age he was when I took over the family businesses from my father," Jason admitted. *He knew?* "Lucien is a very powerful ally, one our family has relied upon for generations. He sees things even you cannot."

"Then what is he?" The burning question, the one I needed answered more than anything. If I knew what Lucien was, maybe I could figure out what this was all about.

It was like he didn't care at all. It had been driving me crazy for two days, and he'd apparently known all his life and couldn't be bothered to look into it. "I haven't the slightest. What Lucien sees, when he looks to the future, is complete. He is never wrong. He can latch on to a future years down the road, and trail it all the way back to the events that cause its inception. There isn't another seer with his power in all the world. I've looked."

"And you don't think that's strange? A seer that lives forever? That's not normal."

Jason dipped his head. "Not any more than a child that can see the world's secrets, and unravel spells with just a look."

"Then why would he be fighting with Uncle John? If Lucien knew how things were going to turn out, why would he need to fight with him on the phone?"

Jason shook his head. "My brother," he said, nearly spitting, "barely spoke with Lucien. Only offering the occasionally vague update."

That wasn't true. I'd gotten the hang-up phone call dozens of times. "Then Lucien's been lying to you."

Attacking the lawyer didn't really get me anywhere. Jason let the words wash right off him, like he was totally unconcerned. "Lucien's been doing this for a long time, Braden. He knows what needs to happen for you to survive."

I have an agenda. The words rang in my ears again. "You said he introduced you to my mother. She was from a witch family. And two witches always have children with stronger powers than either of the parents." I could barely force out a whisper. "It really was about me all along."

I was starting to really understand now. Lucien didn't

just want a war. He wanted destruction. If I went after Catherine, I couldn't even begin to imagine what would happen to Belle Dam.

What I couldn't figure out was why. Destruction for its own sake didn't strike me as Lucien's style. So why was he pushing me into some sort of fight?

Everything Lucien had done had been to get me here, now. He'd set me on the path to learn about Grace, and try to find out her secrets. A woman who lived her life obsessed with keys and locks. So obsessed that the town had started a festival in her honor, and her tombstone made sure that no one would ever forget.

Fragments of things were coming together, like a jigsaw puzzle in my brain. It was like if I squinted, I could *almost* make out the bigger picture.

"He wants the door unlocked. The door that no key should open," I whispered.

Jason's movement was sudden and shocking. His hand jerked out, knocking the coffee mug to the ground and spilling its contents everywhere.

"Where did you hear about that?"

Twenty-Nine

I watched as Jason gestured with his left hand. Powerful, explosive magic gathered itself up and bent around the broken mug. The pieces reversed their trajectory, bonding together and falling upwards until the mug was back on the table, whole and full of coffee.

There were dozens of ways he could have repaired the mug. Jason had bent time itself, twisting it around like it was the most casual of spells.

I was equally envious and afraid. If Jason could do that, then I could only imagine what else Catherine could do. I knew I was strong... but not that strong. Messing with time or space was the most powerful stuff, miles beyond summoning things from the other side.

How strong is he? And Catherine?

"I asked you a question," he said.

"I... I don't know." Where had I heard it? "It's important, then?"

"Just a local legend. A story from our childhood, the kind of things grandparents delight in talking about over a roaring fire. We were young and stupid, thinking that there really was some secret treasure hidden here."

I leaned forward. "So you didn't find it? What happened?"

"We weren't much older than you and Jade at the time. Still in high school. We knew the stories, and we thought that if anyone deserved to know Belle Dam's secrets, it was the three of us: Catherine, Bennett, and I. A history that we traced back to Grace Lansing."

Listening to him talk, it didn't surprise me to hear the links between us. Everyone searching for Grace's secrets, without a clue as to what they were.

"So what happened? Something changed, right?"

Jason nodded. "Bennett Armstrong happened. He was the third part of our little covenant, and then he…changed."

"Changed?"

"He turned against the rest of us. Becoming increasingly paranoid. Dangerous."

"So you killed him?" I steeled myself for the answer. I don't know why it was so important to hear, but I wanted Jason to tell me what he'd done. "Aren't you supposed to be this magical badass? And the only thing you could come up with is killing him?"

His eyes narrowed. "We didn't set out to kill him." He spoke with calm force. "He lost control, and came after us. In a split second, there was a choice. We chose to live." Jason's hand reached for the coffee mug, but instead of grabbing it he held his hand over the mouth of the cup. "Pray that you never understand what that's like, Braden. To have to make a choice, in just a fraction of a second, knowing that someone's life is in your hands."

"Isn't that what you're asking me to do?" I asked coldly. "It's what Lucien's been pushing me toward since I got here."

"Things aren't so black and white, Braden."

I didn't give him the chance to go on. "What happened next?"

"Afterwards, Catherine was different. Colder. Like she hadn't played a part in Bennett's death. From there, the path to now got easier. We knew which sides we were playing for."

"And then it's all Welcome to the Mob," I muttered. Something Jason had said struck a chord in me. The vision I'd had of Grace, the night I stopped the hellhound, had talked about power locked away.

Jason was still talking about how the feud had started, but I interrupted. "Tell me everything you know about immortality. If you had to make an educated guess, what would Lucien be? He's not a vampire, and there's no way a curse could give him the magical Botox for this long. So what would it be?"

Jason was startled, but I was too busy trying to work it all out in my head to worry about it. "I couldn't say," he said with a frown. "He could have struck a bargain with something, but those kinds of deals always leave a mark.

The most obvious choice would have been a demon, but that's simply not possible. Demons cannot be anchored here permanently. They're too powerful."

Power. That was it. *That was what Lucien was after and what Grace had. That's why she was so important, and why he wanted me to look into her history.*

I bolted up out of the booth. "Thanks, but I've got to go," I said, slinging my backpack over my shoulder.

"You haven't eaten anything," he said, glancing pointedly at the tray of sandwiches. He failed to notice he hadn't eaten either.

"Not hungry," I said. "And I've got class."

"You need to focus your attention on the real problems, Braden," Jason said sternly. "And Lucien Fallon isn't it."

I was backpedaling all the way to the door. "I know," I said hurriedly, "and you're right. I totally will." And then my hand brushed the metal handle of the door, and I was outside.

¤   ¤   ¤

Despite what I'd told Jason, I couldn't go back to school. Our conversation had filled in a few details, but I still needed the rest of the picture. I needed the information that Gregory had.

The shop was open, surprisingly busy when I walked in. Trey's friend Kayla was behind the counter, and paused in ringing someone up long enough to give me a curious glance.

I bypassed her and the counter, and headed for my part of the store. I wasn't interested in shopping today. When I walked in, I saw that I wasn't the only one who'd ditched school. Gregory was already there, but Drew and Riley were with him. I halted at the door, waiting for some sense of what was going on.

Drew glanced over his shoulder at me, and I could see the irritation on his face. "Too late, new kid. Gregory already went and spilled his guts to your boyfriend's mommy. We walked in on him turning back to the dark side."

"That's not what happened!" Gregory heaved himself out of his chair, staring daggers at Drew.

"Then what happened?" Riley's voice was calm, for her, and her body language suggested she'd been trying to calm the two of them down before I got there.

"You talked to Catherine?" I wasn't sure what to say to that.

"She called." Gregory looked to me then, his eyes pleading. Then, as if he realized who he was talking to, he looked away. I'd already spelled him once for annoying me.

He doesn't know anything; it'll be okay. But reassuring myself only worked up to a point. "What did you say to her?" I tried to keep my tone light.

"She called. Asked if I knew anything about you—"

"—and you sang like a bird," Drew jumped in. "Don't try to spin this like one of your stories for the D&D group."

"When the hell did you get on my side?" I turned to Drew with curiosity.

"I'm not," he snarled. "But pissing Catherine off's just going to hurt other people." He met my eyes, more or less, before looking to Riley.

Oh. Right. Moving on.

He didn't know about Jason, and he didn't know that I'd been dealing with Lucien. I leaned forward. "What did you tell her, Gregory? What exactly did you say?"

"Just that you were pretty strong," Greg said, going so far as to shuffle his feet.

"And that's it?"

Drew shook his head. "When I walked in, he told her how you were messing with Grace Lansing's monument. Said he took pictures of what the headstone looked like now."

Would Catherine remember those conversations with Jason when they were teenagers? Would a passing memory of Grace be enough for her to put the pieces together? I couldn't take the chance. "So I'm looking into Grace's history. Big deal. If you dig deep enough, everything goes back to her anyway. It's not like I'm covering new ground, right?"

Riley looked uncomfortable. "Catherine might think you're stepping on her toes. Grace was a Lansing, after all." She paused, glancing at me. "What'd he mean, about Gentry? You're not…"

I didn't have time to walk through even a normal secret

like that right now. "Is that it?" I demanded. "That I'm strong, and I've been looking for information on Grace?"

"That's it, I swear," Gregory said, looking from me to Drew.

"He made it sound more sinister than that," Drew added, his eyes narrowed. "Kept using words like 'nefarious' and 'dark side.'"

"Whatever. I don't have time for that." I walked through the room and grabbed his laptop. Gregory immediately sat up, fear in his eyes, but I pointed at him and he slid back down.

I turned the laptop around and set it in front of Riley. "Can you pull up anything he has on Grace Lansing?"

Riley looked at me like I'd lost my mind. "What?"

"I can't trust him to do it," I said, gesturing across the table at Gregory. "Not if he's going to be thinking about all the ways Catherine's going to string him up when she finds out he's a double agent."

"Double agent!" In any other situation, Gregory's squeak would have been funny. Now it was just sad.

"I don't know, Braden," she said, glancing down at the computer.

"She won't find anything without the password," Greg announced. "Besides, she's definitely no Angelina Jolie."

I glanced at him in confusion. "Huh?"

"Hackers reference," Drew supplied. "Angelina played this hot teenage hacker badass schoolgirl chick."

"Didn't we talk about you being offensive?" Riley said, actually sounding caustic for once.

"I could try harder, right?"

"Guys." I rapped my hand against the countertop. "Focus." I turned to Riley. "Can you find what we need or not? Try that website you were telling me about."

"I'll try," Riley said with a little hesitation. All that evaporated after a few seconds of typing. "You're still logged in to everything," she said, glancing up at Greg. "No passwords required."

"Do you have any idea what will happen to me if Catherine finds out?" Greg leaned back in his chair, craning his neck toward the window. "She's not exactly forgiving."

"Drew?" I waited until his attention was on me. "Go downstairs and see if you can dig up a street map of Belle Dam. I want to check something."

"Found something," Riley announced while Drew headed back down the stairs. She turned the computer to face me. There was a whole website, complete with pictures, about Grace. The picture of her he'd shown me the other day was scanned on there, and a portrait I'd never seen before. In both, her entire face was veiled. In the painting, the artist had taken the time to shade the veil with dark and light, giving the illusion it was lit from within.

I scanned the page, finding only a little more than he'd told me before. "This is everything? There's not something you're keeping for Catherine?"

Greg shook his head. "No, no, of course not."

I glanced at Riley, and she shrugged. "This is all I can find. I did a search for Grace, and the only things that came up were the pictures he put on the web."

I nodded, and kept reading over her shoulder. *When Grace Lansing came to the coast around which Belle Dam would be founded, I believe she helped those traveling with her to sketch out a plan for the city. A plan that continues to this day. Property was divided, and the first cobblestone streets constructed within weeks.*

Belle Dam by-laws prohibit changing any property listed as residential into a commercial zone, and vice versa. I tapped the monitor. "What's this mean?"

Gregory leaned across the counter. "Most cities have some sort of process to change zoning, but Belle Dam's never allowed it. That's why there aren't any strip malls in town—the city council won't let them tear down the smaller business buildings."

Drew came back in with the map. It was one of those folded street maps they sell in gas stations. I moved the laptop out of the way, and we opened it across the table.

Belle Dam was laid out before us in tiny fonts and lines representing streets. The town angled along the coast to the north, and right from the start I could see how uniform the solid green parks were.

I closed my eyes, picturing the image of Belle Dam from above, the raging tempest of lights and impressions. Everything moving, almost like clockwork.

Fingers of ice pressed themselves along my spine as I

opened my eyes. "I get it." Belle Dam, the map, all of it. "The town is the spell."

Whatever power Grace had taken, the town was a giant-sized version of Catherine's restaurant. Everything had been arranged and built up right from the start. Angles and lines that drew the eye inward, and kept something trapped inside.

"You really are a witch," Riley exhaled. Her eyes were nearly going to roll out of her head.

She stopped clicking long enough for Gregory to lean over the computer and gasp. "What do you think you're doing?"

Riley grabbed the computer and pulled it off the desk entirely. "None of your business."

"You were changing passwords," he shouted. "You're plotting some sort of coup against me!"

As their bickering intensified, I glanced at Drew and he nodded toward the stairs. He followed me downstairs, which was nearly deserted, and crossed his arms in front of him. "What do you mean, the town's the spell?"

I started explaining, starting with the day at Catherine's restaurant, where I'd noticed the geometry of the place. Then I mentioned some of the things I'd figured out about Grace, and how deeply she was ingrained in Belle Dam.

"So Grace turned geography into magic? How's that even possible?" he asked, sniffing the air.

"I don't know," I said helplessly. "I know it's possible, but actually doing it? That's like stopping the sun or something. Just because it's possible doesn't mean you just wave a hand and it's done. It's not that easy."

"So what's the point?" Drew looked anxious, tapping his feet on the ground.

"To keep something trapped. To stop it from escaping." The only explanation I could think of dressed in designer suits and called himself a lawyer. "Grace took his power from him, and locked him away in Belle Dam."

"Who? Fallon?" Drew's feet stopped tapping.

I nodded. It made a twisted kind of sense. "He's not a vampire. He's not an *anything*. Jason said the only thing that makes sense is if he was a demon. But demons are too powerful to stay in our world."

"I don't understand. You're saying Grace trapped Lucien here? Why?"

I shrugged. "Maybe she thought he was a threat. I don't know. You'd have to ask her." I'd tried once, and I wasn't about to do that again.

"Guess that just leaves the lawyer. Or Thorpe. But the lawyer's not gonna help you, is he?"

"Unless there's something in it for him," I said. And maybe I was the only one who could offer it to him. Offer him his war, in exchange for answers.

"Oh this should be fun."

Something in the way Drew said that set off alarms in my head. I looked up and followed his gaze toward the door.

Trey was just about to walk inside, with Jade in tow.

Thirty

They saw us a moment later, and I watched Jade grab onto his arm. Trying to restrain him. It wasn't a bad plan, actually.

Could today get any worse? I barreled my way to the door and pushed at Trey. I didn't have much chance to move him any other time, but for once he relented and let me lead him outside. Jade followed us.

"What are you doing with Drew?" she asked.

"Jade, can we have a minute?" Trey looked about ready to explode, and the least I could hope for would be to have that happen in private.

"Huh? Sure?" Jade looked dazed.

It took him some time to get his temper in line. "What the hell are you doing? My mother doesn't need another reason not to trust you," Trey said, measuring his words with force.

"I know what I'm doing." My response was quiet. I *hoped* I knew what I was doing was a little more accurate, but I had a good head start.

Trey grabbed me, pulling me close. "How am I sup-

posed to protect you if you're trying to make this a fight."
His eyes kept shifting left and darting right, like he was
trying to figure out where to look to meet my own.

Impulsively, I pushed myself forward, forcing a kiss
that he wasn't expecting. Electric fire ignited in my body
instantly, lines of fire that started in the veins on my hands
and burned their way down. Trey's mouth was hard at
first, unyielding to the pressure. Eventually, he softened,
muscles relaxing.

"I know what I'm doing," I said once the kiss was broken.

"You can't mess with him." Trey's eyes were dazed, but
his tone hadn't changed. "Drew's a monster."

I shook my head. "We have an understanding. Besides,
he's not a threat."

"He attacked Jade! He's a menace!"

I'd forgotten about that. Attacking Jade was the reason he'd been kicked out of school, although Riley hadn't
believed that was the way it all happened. "It doesn't matter right now," I said. "He was just watching out for me."

"Watching out for you? Are you insane?"

I tried a different tactic. "I can't do this anymore. Not
with you," I said slowly, pulling myself free of Trey's hold
on me.

"Because of Drew?" The anger flared in Trey's eyes
again. It turned the normal blue-green dark, like lightning
about to strike. Was he jealous?

There wasn't time for that now. "No. It's just…not in
the cards. We're not supposed to be together, Trey."

It hurt to get the words out. It hurt more when I saw the changes to Trey's face. The muscles had gone slack, the mouth dropped open.

"You're not thinking straight." Trey started shaking me, his face reddening like heated iron.

"Stop! Don't you get it?" I was shouting, but I didn't care. He had to understand. "I'm not your boyfriend. I'm not your anything. So just stop! Your mother isn't the innocent bystander you think she is." I tried to sound as hard as possible, as strong as I could be. "She's just as guilty as Jason." Trey opened his mouth to argue, but I didn't give him the chance. I just kept barreling along, digging myself deeper. "That's why we can't be together. Because you won't see the truth about her, and you refuse to see the truth about him. You're just...blind."

I walked away then, and he let me go. I think he was in too much of a stupor to actually do anything at all. I couldn't give up yet. I decided to forgo the hotel and try and talk with Lucien. Nothing I'd learned had pointed me toward an answer. But maybe he'd let something slip, if I could catch *him* off guard for once.

¤   ¤   ¤

"Mr. Fallon's in a meeting." It wasn't Candy today. I wondered if Candy even still worked here—if Lucien went through secretaries as often as they said he did. I kept walking, straight into the doors to his office. I turned the knob and shoved the door, but the office inside was empty. There was no sign of Lucien anywhere.

"I told you, he's is in a *meeting*," she reiterated, her voice getting higher.

"A meeting where?"

"I don't know," she said, sounding perplexed. "He just called, and said he'd be in a meeting all day. That I should reschedule all his appointments." Her eyes brightened. "Did you have an appointment? I can reschedule that for you."

I left the office after shaking my head. Lucien could be anywhere. On the elevator ride down, I wondered about Grace. Had she felt pulled in all these different directions? Is that why she vanished?

If only it were that easy. Maybe I'd like to disappear too.

¤　　¤　　¤

"You're not listening to me. This was never about the feud. Lucien wanted a weapon of black mass destruction, and you gave it to him." I cradled the phone in my ear, waiting for Jason's reply on the other end.

Hours had passed, but I still didn't have any more of an idea where Lucien was. There was no sign of him around town, and the office didn't expect him back until tomorrow.

I headed back to the hotel and took the stairs. I needed the movement to help clear my head.

If he's with Catherine, he could be telling her right now. I knew it was risky, but if Lucien knew I was onto him, then he might do whatever it took to start the war.

"Lucien Fallon has worked for the family for over a hundred years. He's an employee. An asset. What you need to do is calm down. If you keep acting as irrationally as you have been, the truth is going to come out." Jason, on the other hand, was quite composed.

I rounded the third floor and stepped out into the hallway. My room was just down the hall.

"It's going to come out anyway. Don't you get it? This was all part of the master plan."

The line crackled, a series of clicks and static bursts before dropping the call. "God!" I slammed the phone together and opened it back up to redial when I saw him standing in front of my room.

"Why don't we take a walk," Lucien said.

¤   ¤   ¤

Lucien's idea of a walk was to head up to the roof. While one half of it was framed by much taller, older buildings, the other offered views out over the city and waterfront.

"It's breathtaking, isn't it?" He stood by the railing, palms pressed against the brick ledge as he leaned over it.

"The city? I've seen it."

He glanced over his shoulder and winked. "Of course you have. You've seen a great many things so far, haven't you? To grow up, seeing the world in a way that no one else does. That they couldn't understand."

"I know what you're after," I said, feigning a confidence I didn't have. He still had all the power here, and it wasn't like I could just kill him. "She ripped you open and took out all the stuffing, didn't she? Took the big, bad demon and neutered him. And now you're stuck here."

"You've been busy," Lucien murmured. "Who's been telling tales outside the classroom?"

I shook my head. "Wasn't I supposed to figure it out? All the pieces were there."

Lucien tilted his head to one side. I still couldn't get a good read on him. "If you're wondering, I haven't said a word to Catherine about you-know-what." He was amused, like he could read my mind even now.

"Why not? Doesn't that fit in with your goal? I thought you wanted this feud taken to the next level?"

Lucien turned away. I could hear the sound of him inhaling. "There is something intoxicating about violence," he said, savoring the words, his eyes nearly closed. "But you're…hollow. Wasteful. I thought I saw the potential in you, but there's nothing but empty spaces. You've squandered a perfectly good annihilation."

I shook my head, surprised to find myself walking toward the ledge. Closer to him. "Then what do you want from me?"

"Haven't you learned anything by now? Coming home like the prodigal son, baby-stepping your way into our world. I want for nothing, child. But I have something I know *you* desire."

Thirty-One

"You don't have anything I want," I said immediately.

Lucien's only response was a cocked eyebrow, like he knew something I didn't.

"I'm not involved with him anymore." I tried to keep my voice steady. Lucien knew about all about Trey, thanks to Catherine. "I can't be."

He waved his hand through the air with a dismissive gesture. "As poetic as your love connection was, I'm afraid I'm not much a fan. I suppose Gentry Lansing made excellent eye candy, but he isn't quite what I'm thinking of."

"Then what? I've already got a father, and you can't bring my mother back. My uncle's never coming back here, and pretty soon everyone's going to know about me anyway." Lucien was already too late. "I'm not running anymore. And if I have to do this on my own, then I will."

Lucien turned back toward me, his elbows still resting on the ledge. "I'm resourceful, Braden. I think I can find something to give you." He glanced over a shoulder at the city, and then back to me. "Don't you remember the night at the cemetery? The night you uncovered Grace's Lock?"

I shook my head in annoyed confusion. "Grace's what?"

The smile widened a fraction. "Oh, you remember," he said, as if I was just being modest. "The night you unleashed the hellhounds, you also turned a key. Why else do you think Grace would have gone to such lengths to lay down a trap?"

"What about it?" More talk about locks, and keys. Grace really needed a hobby.

"Don't you remember how free you were that night? How the power that has ravaged your life so thoroughly was suddenly so docile? Everything flowing inside you as smoothly as water?"

I couldn't forget. That was the first time in my life the witch eyes hadn't felt like a curse. "What about it?" I repeated.

"You think that was just a happy accident?" His words drawled out, hanging on his lips as he enjoyed the taste of them. "A taste of what it could be. Your life, your gift. It was always possible, you know. All I had to do was bend the natural law—just for a bit—and you were all better, weren't you?"

Lucien was saying *he* was responsible? "Y-you couldn't have done that. It's not possible." The hair on my arms stood on end, and I looked down to see a tremor in my hands.

"You should know what I am by now," he said, and I nodded.

"You're a—"

"Demon," he said, cutting me off. "I suppose that's close enough."

"Aren't you?"

"I am so much more than the word can even contain. I am the one who deconstructed the primal forces of this world, relegated to being some sort of modern-day monster under the bed."

He could fix me. I could see it in my head. Never again suffering the migraines, using a little illusion to hide the supernatural, shifting colors of my eyes. No more sunglasses, unless it was bright outside. Normal.

"Take off your glasses, Braden. Let me show you," Lucien whispered, his voice husky in the night.

My hands moved by themselves. I closed my eyes by instinct when I felt the plastic above my ears fall away. His hands never touched my skin, but I could feel the pressure of them as they got close.

"Open your eyes. See what the world would be like."

I did what he said, feeling rebellious hope stirring in my chest.

Belle Dam laid out before me, a painting that surged with lights and colors. The city came into focus wherever I looked, allowing me to pick out each individual pine tree lining Park Street. I could see all the way to the ocean, where boats had once sailed thanks to the lighthouse, free of worry.

Everywhere I looked, there was a story. A memory,

secret imprints that were just begging to be told. But the choice was mine.

"Look to the cemetery. See what remains of Grace's treachery." Lucien's voice in my ear, seductive and powerful all at once.

I saw the monument—the dark, charred remains where the lightning had struck. And beneath it, I could see something that was buried deeper than any coffin. Hidden deep within the earth, behind a door that was still opening. As much as it yearned to be free, Grace's spells had gone far deeper than the hellhounds. But every hour, more power slipped through the cracks. Pushed it further. Wild, raw magic woven so tightly, so full of all colors that it was hard to pick away at any of them.

"You did that. You opened the way. Can you feel it?"

There was a hum to the magic, a vibration that only I could see and feel and touch. I reached out a hand, feeling it flow through my fingers from miles away. Pure, raw, and channeled in some way I couldn't understand. I didn't want to; it was so beautiful.

"Feel the others. See them. Where are they hidden?" His voice cajoled me from across a great distance, but I knew I could do it. His voice lulled my mind, and I found myself wanting to do it.

I stretched out my vision, seeing everything in Belle Dam at once. I held on to the impression of the door, and the secrets hidden behind it. Faint at first, but growing stronger, I felt an echo, and then another. Like ripples in a pond, three points where the magic buoyed outwards, hidden from even the most sharp of prying eyes.

Power. Greater than normal magic. Something far more severe. Deadly, but a beautiful kind of strength. I could do anything if I had that kind of power. All of them connected with one another, three pieces of the whole.

"Your salvation, Braden. I can give that to you. Look at me."

I pulled my eyes back and focused them on just one direction. It was hard, losing that sense of everything. The rooftop slowly came into focus, and Lucien had his hand over mine. He lifted it up, helping me to settle the glasses back on my face.

I didn't want to lose this. This control, this power. This was the way it should have been all along.

"And all you have to do is help me unlock the rest of Grace's secrets. You're my skeleton key, Braden. I've been waiting a *very* long time for you."

"And then you go back to wherever you came from?" I asked, my voice wooden. I felt hollow inside, like something had been taken from me. In a way, it had.

Lucien looked me up and down, all fluid movements and shifts. "Where else would I go?" He nodded his head. "I can see you need some convincing. Come."

¤   ¤   ¤

It was a surreal feeling to get into a car with Lucien. It only got worse when I started interrogating him.

"Why all of this? Why try convincing John to let me come? Why keep my father a secret?"

Lucien's driving was smooth and controlled, just like the rest of him. "You still don't understand. I never tried to convince your uncle. I told him you were coming. There was never any doubt. But he seemed to think otherwise."

"I never had a choice?"

Lucien shrugged. "There were possibilities. Minor probabilities that became moot after your episode at the convenience store."

"So there were other paths." How many mistakes had I made since coming here? Maybe I'd cut off a whole path where things had never gotten this bad.

Lucien looked over at me, his eyes shrewd. "No. All roads lead to Belle Dam. You could have lived a thousand different lives, and all of them would have brought you here in the end. You are bound to this city."

I didn't want to believe him, but I did. Lucien saw the future, and the knowledge was enough for him to forget his tendencies as a liar.

"Sometimes you surprise yourself," Lucien continued, "with the things you learn to do. Your witch eyes are a powerful gift. But they were given with strings, as the best ones always are. Grace used hers to build this town, and tucked secrets away in every building and sapling. And now her successor has arrived."

"And how did Grace get involved in all of this? What's the story there?"

Lucien's voice lacked any of the heat I would have come to expect. It had to be a sore subject, but he was as nonchalant as ever. "Grace took something that didn't belong to her and hid it away beneath the town."

"Why?"

Lucien shrugged. "Why do the Lansings do anything? Because they can. But alas, Grace vanished, and her hidden magics vanished with her."

"Because of the witch eyes?"

"Of course. You've only scratched the surface on what they can do, my boy."

"So Grace found a way to separate you from your power. She locked it away, and you were stuck...what? Human?"

Lucien snorted. "I am a prisoner of war. This world brims with weakness and death. Where I come from, death hums like a lullaby."

And he'd been waiting to go back. "There's something you're not telling me."

Lucien laughed. "Of course. But what other options do you have? This way, we both get what we want."

I thought about that on the rest of the ride. Demons couldn't remain in this world, so maybe giving Lucien what he wanted wasn't the wrong choice. Instinct told me it was, but that was just because the idea of being free from the visions was...indescribable. But helping a demon...that was always the wrong choice. Wasn't it?

We pulled up in front of Lucien's office building,

and he got out while I sat in the car. I had a sinking feeling in my stomach. Somewhere, out of the corner of my eye, I could sense a stirring of color that seemed familiar. I refused to look, to subject myself to the visions. Right now was not the time.

"Come along then. Only one item left on the agenda."

I got out of the car and followed him inside.

It wasn't until we were in the elevator gliding up the floors that Lucien turned back to me. "This has always been your destiny, Braden. Grace was foolish—unraveling dark powers, and learning things a woman wasn't meant to know. But you—you can be this town's salvation."

The office was dark and empty when we walked out of the elevator. Lucien flipped a bank of switches along one side of the wall, throwing light back into the room.

I was like a puppet without strings, blindly going along with Lucien simply because he'd dangled a carrot. I couldn't stop myself; the idea of seeing without the pain was something I couldn't fight.

I followed him into his office, looking out at the city at rest beneath me.

"Who would have thought a week ago you would be here now," he said in a pleasant tone. He'd played his part well, and I'd done everything he'd expected of me.

"I never should have come. I thought…"

His eyes glittered. "You thought someone was coming for you. Just like you later thought that Catherine was responsible."

"But it's been you all along."

He leaned against the desk, exuding serenity like it came with his three-piece suit. "I don't believe in waiting for the future to happen. I believe in taking charge. I taught Grace to master her powers. I can certainly trick a seventeen-year-old into believing that what he saw was the real thing."

That was why the vision was so strange. I hadn't seen a vision of the future after all. Only what Lucien wanted me to see, just enough to force me here. "But why?"

"Because I knew your curiosity would consume you. You'd look for answers from the one man that could not answer any of them. Jonathan had almost escaped with you, after your mother died. I couldn't have you vanishing into the night."

My brain was trying to tell me something, but I couldn't process it. "What did you do?"

"I promised to clean up the mess he left. All he had to do was swear a few oaths, spill a little blood, and never warn you about where you come from, and what I'm capable of."

"What mess?"

Lucien was loving every second of this. Revealing all the elements he'd put into play just to get me here. "After your mother's death, your father was inconsolable. And for the first time in his pathetic little life, his younger brother thought to step up and be a man. He tried to balance the scales. A spouse for a spouse." His smile twisted, becoming something mocking and cruel. "Catherine's husband lived, of course. Your uncle was always a screwup."

"You shut the hell up," I seethed, flashes of red streaking into my vision. John had been my only family all my life. I could accept Lucien using me. But insulting my uncle was crossing the line.

"He let you walk into a nest of vipers. Abandoned you, the same way your father did. And you stand up for him? The man cared more about his life than your own."

I knew he was toying with me, but I didn't care. My body kept flashing hot, and a thousand different spells kept flickering into the haze. Spells to use against him. To shut him up. "He knew he had to let me go. You said that yourself."

The demon in the three-piece suit snorted. "Because if he followed you, he'd be dead. Jonathan knows all about Catherine's desire for revenge. And he's just a wounded calf to her. He stayed away because it kept him alive."

"Then I'm glad he stayed away."

"And left your real father to shoulder the family burden all alone. Oh yes, the man is a humanitarian. At least Jason always understood the need for temporary setbacks."

"And Jason's bought into your 'temporary setbacks' all along? Losing his wife and son, and waiting it out? Did you promise him I'd come back and destroy Catherine once and for all?" I walked toward the window, hugging my arms close to my chest.

"Jason believes what I tell him to. He's your father,

isn't he? The lies you've told your new friends. The hardest of all your new secrets that you've had to bear. Jason Thorpe's dead son, alive and well. And ingratiating himself into the next generation of Lansings. What father could be prouder?"

There was a strange tone to Lucien's voice. A savage clarity. I turned away, only to see Lucien watching me from the desk. And Trey, standing in the doorway.

"Gentry, excellent timing. Braden and I are just finishing up." But Lucien didn't look toward him; he was still staring at me.

"It's not true," Trey whispered, looking to me for confirmation.

This was what Lucien had been after. The "last item on the agenda."

"Why?" I could feel the tears starting to form, and I blinked rapidly, as though it would banish them.

"Everyone loves a sacrifice; at least they do where I come from. You may have squandered the annihilation I wanted…" Now, finally, his eyes moved and he looked to Trey. "But a good agenda always has a contingency plan."

Trey was still standing there in shock. But I could see the way his mind was working furiously, putting together pieces of the puzzle. My arrival, and Jason's return not long after. The fear of Catherine, and the way I'd reacted when I found out he was her son.

"Trey, it's not what you think…" But it was.

He straightened in front of me, all that Lansing ego

steeling his spine. "You don't look a thing like him." His hands gripped into fists, every muscle in his face clenched up. "This is just some trick... you're being manipulated, Braden."

"No I'm not." I didn't want to tell him, but it was already out there. There wasn't any taking it back, or hiding it now.

"You don't look like him!"

"But he does look remarkably like his mother, doesn't he?" Lucien stepped aside, standing directly beneath the painting I'd noticed the first time I came in here. A dark shape hovering over a young woman. A shape with features I could see now. A man, with the same dark hair and upturned nose as Lucien.

"They're manipulating you. That's all this is, some giant plot to get back at my mother." Trey was heaving now, his breath coming in furious bursts of energy. "Because of what you can do."

"Not everything's about your mother!" I screamed, reminded again of all the reasons we would never work out. His blind faith, his arrogance, my lies... and our families.

"Boys, boys. Keep it civil. You're not Romeo and Juliet, and this isn't the stage. Don't get any ide—" In the middle of speaking, Lucien whipped his hand out suddenly. His eyes zoomed onto Trey.

Trey had been reaching behind him with one hand. I

didn't have to see it to know what he was reaching for. A weapon.

Everything started happening all at once. The atmosphere in the room intensified as the lights flickered, then dimmed. Trey jerked upright in the middle of his movement, flying backwards against the wall next to the door.

I ripped off the glasses an instant later, but there was nothing for me to see. Only a hint of shadows where I expected to see magic. The room was empty of visions, of memories to cling to. It was a blank canvas, but brushed with a tainted feeling.

Trey struggled on the wall where a force pinned him several feet above the ground. A trail of shadows, darker than the rest, ran between him and Lucien like a cable line.

There was something in the lawyer's eyes, a swirl that hadn't been there before. At first I thought I was imagining it, but the closer I looked at him, the darker the fog in his eyes grew. It flowed through the iris, a cloud that smoked through everything until there was nothing left but solid obsidian.

"Wh-what are you?" Trey choked out.

This was it. The darkness and shadows I'd seen before. The demon hidden inside the body of a man. The traces of darkness that had been watching me since I came to town. The shadowy eye revealed by my spell.

Hidden inside, but where I couldn't see. Only coming out when Lucien tapped into his powers. He'd been spying on me since I came to town, stalking me.

Now that there was something to grab onto, my mind did what it was best at. It soaked up everything it could.

Naked pain and fear no light even the moon grows dark please stop I don't want this anymore what is that boy doing now with empty hollows where there should have been fire that burns inside I'm never going to do anything worthwhile with this concrete void like a whirlpool I can't look away but god it hurts.

Lucien's eyes continued to grow in front of me as I struggled against the snapshots, pictures, and voices that hurtled out from him. Hundreds of them, all sounding so terrified before the apathy set in. Soon the darkness swallowed his face, until all I could see was a pair of shadowy eyes across the breadth of my vision.

And then they swallowed me up, too.

Thirty-Two

"Of course it doesn't hurt, my darling. You should know by now that I'd never want to hurt you." My mouth opened to the words, but it wasn't my voice that came out.

We were in Lucien's office, but now it was daytime, and I was seated behind his desk. And seated in one of the client's chairs was a young girl. Long dark hair was pulled back in a ponytail, and she was dressed conservatively. She looked nervous.

Fear always makes them smell so much like roses. I reached out my hand, realizing it was Lucien's hand I was looking at, and touched her cheek. This wasn't me. It was Lucien. A memory?

"Soon it will all be over." My own voice had never sounded so husky. Energy vibrated around her—an aura only Lucien could see. As he grazed her skin, the bright colors muted, replaced by the night sky drawn to his fingertips. Darkness and sparkling lights, only the sweetest stuff, collected where he touched. Faster and faster it gathered, stealing the color from her cheeks.

She would have touched the heart of a small boy, inspiring him to write a legacy of children's books. The more I drew it out of her, the more lightheaded I felt. Contentment washed through my body, and I felt...satiated. Lucien's thought, not mine.

Feeding. That's what he was doing. Drawing out her potential, her destiny, and feeding on it like some kind of vampire. That's why so many girls worked here. And why they never lasted long. He was using them as some sort of food source, taking all that potential, all that talk of destiny, and feasting on it. How?

I wanted to gag—to take this dark act and expel it out of me. To forget it had ever happened. But I wasn't in control of this body; I was just a visitor. It happened fast, all that potential sucked dry. The girl slumped in the chair, looking winded and vacant.

An entire path of her life, a path full of goods and bads, sucked away, leaving only a gnawing emptiness. *This is how demons exist,* the mind around me explained. *Sating the hunger, however they can. Stealing innocence, purity, and potential.*

The image shifted and the office blurred away until I was seated outside on a garden bench. A house behind me stood three proud stories tall, a glimmer of something I recognized.

"You'll never find it. I know your games well enough." A woman was speaking, draped in layers of silk veils that did nothing to hide her features, but managed well enough to mask the truth that those eyes saw.

I glanced down, studying the cuticles on my—his— hands. *Funny how the skin looks so shiny, like marble.* I tested a nail against the palm, but felt nothing. The skin didn't shift at all, as though it were iron and not flesh.

"You'll forgive me someday." My voice was pleasant, belying the rage that boiled inside. *Arrogant witch!* "All I did was adhere to the nature of our agreement. Harming you was the last thing I ever wished."

"A different story you spin, now that you've lost your edge." The woman chuckled, her form fading into mist at the edges. He hadn't seen more than a projection of her in months. Hiding away, somewhere he couldn't find. "How has humanity been treating you, Lucien? Trapped inside your cage of blood and bones. Never say I wasn't the most attentive of students."

She was staring at me so long, and so hard, I wondered if she could see me. The real me, trapped inside this vision out of Lucien's mind.

Everything sped away again, and with force I pulled myself back. Back into the office, where Trey hung with Lucien staring him down.

The connection with Lucien was still there, linking me to him. Though the room was empty of the things I normally saw, there were threads spilling out everywhere. Each one vibrated a different color, humming and glowing with the need to be seen and be made real. Futures.

And behind them, the dark swirl of energy I barely saw, thick like fog. Power that was magic's other half, invisible to witches the way magic was invisible to normal men. Demonic power.

The threads were like the images and symbols I saw, but spread out over a hundred different stretches of yarn. And wherever I looked, they throbbed.

My eyes rested on one for a moment too long, and I could see inside. A path where Trey pulled out his gun and fired. Different threads, all nearby, said much the same. I flickered my gaze between them, and saw the bullet's arc shifting just a fraction of an inch. Each a different possibility.

"As I was saying." Lucien seemed oblivious to the trip I'd taken through his mind. Images flashed around me, but I tried to push them aside. "Neither of you is fit to accomplish his destiny. That leaves me little choice in the matter."

The threads started to pulse all at once, shrieking their tales at me.

"Braden... help me."

"Braden... help... "

The timing is always different, fractions of a second in some cases, but he always calls out for me.

"Braden!" Trey's voice, his real voice, drew me out of the threads and back into the room. Lucien was clenching his hands now, tightening them into a fist. Trey's body was constricting, the shadows shrinking around him.

"Stop!" Even if I couldn't see it, there was still a lot I could do. Coming to Belle Dam had shown me that.

Lucien didn't even look my way. "The boy will betray you. Weaken you. *This happens.* Deal with it." He spoke like the future was already written. Killing Trey meant nothing to him.

But I cared. I cared a lot.

"I told you to stop!" I looked around, but there was nothing to help me. No Jason. No John. And no Trey. I was alone.

Lucien's hand closed tighter, and Trey writhed against the wall. "I don't work for you. You don't own my leash."

"Put. Him. Down." Visions and feelings and memory collided into me, swept up in a hurricane of power and trauma. Everything that Lucien kept hidden was slipping out, spilling his secrets into the room.

Embrace the pain, Jason said. *Stop running,* Trey said. Everyone always telling me what to do. For once, I listened.

I drew on the magic, without words, and without any sort of safety net. I took everything that was building around me, and took the power from it. I didn't have to speak; my vision was a crystal voice, drawing as much magic from the city as I could. I could totally do this.

As flames and energy crashed around me, the link with Lucien severed itself and returned the room to its normal emptiness. Too much, and too fast. The last time I'd channeled this much energy, I hadn't been able to control it when it got loose.

I knew where the shadows were, where the trail of Lucien's power was arcing toward Trey. Even if I couldn't see them, they were still there. I thought of the sun. Shadows and sunlight never played well together. I just hoped it was enough.

I twisted the magic in on itself, honing it into sunlight and filling it with purpose. Destruction. Once the magic had a direction, it lasered out of me. When it reached the center of the room, it suddenly stopped.

Then, it swallowed everything.

It was like a supernova had been unleashed. The tiny little ball of magic fell in on itself until it pulled a Big Bang. Dazzling sunlight flared through the room.

I could handle a lot, and most of the things I saw were hard to perceive but still possible ... but this much light was agony. My exposure to real, unfiltered light had always been taken in short, sickly-sweet sips. And now I was drowning.

I tried to close my eyes, but couldn't. I saw every bit of sunlight that tore through the room and eviscerated the shadows.

I heard Trey fall to the ground, or at least I heard a thump that might have been him. But my vision was a solid wall of white, and my head pulsed with a seventeen-hammer orchestra.

"What are you doing?" There was no mistaking Lucien's snarl. What kind of future was he seeing now?

Using that much magic, and seeing it in action, was

worse than any normal vision. The pain still thrusted in my head—an arrow that wouldn't remove itself. It just ground against the insides of my skull, etching in grooves and lines. More arrows joined the first, all scrawling secret messages inside my skull.

"Don't be an idiot!" I couldn't see what Lucien was doing, but I knew I still had to act. If I didn't, he'd kill Trey.

I gathered up the magic, picturing it as it dispersed all over the room. I took it back, recycling the power and hardening it into steel.

It wasn't as neat as the binding circle John had trapped me in, but the core of it was the same. I slammed a wall into the room, a force of air that warbled and wavered even as it tightened around Lucien. The wall was tenuous at first, slowly hardening from something fragile like a balloon into something like steel. Boxing him in.

It was the first thing I saw when my vision started to clear. A silver and blue bubble, barely more than five feet across.

I was rattling so hard it felt like even my lungs were shuddering in my chest. My knees gave out from under me, and I fell.

On the other side of the room, I saw Trey rise up.

Lucien's eyes didn't glow so much as they gloomed, shadows that were growing darker inside the bubble. He reached out to press his fingertips against the edge of the shield. The blues and silvers arced like bottled lightning, separating from each other and slowly tearing apart the shape. The harder he pressed, the faster the lightning arced around the shield.

I drew more magic through my body and into the spell. *Harder. It has to be stronger!* I was just the conduit—the focus to keep the magic stable. But the harder I pushed, the harder Lucien pushed back. And the faster the spell continued to crumble.

"You're making a mistake, boy."

I couldn't keep this up. But I wouldn't back down, and I wouldn't give up. Sweat poured down my face, so cold I thought for sure it must have been freezing against my skin. "I won't let you hurt him."

As far as intimidating voices go, mine was not one of them. I was lucky I could still make audible sounds.

I'm pushing as hard as I can, and it's not enough. A half hour ago, I'd been willing to make a deal with Lucien, knowing what he was.

Now, he wanted to kill Trey. And maybe me, too.

Then Trey surprised the hell out of both of us.

¤ ¤ ¤

"I'll shoot him, Fallon!" The gun was pointed at me, and there wasn't an ounce of hesitation on Trey's face.

Lucien's manicured fingers hesitated, and gave my spell a much-needed chance to regroup. "You wouldn't," he said, his tone musing as his eyes flickered left and right. Reading, the way he'd read me when we first met face to face. Just as abruptly, his voice changed to a certainty full of wonder. "You would."

The guy I'd fallen for, the one who'd made Belle Dam a more comfortable place to be, was gone. As I looked at him, all I could see was cold, hard lines of icy loyalty and purpose. He wouldn't look at me.

Trey would shoot me. After all, I was the enemy. I was the one who'd played him. I'd used him.

But I didn't want to die. "Trey, you can't—"

"Shut up!" Trey's aim never hesitated; it was locked on me.

"I saved your life, you asshole!" This was the thanks I got. I was pushing as much magic through me as I could. There wasn't an ounce left to try and defend myself. Release it, and Lucien would finish the job. To save me?

It was getting hard to breathe. With every pump of my heart, my head throbbed, and in the space between, more images continued to shove themselves inside.

I wouldn't even die in peace.

"I thought you could take care of yourself?" Trey's voice was like steel, but at the moment his voice died, his eyes met mine, and I saw through him.

I can't shoot him but I have to blue agony and rose colored remorse so desperate Fallon will kill me him us but he's shaking little Braden like rabbits. Something bad will happen he can take care of himself but must stop Fallon this is agony hell despair.

Flashes of reds and pinks hidden under a silver shroud

of determination. Heat, and desire, and pain. I only saw through him for a moment, but it was long enough. Trey was the one who always followed through. Determined. Never wavering from what he wanted. He didn't want to, but he'd shoot me if he had to. Unless I could stop Lucien.

"Put the gun down, Trey." I could feel the strain on the binding spell ease, as Lucien watched us both. Waiting to see how this all played out.

"You're Jason's son?" The cords in Trey's arms flexed as he gripped the gun tighter. "You're working with *him?*"

There was no sense in denying it. "I was." Vertigo was starting to set in. All that magic, rushing into me and out into the barrier surrounding Lucien, was starting to sweep me away with it. It felt like my feet were falling asleep, tingling slowly as sensation struggled to assert itself.

"My mother was right about you."

He had to know the words would sting. Had to know just how bad it would hurt. But he didn't care. And in that moment, neither did I. I was as much a part of the magic as I was the container, and before I even realized it, cords of power were extending out from me, wrapping around Trey. My anger pushed at the magic, demanding pain in return. The spell Jason had used on me, but far stronger.

His hand with the gun dropped, his muscles going slack. I could feel the way it affected him, vertigo that was quickly setting every nerve ending into a screaming frenzy. Pain, and lots of it.

He gasped, and the sound drew me back. Oh god.

What was I doing? Hurting *Trey*? Even if he had been pointing a gun at me, this wasn't me.

To my right, Lucien cleared his throat. It felt like my head moved in slow motion. Inside the binding wall I'd thrown around him, the air had gone black. I couldn't see inside, nothing but the flaring sparks of light where my spell held.

Then it erupted, raining magic down on me as I was thrown to my knees.

"Let me make something clear." Lucien strolled toward me. "I can take the pain from you." Looking down on me made him seem even more smug. "Or I can make it worse than you've ever felt."

My skull exploded. Shrapnel dug into every single part of my consciousness. Every thought I'd ever had was lanced and filleted and set on fire. My mind was torn apart, shredded into tiny pieces only to pull itself back together long enough for the cycle to continue. I was screaming. Dying. This wasn't fire, and this wasn't pain. It was hell.

Just as quickly as it started, the pain vanished. But I'd never forget the feeling. My whole body was shaking now, a broken mess of muscles that didn't understand a single thing I wanted them to do.

"The boy has to die." Lucien stood above me, but all I could see was a corner of his shoes. My stomach revolted, choking gasps of icy air punctuating the dry heaving.

"W-why?" I croaked between heaves.

Somehow, I managed to look up. And I saw the rest.

Fear like stinking humanity clawing against the holes in this body, the boy has to die. Everything centers around it. So much power in a new war, feasting for generations to make myself powerful again, and mend what she broke. That bitch, if I ever find her, I'll carve her soul into diamonds.

And I saw flashes of images. Visions and impressions and feelings all wrapped up into one.

Trey and I, together, bound together by things deeper than physical touches and feelings. And in our wake, fires raged out of control, battles and feuds that were yet to come, and Lucien, kneeling before me.

I watched half in fascination, half in horror. He begged for mercy, but I had none. This other Braden—future Braden—was so cold. Ice and steel, not blood and bone. Lucien cowered beneath us, and I unraveled him … somehow. Finished what Grace had started and left him nothing but ash.

That's what this is all about, I realized. "You're scared of us," I whispered. "What we're going to do." He needed me, but he couldn't risk Trey and I together.

It gave me hope, at what was the worst possible time. Maybe we had a chance after all.

Lucien's eyes narrowed slightly, the first shadow of disbelief crossing his face. "You know nothing." He started to raise his hand.

I felt the power calling from the cemetery, the door I hadn't fully opened. I pulled at it, calling it to me with every ounce of willpower I had. The moment I started, Lucien's hand stopped again. He hesitated.

I didn't try to think it through. Didn't have that luxury, and the wrong twitch might reveal the deception I was planning.

I threw myself into the spell and into the energy I had raised. The moment the energy peaked, I hurled it toward Trey, a spell with no words. No tools, no limits.

My body was nearly useless, ravaged so hard I couldn't even stand. But Trey's wasn't. And that's what I was counting on. My mind soared out of my body, riding on the tip of the spell as it slammed into Trey. There was only a second of resistance before I flowed inside of him like water.

Trey's mind was full of rigid lines of obedience, hard edges where he'd had to develop a thicker skin, and corners that kept out the light. There wasn't time to explore it all, as much as I wanted to.

Shock assaulted me, an alien presence that pressed against my control. There wasn't any time to explain to Trey that I'd hijacked a ride on the spell and shoved him out of his own body's control. I pushed it down, pressing on bits of spirit and thought that radiated *Trey.*

Everything looks so drab to him. Seeing the world through Trey's eyes was anticlimactic. No matter how many times I'd wished to be free of the witch eyes, I'd never pictured it would be so... unimpressive. Bland.

From here, I could have stopped Trey's heart, shut down his nervous system. Anything I wanted. Trey's body and mind were at my disposal, and there was nothing he could do to resist.

I pivoted to the left and fired the gun in his hand. Right into Lucien.

Trey had training with the gun that I couldn't have duplicated without years of practice. I'd never even fired a gun before, let alone fired a gun at something. But Trey's muscle memory was strong, his body knew what I wanted, and the gunshot barely caused his arm to snap back in recoil.

The moment the gun fired, the spell faded and I snapped back into my own body.

As I straightened my head, I caught a glimpse of Lucien right before he fell out of my sight, hidden on the other side of the desk. A single bullet had taken him through the eye, leaving a bloody and violent hole in its wake.

I managed only a single, racking cough before everything in my stomach made its way to the surface. I couldn't be sure, but I thought there was blood.

As I knelt there, heaving my guts out, I heard Trey walk around the side of the desk and crouch down in front of me.

"He … he saw … " I could barely think, but the one thought that came clear was that I had to explain to Trey. I had to make him understand.

"It's okay." He touched his fingers to the back of my

head, and I flinched. "Here." He was so gentle I had to strain to hear the words.

The splotchy mess on the ground under me was soon punctured by pure red drops. Slow at first, it started to grow into a steady stream as my nose released everything. I whimpered, and felt fingers slide around my eyes. Cold plastic found its home as the glasses settled, and even as my vision dimmed … it still wasn't enough.

"You have to go." I couldn't think straight, but I knew if Trey stayed, it would be bad. Jason would blame him. Maybe try to kill him, too.

Just as quickly as the moment happened, it was over. "I'll call your father. Will you be okay until he gets here?"

The migraine kept growing, like a train coming out of a tunnel. I started whimpering. Nodding was out of the question, but I tried.

"He'll think I did this to you."

I felt him move away, and I curled up in a ball behind the desk. I think I might have been lying in breakfast, but it didn't matter.

"You did great, Cyke."

Days could have passed, and I wouldn't have known. I tried to focus on something, anything other than the pulsing, but the pain was merciless and wouldn't let me forget.

Finally, someone came for me. I never even opened my eyes. All I knew was that it wasn't Trey.

Thirty-Three

One week later

"You're out of bed, that's a start, right?" Jade's voice was quiet. She'd been here every day, the nurses said. They thought she was my girlfriend.

Riley had only visited once, and only stayed a few minutes before she darted out of the room. The whole time she was there, I didn't hear a single clacking sound. It freaked me out.

Jade wouldn't tell me what was going on with Riley at first. She changed the subject every time I brought it up. I kept pushing.

"I think she's scared. Not that she'd tell me if she was. But she thinks Catherine did something to you. Maybe she thinks she's next," Jade had whispered, resting her hand gently over mine. I knew there was something more to it, but nothing huge. There had been some whispered fight between the two of them out in the hallway before Riley had come in. Jade refused to talk about it.

For the first few days, I'd spent almost all my time dripping with as many drugs as Jason could order the doctor to give me. By the second day, the headaches still hurt, but I was so drugged up I didn't even care anymore.

They told me, eventually, that I'd started having seizures after being admitted. Despite giving me pills they thought would stop them, the seizures kept coming and there was nothing they could do but let me ride them out. They still weren't sure how much damage had been done.

I had a dream, at least I think it was a dream, where Jason talked to one of the doctors. The words "permanent" and "possible blindness" came up often.

My eyes had been bandaged up with thick rolls of cotton, siphoning off every last shred of light that might have opened me up to the visions. It pulled at my hair, and made my skin itch, but they wouldn't remove it. Everything to keep me safe, Jason had assured me.

"Why are you here? Isn't your mother going to find out?" Finally, I'd pushed the nurse to let me out of bed. A struggle of words quickly turned into a struggle to control my legs, which shuddered and threatened revolution at the first sign of strain. It was like I hadn't walked in years, instead of days. Finally, I pushed my way into the chair. I could feel sunlight on my face. But the world was still black.

"She knows Jason's taking care of you. I don't think she knows the rest yet. It's just a matter of time," Jade admitted. When I'd woken up, I'd found out that Jade knew the truth. Jason was my father. "She's not talking to me much right now. Gentry either."

I swallowed. Every day, I hoped to hear his footsteps in the hallway, to hear his voice in the room. But that never happened. "How is he?"

Jade pulled away, her fingers resting against my palm for only a moment. "I don't know," she said in a quiet tone. "He's off by himself a lot." The truth of it all hurt. Stung, actually. I'd hoped for something more.

She touched my neck, fingering the cool silver of the necklace John had given me in another lifetime. Her fingers touched something new, a weight I hadn't felt before. "Trey gave me this. I put it on the chain when you were still asleep."

"What is it?"

"Just a little star. He thinks it'll keep you safe."

A pentacle? I traced my fingers over it, and felt the circle surrounding thick lines. It was big; at least I thought so.

"Time for you to leave, Jade." Jason's voice echoed from the hallway. Even though I couldn't see, I knew he was in the doorway watching the two of us. Whatever his real feelings about Catherine, Jason tolerated her daughter's visits. I think it bothered him that she was the only other person who visited me regularly, but he never said anything.

Jade's voice was slow in coming. "Okay," she said, in a subdued tone she'd never taken with anyone else before. Jason had that effect on people. I could feel her get close again, as her arms wrapped around me. "Be careful," she whispered in my ear.

Once she was gone, Jason settled himself against the edge of the bed. I heard the shift of the paper-thin sheets as Jason tried finding some sort of comfortable balance. "It's about time for you to come home. Are you ready?"

I curled up in the chair, straining my body toward the light I could feel, but not see. "I don't know. It's been awhile since I had one."

"You're stuck with me, Braden. Maybe it's not ideal, but there's still a lot we don't know about each other. I can help you." Jason again tried the concerned parent routine, which seemed to be just another mask that was slipped on as the day went on. Sometimes, I caught a glimmer of the man underneath. That was the thing. I was never really sure who he was.

Stuck. Trapped. I had the school; I could go to the football games. I could fail Algebra just like everyone else. I just couldn't be friends with my friends.

"When do the bandages come off?" I turned away from the window. Sunlight wasn't something I wanted to see now anyway.

"We'll take them off before we leave. I've got your glasses right here." Jason wasn't taking any chances.

"Then let's go."

¤   ¤   ¤

The sun was just starting to set when I started swinging. Two days in Jason's home, and everything was still so surreal. It was like a museum. Even the furniture looked like antiques. I was supposed to be on "strict bed rest." Jason thought it was for the best. "This way, things can settle down," he said.

The fact that his almost-blind son had managed to sneak out of the house and slip away to the park was probably going to royally piss him off later. But I had to get away. More importantly, I had to see him.

While I still could.

Trey crossed the park slowly, dressed in thick layers. During my week in the hospital, I'd missed the day when fall really hit the town, and leaves started falling everywhere. Now, there was a solid crunch-crunch as Trey made his way across the leaf-covered grass.

"You showed up." Somehow, I managed to conceal just how scared I felt at seeing him again.

"Hi." Short and sweet. Trey sounded and looked tired. There were thick, dark circles under his eyes, and his hair was scattered and limp.

I wanted to say any number of things. Anything. I wanted to see him smile, to roll his eyes and admit that maybe I could take care of myself after all. "Did you tell her?"

That had been my argument for seeing him. To find out how much Catherine knew about me. If Trey had told her my secrets.

Trey's jaw flexed, but he shook his head. "I should have, but I can't."

"Jason thinks Lucien might have told her after all." I was giving him an out, a way to tell his mother and know that Jason would never find out about it.

"What about him? Does he know about you and me?"

Jason refused to discuss the feud with me. It had taken days to convince him of the truth of what Lucien had been up to. Even now, I don't think he believed me. I was asking him to believe my story—that Lucien had been playing both sides against each other.

A demon wouldn't have died, but Lucien wasn't a demon anymore. When Grace had ripped the power out of him, he must have been left as something close to human. All humans die eventually.

"I told him. He thinks it was a *bold, strategic move*," I said, emphasizing his exact words. "I think he's not very comfortable talking about it, because of the gay thing. He wasn't expecting that."

"How long have you known?" Trey looked up at me, and I saw the hurt I'd put there. He'd wondered the same thing, thinking I was using him. We didn't have to talk about it to know it was true. Suspicion was one of the building blocks of our relationship.

"That he was my father?"

Trey nodded.

Lying didn't even cross my mind. "The day you picked me up, when it was raining."

He grunted. I'd known the truth almost as long as I'd known Trey. Had it really only been a couple of weeks?

"Lucien?"

I closed my eyes. "Jason covered it up. No one knows what really happened that night. They're saying Lucien booked a flight out of Seattle a few days ago."

Jason wouldn't tell me how he'd cleaned up the mess. The body, the damage to Lucien's office, any of it. Lucien had vanished. One of the nurses claimed he'd taken a better-paying job in Massachusetts somewhere.

"I miss you," I whispered.

I thought he might walk away then. But instead, Trey held out his hand. He looked so scared, like a little boy instead of the man I knew.

I threw myself off the swing and into his arms. Arms that wrapped around me, so tight I could barely breathe.

"She'll tell you to kill me someday, won't she?" My words were muffled against his jacket, but I had to know.

I felt him nodding, his cheek rubbing against my hair. "She'll expect me to try."

"What do we do?"

Trey disentangled himself from me and turned away. He cleared his throat as his hand moved to his face. "Just be careful, Braden. Everything's different now."

I watched him go, my eyes welling even before Trey was out of sight. All the times I'd tried not to cry, and now all I could muster up was a few tears.

I got back on the swing, rocking back and forth for over an hour as I tried to process everything. Everything that had happened, and where I ended up. I'd tried to find a normal life, and everything crumbled down around me.

When I finally looked back up, I saw that the sun was about to set. Jason was parked on the street in front of me. Of course he knew where I was. He didn't get out, and I didn't make him wait.

"You said everything you needed to?" Jason asked, turning up the heater as I shivered. He didn't even mention that I'd snuck out.

"More or less."

Jason pulled off into the street, driving us back toward his house. "It gets easier. Just remember, you're safe. You don't have to hide anything. I'll take care of you."

All the right words, just the wrong person. But Jason was trying. I knew that, and knew I had to give a little, too. "I know."

At the light, he turned to me. "You can't see him anymore. You know that, right?"

I thought about that on the rest of the drive. Looking out the window, I saw Belle Dam laid out around me, a town still full of secrets I'd barely glimpsed. It was like a game. And the only thing left to do was to make it my own.

"It's like Trey said. Everything's different now."

THE END

About the Author

Scott Tracey aspired to be a writer from a young age. Today, he is a member of The Elevensies, with his debut novel *Witch Eyes*, and is an active blogger and vlogger alongside fellow YA authors at TheBookanistas.com and YouTube .com/YARebels. Tracey lives near Cleveland, Ohio, and can be found online at his home site, www.Scott-Tracey. com.

Acknowledgments

First and foremost, there wouldn't be a book without Colleen Lindsay. Gratitude doesn't begin to cover it. And many thanks to Leah Clifford, the first person to read, the first to tear the book to shreds, and the first to declare her love for it. I will never forgive you for the tiny pine trees, but at least this is an easier way of making an impact.

Thanks to the good friends who've been there for me along the way: Tiffany Schmidt, Gretchen McNeil, Karsten Knight, Lisa and Laura Roecker, Courtney Summers. You're always there when I need something—thank you. To Jessica and Lee Verday, the best cheerleaders ever when I suffered from Panic Face. Patrick Mac-Donald and everyone at Querytracker, who helped me refine the query that landed me an agent.

My editor Brian Farrey, for resonating with Braden's story from the minute he read it. And thanks to Steven Pomije, Marissa Pederson, Ed Day and everyone else at Flux who has been so supportive since day one. To Ginger Clark, thank you; you make my life easier on a daily basis.

My appreciation to all the friends who never understood the writing process, but were supportive anyway: Jacinda Espinosa, Daniel and Ryan (the brothers Burnett), Erin Saar-Hanes; to my friends from Team Sparkle and the YA Rebels, thank you so much. The English teachers who always chided me for reading in class: Mary Primm, Elaine Hurst, and Kathy Knox; all of you encouraged me to write and taught me how to do it well.

Last, but definitely not least, to my family, who believed in me when I said, "I'm going to write a novel," and supported me when I could not support myself.